Division
Denise Kawaii

For my son, who wanted to know everything about the story, even if he wasn't old enough to read it.

ACKNOWLEDGEMENTS

I was hoping to thank a bunch of government people for getting me onto Hanford's former Manhattan Project site to help make *Curie* and *Division* as believable as possible. I anticipated a long, boring trip through the now-defunct desert site so I could get the landscape "just right." Had that happened in the two years since I applied for a visitor's pass, this is where those thanks would have gone.

Sometimes, you just have to wing it, and hope for the best.

In any event, there are people to thank. I'm grateful to Vikki Carter for inviting me to participate in the 2018 NaNoWriMo write-in sessions at the Longview Public Library, and for the librarians who made the space available. Many of these chapters were contemplated during those writing sessions, even if not much actual writing got done. I'd also like to thank the Wordfest group for being kind enough to let me read several pages of Division's rough draft over the microphone. I know none of you had a clue what was going on in my story, but I appreciate you for humoring me.

As always, thank you to Keith for believing in these books, and for pushing me to share them with the world. If you're reading this, it's because he forced me to keep writing even when it seemed like being an author was a terrible idea.

Denise Kawaii

CHAPTER 1

The hills lay before 62 like the rows of an oversized graveyard. Death screamed out from the landscape and he wondered how he and his friends could possibly survive in the brown on brown monotone spread out before them. Hanford wasn't pristine by any means, but it was a lush oasis compared to this. Blue's mottled blue facemask turned to look around, then his hand waved 62 forward. Blue pushed the wheelbarrow full of computer parts toward a crease between two of the giant mounds. From a distance, it looked like nothing but a crack in the desert, but as they drew closer 62 gaped over the green seams around the lens of his own mask at the deep canyon that revealed itself.

The base of the canyon was level enough, but it was riddled with boulders exposed by the harsh winds at their backs. 00 dropped the handle of his wagon beside one of the rocks. His black mask was so covered in dust from the trail that the stitches were outlined in brown. He turned to eye the narrow path that curved around the boulders. He shouted at Blue, "Are we really going to drag this stuff in there?"

62 stopped next, his route blocked by 00's wagon. He, too, looked over the narrow trail. "I don't know if I'm going to be able to manage this," he admitted.

"We aren't too far off from the building," Blue said, looking at the map. The trio had been walking for as many days, luckily without much incident. Despite the weight of the computer parts rattling around in the wheelbarrow and the heft of food and supplies pilfered from Hanford's stockrooms, the friends had made good time.

"Can we leave it here for now then?" 62 suggested. "Maybe we could hike the rest of the way up and check things out and come back for this later."

00 looked with worried eyes at the prized computer parts. The pieces were a jumble of wires, tossed into the wheelbarrow in a hurried attempt at making it look like useless scrap metal as they'd made their escape from Hanford following 62's banishment. "If we keep the bot covered, it should be okay," he said in a reluctant tone.

Blue nodded, "Sounds good to me. I've got enough food in my pack for dinner, and there's beds and blankets already up there. If we're too beat to come back for the rest of it tonight, we can get it in the morning."

The Boys pushed their supplies off the path, covering them with tarps that Auntie had given them. At Blue's direction, they pulled some dry brush from nearby, piling it on top of the gear and making it less visible. Not that there was anyone who would stumble across it on this desolate stretch of land. "Better safe than sorry," Blue had muttered when they'd questioned him about it.

Tired, dirty, and coated in several days of sweat, the Boys picked their way through the canyon. Blue clambered over obstacles with ease, stopping frequently to poke fun at the others while he waited for them to catch up. The sun dipped below the lip of the canyon by the time the structure they were looking for revealed itself. It looked like an exact duplicate of the dorms in Hanford, although it was surrounded by high walls of dirt and stone instead of a bustling town full of people.

"Someone's been here," Blue said. "I was expecting to have to break in, since Joan didn't give us a key when she kicked us out. But look." He pressed down on the door's handle and the door swung open a crack. He stopped it abruptly when the hinges started to squeal. "Dang rust," Blue whispered. "I hope nobody inside heard that."

"Who could be here?" 62 whispered as he looked around the entrance. There didn't seem to be a living thing in sight.

The skin around 00's eyes paled through the lens of his mask. The anxiety in his voice made him stammer. "M-maybe they forgot to lock the door when they left last."

"Doubt it," Blue said, shaking his head. "But, there's only one way to find out." Blue reached over to 62's pack and unstrapped the machete that was tied there.

He pushed the door the rest of the way open, holding the weapon out in front of him. "Hello? Anybody home?"

A clatter sounded from deep within the building, echoing through the empty lobby ahead of them. When Blue took a step inside to investigate, both 62 and 00 grabbed the back of his jacket to pull him back outside.

"Are you crazy?" 62 whispered. "Somebody's in there! What if it's an Adaline patrol? Or the Oosa?"

"Or a bear?" 00 hissed.

Blue rolled his eyes at 00. "There's no bears here. That's just fluff grownups tell kids to make them scared to go outside."

"What about—" 62's question was cut off by the sound of shuffling feet somewhere inside, out of sight.

Blue tapped the machete against the door frame. He cleared his throat and spoke loud and clear, sounding older and more commanding than the ragamuffin that he was. "Hello? If you're a friend, let's have a quick introduction. If you're not, well, let's have a different conversation."

The footsteps came closer and all three Boys took a few steps back from the doorway, instinctively wanting to be out of arm's reach of whoever emerged from the dark interior of the secret building. The door peeled back, exposing someone wearing the same basic smock that the medical teams back in Hanford wore. There was something odd about how they looked, and the Boys drew back again as the person stepped bare-faced into the late afternoon light.

The buzz of anxiety faded as 62 looked the stranger over. They were thin; thinner than anyone 62 had ever seen before. Lanky limbs crossed over a flat chest and sharp angles pressed against the too-large smock that hung on the stranger's frame. Their hair was long and matted, greasy strands covering much of their face.

"My name..." the small voice creaked. A hand pushed back a clump of hair and the wild eyes beneath looked surprised at the sound of their own words as they hung in the air.

Blue dropped the machete to the ground and rushed forward. "Sunny?" He pulled a cloth out of a pocket and rushed to wipe his hands before grabbing the frail Woman's shoulders. He looked down at the flatness of her body, a look of intense worry in his eyes.

"Yes," her chapped lips curved into a broken smile. Her vacant eyes passed over the hands gripping her, and then suddenly drew a sharp focus when they landed on Blue's eyes within his mask. "Oh, Blue," she whispered, "you found me."

CHAPTER 2

The hideout looked weather-beaten, but inside, it was well stocked. 62 marveled at the equipment. Blue explained this was where the Adaline-born residents of Hanford hid when the Oosa came each year. The first place they stopped was the detox room, just inside the front doors. There were no medical staff to help with the equipment, but big paintings on the walls showed the detoxification steps from start to finish. They unloaded their packs, set their bags in the laundry bin to be washed, and put their belongings into boxes Sunny had brought them. They discovered racks of medical smocks like Sunny was wearing, but decided to skip donning the smocks in favor of their own clothes.

16

By the time they got through the detox process, Sunny had disappeared back into the rooms upstairs. 62 and the others tried to find her, hoping to find out more about why she was in hiding, but there was no way of knowing exactly where in the building she'd gone. They gave up their hunt for her, deciding that she'd find them when she was ready to talk again.

After abandoning their search of the living quarters, Blue gave 62 and 00 a tour of the rest of the building. They started at the greenhouse attached to the south side of the barracks. It teemed with root vegetables, lettuces, and a couple of fruit trees. Blue showed them the automatic watering system that kept plants thriving while unattended. As long as someone came to harvest and replant once or twice a year, Blue said the greenhouse would keep the garden green and growing.

When they left the greenhouse, they entered a massive pantry. It was more like a storeroom than anything, full of dried fruits, powdered potatoes, grains hauled from Hanford, and seed packets for anyone staying an extended time to plant and harvest. The pantry was attached to the kitchen, which was clean and stocked with salt, pots, pans and utensils, and hundreds of kiln-fired clay plates to eat on.

The cafeteria where 62, 00, and Blue finally settled was a smaller version of the resident's meal area back home. The furniture looked newer, owing to its limited use. Although the sun had already disappeared over the mountain's crest, the area surrounding them was brightly lit. There was plenty of power, enough for a hundred people or more, and Blue vowed he was going to use it all. He'd flipped on every light switch they'd found on their tour of the main floor, and Blue joked that he'd like to keep them on until the day they left.

Although the building was well lit and would be comfortable for the foreseeable future, 62 couldn't seem to feel happy about the place. He looked up from the loaf of bread he was sharing with his friends and took in the cafeteria one more time. "It's so empty," he said.

00 nodded, swallowed his bite with a gulp, and answered, "It's kinda creepy, isn't it?"

Blue's eyes were fixed on the doorway that led to the building's main lobby. He had only eaten a bite or two before giving the rest of his meal to his friends. Now, his mind seemed to be a million miles away, totally unaware of the conversation going on around him. 62 leaned across the table and shook Blue's elbow.

"Hey, is this place giving you the creeps, too?" 62 asked.

Blue blinked his eyes several times and shook his head. He pulled his attention back into the room. "What? Oh, no, this place is fine. I've been up here loads of times."

"Have you ever been here without the others though?" 00 asked.

"Once or twice," Blue answered. He tried to give a cocky grin, but the confidence that normally filled his features failed to appear. Blue looked back at the doorway.

62 followed Blue's gaze and then tapped his elbow again. "Hey, are you okay?"

Blue gave a half-smile. "Yeah, I'm fine. Just a little surprised Sunny's here."

"Yeah, whu up wit dat?" 00 asked through a mouth full of bread.

"I'm not sure." Blue dragged his hands through his hair, looking suddenly exhausted. He looked at the table, forcing his gaze away from the door. Sunny had gone to bed nearly as soon as they'd arrived, hardly speaking a word to any of them. "She's so different from how she used to be."

"What do you mean?" 62 asked.

"She was so happy. She hugged everybody. Today, she barely let me touch her. It's not like her at all." Blue shook his head. "And I've never seen her look like that before."

00 swallowed his bread and grabbed the last slice from 62's plate. Before he took another bite, he said, "She did look pretty worn out. Maybe she's sick."

"It's not just that," Blue said with a shake of his head. "Did you see how thin she was? Her whole body's flat as a pancake. She didn't look like that the last time I saw her."

"Why do you think she's here?" 62 asked. "I thought that when the Oosa let people go, it was because they were pregnant and going back to Hanford. I don't remember any of the Women in the nursery looking like that."

Blue shook his head. "I don't think she's got a baby hiding under her clothes. She'd have been sent back with the other mothers if she was. And she'd be huge by now." Blue puffed out his cheeks and grabbed an invisible round belly in his lap.

00 finished the meal and stretched his arms over his head. "Well, I don't think we're gonna unravel her mystery tonight. Maybe we should wander up and find a place to sleep?"

"Sure," Blue said with a reluctant shrug. "Let's clean up these plates in the morning. I'm too worn out, now. Follow me, I'll show you the rooms." The trio got up from their seats, picked up their boxed belongings from a nearby table, and made their way out of the cafeteria. They trudged across the lobby and through a side door marked *stairs*. Blue opened the door and reached up to find the switch to turn on a couple of bare light bulbs hanging from the ceiling. "There are elevators on the other end of the building, but they're ancient and not exactly reliable," Blue explained. "We'll turn them on when we bring N302 and the rest of our gear in, but then it's probably best if we turn them back off again."

"That's okay by me," 62 said. "Every time I get into an elevator, something bad happens. I'm fine taking the stairs."

"Speak for yourself," 00 complained. "I like pushing the buttons."

They reached the first landing. Blue lifted a leg, resting his box on his knee while he placed his hand on the doorknob. He leaned back from the door briefly and nodded toward the staircase that continued to rise through the building. "There are more rooms up there. Every floor from here to the roof is full of 'em. Do you want to keep going, or are second floor rooms good enough for you?"

"I'm used to the view from the first floor," 62 said. "Doesn't matter to me."

"I want to see the rooms before I make a decision," 00 said. "Maybe the beds upstairs are nicer than the ones down here."

Blue pushed the door open and they entered the center of a dark corridor that stretched past a dozen doors in either direction. Blue found another switch and flicked it on. "I doubt any of the beds upstairs are better than the ones here," he said to 00. "Most everything here is barely used, so it's pretty much the same no matter what room you're in."

Blue walked a few steps, stopping at the door closest to the stairwell they'd just come from. He adjusted his box so he could knock, just in case Sunny was inside, but there was no answer. He turned the knob and swung the door inward. Blue entered, dropped his box on the floor, and turned on the ceiling light. The room looked nearly the same as the dorm rooms in Hanford, aside from the bars inside the room's single window. 62 set his box on a shelf in the open closet and walked to look through the bars at the darkening sky and shadowy hill just beyond the glass.

"What's with the window?" 62 asked, placing his hand on the cold steel encasing the glass.

"This used to be Hanford's jail," Blue answered as he flopped down on the bed. "The jail on Rattlesnake Mountain. That's what they called it, back before whatever wrecked Curie."

"What's a jail?" 00 asked from the doorway.

62 answered, "I've read about them. They're places where bad people are sent to be punished for rules they've broken."

"That's fitting then," 00 said. "Since we broke all those laws building N302."

62 thought back on the computer parts waiting for them at the bottom of the boulder-covered trail. 00 and Blue had been on the recovery team that discovered the bot's memory and hard drive. And it had taken both of them, plus 62, Mattie, and Auntie, to put a computer together that could run the program. Although it was 62's dreams that got him banished from Hanford, he hoped his exile would give them a chance to discover more of what N302 had to tell them.

62 turned from the barred windows and looked at his brothers. "Hey, before we split up for the night, I just want to say thanks."

Blue folded his hands behind his head and reclined on the bed's pillow. He closed his eyes. "Thanks for what?"

"For coming with me." 62 looked down at his feet, which shuffled nervously on the floor beneath him. "You could have stayed in Hanford, you know?"

"And leave you out here all alone?" 00 shook his head. "Fat chance."

Blue cracked one eye open and tilted his head up to look at 62. "Besides, if you'd been on your own, what would you have done when you found out Sunny was here?"

"I don't know," 62 said with a nervous laugh. "Ran away, I guess."

"To where?" 00 demanded. "You can't go back to Hanford, and there's no way you'd survive if you went to Adaline. N302 definitely wouldn't last getting pushed around the desert in a wheelbarrow forever."

"Oh, I see," 62 rolled his eyes. "You aren't here for me. You're here for the bot."

00 grinned. "Basically."

"Well, thank you all the same." 62 set his jaw and took a deep breath to keep the tears that stung his eyes from falling. He knew he was lucky to have friends who would leave the comforts of home for him. He cleared his throat, hoping his voice wouldn't crack when he spoke again. He walked over to retrieve his box of things, then moved toward the door. He shifted the box in his hands to motion back into the hall. "Well, it looks like Blue's taking this room. Suppose we should find our own?"

Blue had closed his eyes again and didn't say another word as 00 and 62 left, leaving the light on and closing the door behind them. 00 walked away, not stopping at any of the doors between Blue's room and the end of the hall. "Why aren't you checking any of these other rooms?" 62 called as he followed behind.

00 set his things down and knocked on the final door. He rested his hand on the doorknob. He looked over his shoulder at 62 and listened at the door for any sounds before answering with a single word. "Privacy."

00 swung the door open and searched for the switch. The light flickered on in a room decorated in the same bare, utilitarian manner that Blue's room had been. There was a neatly made bed, a barred window, and an open closet with bare shelves. 00 meandered over to the window, trying in vain to look through the bars into the now-dark evening. "Not sure there's much of a view from here," 00 muttered.

"What do you want a view for? There's no Girls here to look at, you know." 62 leaned against the open doorway and watched his friend pull on the bars bolted to the inside of the window frame.

"Did you notice how surprised Sunny was to see us?" 00 asked. "It might be worth having a room where you could see down the hill. It'd give us a chance to know someone's coming before they got here."

"Maybe," 62 considered. "But are you really going to be sitting in your room looking out the window when we've got a bot to build?"

"I might," 00 said with a shrug of his shoulders. "Depends on how uncomfortable I end up feeling out here." 00 walked back across the room, pushing past 62 in the doorway. "It's gonna be too low here to see much. I'm heading upstairs. You can have this one if you want."

"Okay," 62 said. "How high up are you going?"

"All the way to the top." 00 grinned. He picked up his belongings and started back down the hall.

"I thought you hated stairs," 62 called after him. Without turning around, 00 waved a hand over his head in farewell.

62 plopped his box of clothes and knickknacks on the floor just inside the room. He pulled the door shut and took a step toward the bed. Then, he shook his head and turned on his heel, going back to slide the thin chain lock that dangled from the doorjamb. 00 was right. Out here, there was no telling what could happen, or who might show up unannounced. It was just like Blue had said when they'd left N302 and the rest of their supplies under tarps and brush earlier that day. Better safe than sorry.

CHAPTER 3

The sun was high above the window's edge before 62 stirred. Days of hiking through the wind-blasted desert had drained every ounce of his energy and as he wiped his eyes, he wondered if he'd ever get it back again. His stomach gurgled and he wrapped his arms around himself to quiet it. He sat up slowly, taking in his new surroundings. Today they'd hike back down the hill to retrieve the rest of their things. 62 groaned, plopped back into bed, pulled the covers over his head, and went back to sleep.

It was mid-day before a knock at his door roused him from his slumber. His voice sounded raspy and broken when he called out, "Hello?"

The door opened just a crack, the latched chain keeping it from moving any farther. A blue eye peered through the narrow breach. "Hey, you coming down? Sunny's making us something to eat before we go."

62 felt even more exhausted than he had the first time he woke up. He sat up slowly, marveling that the rest seemed to be making his tiredness even worse. He nodded at Blue, then got up and shuffled across the room to unlatch the chain holding the door. Once the door was unlocked, Blue pushed it open and leaned against the doorjamb. 62 went to the closet and rummaged through the few things he'd unpacked the night before. He pulled a long-sleeved shirt on over what he was already wearing. Socks and boots soon followed. "How is she today?" 62 asked as he dressed.

"I don't know," Blue said with a frown. "There's definitely something wrong, but Sunny won't talk to me about it. She's acting like we're back in town and everything's normal."

62 grabbed his coat and a clean mask, and followed Blue into the hall. There wasn't a way to lock his door from the outside, but 62 figured that there wasn't much in his room to protect, and not many wandering eyes to protect it from. He closed the door tight and walked with Blue to the stairwell. "If there's something going on, I'm sure she'll tell you after she's gotten to know 00 and me a little bit better," he offered. "Or, maybe, there isn't really anything wrong. She might have just decided to not go back to Hanford after the Oosa let her go."

Blue pushed the wild hair out of his eyes, letting their blue irises shine out from his boyish face. "I guess it's possible, but I don't think anyone has ever been found after the Oosa took them, unless they came back to town to grow new babies."

"It's a big world, you know?" 62 said. "Maybe we don't know everything that happens out there."

"You just might be right," Blue said. His smile reached his eyes and he slapped 62 on the shoulder. "Now, let's go eat. I'm starving."

The pair made their way to the cafeteria where 00 was already stooped over a bowl of hot, steaming, fried potatoes. He glanced up as they entered, and spoke with his food rolling over his tongue while he ate. "G'mornin!"

62 gave a shudder at the sight of his friend's open maw. "Hey, can you finish eating before you say anything? Your face looks like a dust devil full of mashed potatoes."

00 winked at his friends, but finished chewing and swallowed before talking again. "You're jealous because I got the first serving."

"Nope," Blue said. "We just know there's such a thing as table manners."

"Pshaw." 00 leaned back in his chair. "Who gives a rat's tail about table manners? There's nobody out here to tell us what to do."

"True enough," Blue said. He looked at 62 and tipped his head toward the kitchen. Leaving 00 behind to maul his meal, the two hungry friends headed into the cook's room in search of food.

"Hey there," Sunny said with a weak smile when she saw them. "I found some lard in the pantry and fried up some potatoes. There's jerky too, if you'd like some meat."

"Potatoes are fine by me," Blue said. 62 nodded and they followed Sunny over to the stove where she served them hearty portions. "Thanks."

62 stared down at the bowl of cooked tubers. "They're orange!"

"Yes. I found a whole stash of sweet potatoes. A bit of fat and salt and they fry up really nice." What little bit of a smile Sunny had was lost as she watched 62's bewildered expression hovering close to his bowl of food. "You do like sweet potatoes, don't you?"

"I bet he's never seen 'em before," Blue said. "He came up from Adaline not too long ago. Parker fed them potatoes, but only regular white ones. Right, 62?"

62 stuck his tongue out, prodding the soft meal with it. He wrinkled his nose. "Right. White potatoes." 62 looked up at Sunny, whose face had blanched. He stammered, "But I'm sure these are great. Thank you for making them for us."

"Parker?" Sunny's whisper was barely audible. She clutched a hand to her neck and leaned back against the stove.

"Yeah," Blue set his bowl down on a nearby counter and moved close to Sunny. He raised his hands as if he wanted to hold her, but when she shrank back he lowered them to his sides, fingers twitching nervously. "Parker took over classes for the refugees after you didn't come back. If you come out and sit with us while we eat, we can tell you all about it."

"No." Sunny shook her head. Her eyes were watery and she trembled where she stood. She gripped the edge of the stove behind her for support with one arm, and the hand around her neck dug into the soft skin around her protruding collar bone. "I don't feel like eating just now. You Boys go on ahead. I think I'd better go lie down."

"Okay," Blue said with concern in his voice. "Maybe later, then."

Sunny nodded, then pushed herself away from the stove and scampered toward the exit like a wounded animal. The door swung closed behind her and they listened to her footsteps fading away into some dark corner of the building.

"That was odd," 62 said. "Do you think she's all right?"

"No. I do not think she's all right. But there doesn't seem to be anything to do about it now." Blue narrowed his gaze on 62. "Good job being grossed out by her food."

62 hung his head. "I'm sorry. It does smell good. It's just new, is all."

"I know," Blue lamented. He picked up his bowl and shook his head. "Let's go eat."

00 passed them on their way out of the kitchen. "Going for seconds!" he exclaimed, waving his fork in the air. They waited for him to scoop himself up another round of sweet potatoes and then all went back into the dining area to eat together. Once 62 had watched both of his friends eat half their meals without retching, he speared a slice of glistening orange potato and took a bite. The exterior of the potato had a light, salty crisp to it, and the sweet center melted over his tongue.

"This is delicious!" he exclaimed as his eyes popped open. He stabbed another bit and shoved it into his mouth.

"Why couldn't you have said that to Sunny?" Blue rolled his eyes to the ceiling and slumped back in his chair.

00's eyes darted back and forth between his friends. "What happened?"

Without looking away from the ceiling tile above him, Blue raised a hand and pointed at 62. "This chucklehead made a face and complained about the orange potatoes right in front of Sunny."

62 dropped his fork to the table. "Well you're the one who brought up Parker and almost made her cry."

00 gulped. "You guys! You can't make her cry. Then she might not cook for us again."

62 glared at 00 and crossed his arms over his chest. "You're not helping. I wasn't trying to be mean about the food. I haven't had this kind of potato before, okay? And with all the weird food that Parker's been throwing at us, I wasn't sure what to expect."

"And, I didn't know that talking about Parker would make her sad. I mean, they were always together before she went to the Oosa. How should I know that she'd cry if I talked about him?" Blue dropped his arms to his sides and slumped farther into his chair, defeated.

"Maybe she misses him," 00 offered. "Sometimes when I think about Adaline, I get sad because I miss it there."

"But if she misses him, why didn't she just go back to Hanford?"

"I don't know," 62 answered. "But what I do know is we've got to finish eating these delicious potatoes she made us. Then, we need to bring N302 back here before it gets too late."

They finished eating in silence and cleared the table. As they were preparing to leave, 62 rested his hand on Blue's shoulder. "I'm sure she'll be okay. And maybe after we've been gone a while she'll be ready to talk again."

Blue pressed his lips together and dipped his chin in agreement. Then he pulled a clean blue mask over his face and secured its straps around his head. His voice was soft and low as it leaked through the filter of his mask.

"We're burnin' daylight, Boys. Let's go get that blasted bot."

CHAPTER 4

It took the Boys the entire afternoon to haul their equipment to the jailhouse barracks. Moving their belongings through narrow trail gaps and over the rocky terrain hadn't been easy. After they'd unpacked and sorted through what needed to go through detox, and what could pass as clean enough to be okay, Blue showed 62 and 00 how to use the high-pressure hoses and scrub brushes to clean off the wagon and wheelbarrow. 62 was surprised that he had fun using the hose to blast dirt and grime off the battered metal of the wheelbarrow. He was disappointed when Blue shut the generator and water off.

"Do you think we'll have to use the pressured hoses to clean off anything else?" 62 tried not to sound too enthusiastic as he wound the hose and put it away.

Blue put his hands on his hips and tilted his head with a curious stare. "Leave it to you to like cleaning. You're a weird kid, 62."

62 shrugged off the comment. It was dumb, Blue calling him "kid" even though 62 wasn't that much younger than him. It was true that with his lengthening limbs and solid torso, Blue looked more like an adult every day. But it wouldn't be long until 62 had another growth spurt and started catching up. 62 rolled his eyes and followed his brothers back into the detox room. They headed to the showers. 62 almost ran into 00 when he stopped abruptly in the doorway. Blue was already in the room, and 62 stood on his tip-toes to see around his brothers.

"What are you doing in here?" Blue asked. 62 leaned to look over 00's shoulder and saw the edge of someone wearing a white medical staff suit. It was the same kind of outfit that the doctors wore back in the detox room of Hanford's hospital.

"I figured out how to use the radiation meter. I figured it might make things easier," came Sunny's muffled voice through the enclosed hood she was wearing.

"I didn't even know they had one of those up here," Blue said. 62 could hear the familiar tick of a radiation counter, just like the ones back at Hanford. "You're sure you know how to use it?"

There was no answer, but when 00 finally stepped the rest of the way into the room, 62 could see Sunny waving the stiff metal rod all over Blue's pants and boots. She pulled the wand up again, tucking it under each armpit, down to his hands, over his shoulders, and circling his head. The box in her other hand ticked with varying frequencies as it searched for the radioactive signature of the poison that appeared outside without warning.

"All clear," she said to Blue. He bounded away from her toward a stash of clean clothes, happy to be skipping the detox wash. Sunny waved 00 forward and repeated the procedure with the wand. She announced that 00 was also clean, and then 62 stepped forward for his turn.

"You're new here," Sunny said from somewhere behind the mask. 62 couldn't see her face through her reflective lens. Sunny lifted the radiation counter box in one hand, and the wand in the other. "Have you seen one of these before?"

"Yeah," 62 answered. "I'm new, but not that new. I saw Geiger use one of those right after I left Adaline."

The oversized hood of Sunny's suit bobbed once, and she waved the wand around 62 in the same manner she had the others. "You're clear," she said. She set down the box and wand, and turned off the device. 62 waited for her to pull the hood off of her suit.

"Thank you," he said.

One side of Sunny's mouth turned up in an attempted smile. "No problem. I hate having to do the whole wash-down routine and figured if we use this thing, we'd all be better off."

62 smiled at her and patted her gently on the arm. "It makes a load of difference."

Sunny nodded. She tucked the medical hood into the crook of her elbow and retrieved the device at her feet. "I've got food on the stove in the kitchen, if you'll take a chance on my cooking."

62 blushed. "I'm sorry about before. I'm still new to the whole food thing. But the sweet potatoes were good. I've never had anything like them before."

"I'm glad you liked them." Sunny's smile widened an inch. "There's some in the stew I'm cooking. It'll make it taste sweet."

"When we were in Hanford, my friend Mattie said that you used to be a teacher. How did you learn to cook?" Sunny moved toward the door and 62 followed.

Sunny shrugged. "I used to hang out in the kitchen. I was friends with a cook and she showed me some things." Sunny's full arms made her fumble the doorknob and her face darkened. 62 reached around her, turned the knob, and swung the door open. "Thanks," she mumbled. She walked quickly through the doorway and scuttled into the main building.

"I'll see you at dinner!" 62 said in his friendliest voice. Sunny didn't reply. He wrinkled his nose as he pondered their brief conversation, hoping he'd been cordial enough to make things right with her. Most of the Women he'd met back in Hanford had been cold toward him, but the way Sunny acted was different than that. She didn't act as if she thought she were better than him, or the others. No, he didn't feel that her distance was because they were clones. Especially not Blue, whom she seemed to have been friends with before. Instead, it was like she'd put up an imaginary barrier for protection. But was the barricade protecting her from their prodding, or was it protecting them from whatever secrets she held? 62 wasn't sure.

62 changed his clothes in silence, ignoring the idle chatter of Blue and 00 in the changing stalls. When they'd all finished, 62 told them Sunny had dinner ready and all

three of their stomachs grumbled at the news that food was coming.

"I've never been so hungry in all my life," 62 marveled. "It feels like there's a baby bird in there, pecking at my insides, waiting for its mamma to bring it a meal."

"I doubt you've ever worked so hard before, either," Blue winked. "That's the thing with work. The more you work, the more you've gotta eat. Your muscles burn up all the energy from whatever you ate before, so you have to keep at it."

62's stomach growled again. "Well, let's not keep Sunny waiting then. I feel like I could eat a hundred potatoes."

The trio marched noisily to the cafeteria and met Sunny in the kitchen. She plied them with bowls of hot stew, bread rolls, and even some fizzy cider to drink. The Boys convinced her to eat with them this time, and soon the four of them were seated around a table with a bounty of food piled between them. 62 and 00 marveled at the stew. Sweet potatoes bobbed in the dark liquid, along with rehydrated jerky, white potatoes, purple carrots, and soft, white apples. It was sweet and savory, filling their bellies with warm comfort.

Sunny was sipping her mug of cider, watching the Boys devour the meal. She lowered the mug to the table, a thoughtful look in her eyes. Her mouth opened and closed several times as she tried to gather the courage to talk. Finally, her low, deliberate voice eked out over the sound of smacking lips and spoons scraping the sides of bowls. "So," she asked, "what was in that wheelbarrow you brought up today?"

62 looked at Blue with questioning eyes. He didn't know if Sunny was someone they could share their secret

with. Would finding out they'd built a computer be the thing to drive her back to Hanford? Even though they were living outside the reach of Hanford's laws, he knew that if anyone found out about the bot, it wouldn't help him have any hope of being accepted by the town again. Blue locked eyes with 62, then glanced at 00 and gave the pair an almost imperceptible shake of his head.

Sunny wasn't immune to the extended silence hanging in the air as the Boys considered how to answer her question. She folded her hands on the table in front of her and looked them over. "It's a secret. I understand."

"It's not that we don't trust you," Blue said. He winced as the words tumbled out. Trust was exactly why they weren't telling her about N302.

Sunny raised a hand to stop Blue from saying anything else. "It's okay. Whatever it is, I won't pry. I only have one question about it. Is it dangerous?" She looked around the table, and the way that 62 and the other's faces dropped was all the answer she seemed to need. "I see," she acknowledged. "I won't pry any further."

The conversation was dropped, and everyone stared at the food in front of them. 62's mind was nearly as full as his belly, and he started picking at his food instead of gorging on it as he had before. He hoped a day would come when he'd feel comfortable with Sunny, but he still couldn't figure out why she was here. He decided not to feel guilty for keeping secrets from her, since she was wrapped in a shroud of her own mystery.

00 was the first to get up, and the rest followed. They cleared the table in relative silence until the last dish was washed and set to dry. Sunny closed her eyes, stood tall, and took in a sharp inhale. She held her breath for a moment and then opened her eyes and looked at the

Boys standing nervously around her. She blew out the held air through her nose, seeming to decide on something.

"I don't know why you've come here," Sunny started. She paused for a moment, carefully considering her next words. "And I can't expect you to tell me while I'm keeping my own story to myself."

Blue looked at Sunny with somber eyes. "You don't have to tell us."

Sunny frowned. "I do. But not now. Tomorrow. For now, I'm going to my room. I'm tired." Her face drooped as she said this, as if simply talking about her exhaustion made it manifest into reality. She patted Blue on the shoulder as she walked past him, then left the cafeteria, taking the weight of her worries with her.

"What do you think she's going to tell us?" 00 asked.

"I don't know," Blue replied. "But I don't think it's going to be good."

"It can't be, if she's been hiding out up here. It's not like we came to live in a jail because we wanted to," 62 said. His mouth twisted to one side for a moment, then he asked, "What do you think we should tell her about the bot?"

"Not much, if we can help it," 00 said, crossing his arms. "She grew up in Hanford. There's no way she's going to think having N302 up and running is a good idea."

Blue squinted. "She might surprise you. Let's see what she says tomorrow. Then, we'll decide what to tell her about the computer."

CHAPTER 5

62 was up with the sun, having hardly slept the night before. When his eyes had closed, he'd had a series of strange dreams. He'd tried to connect with Mattie to tell her that they'd arrived safely, but no matter how hard he tried, he wasn't able to envision her or the library. Instead, his dreams had been plagued with Nurses from Adaline chasing him through darkened corridors. The flaming furnace loomed ahead of him before finally expelling him into the desert. The dreams ended with Joan, the Woman who'd wanted him sent away from Hanford, standing at the town's gates surrounded by a crowd of angry town folk shouting that he'd never be allowed to return.

Now that he was back in reality, he headed down the hall from his room, stopping to knock on Blue's door. When there was no answer, 62 opened it and poked his head inside. The bed was empty, so 62 pulled the door shut and crossed the hall to the stairwell. He listened to the silent air, trying to determine if he should go down to the cafeteria, or up to 00's room on the top floor.

62 tilted his head and strained his ears. He couldn't hear a thing, no thanks to the enormity of the building compared to the four souls living quietly within. He frowned, then decided to climb the stairs to see if 00 was in his room. No matter what Sunny was planning on telling them today, they'd need to find a good place to keep the computer, and 00 knew more about what the bot would need than anybody. He grabbed the handrail and pulled his tired body up the stairs. When he made it to the top of the stairwell, he let himself into the dorm's hallway and headed toward the far corner of the building. Light streamed through the open door, leaving a bright rectangle of light on the floor and opposing wall.

"Hello?" 62 peered into the room. 00 was sitting at the window, reclining in a chair borrowed from some other area in the building. He looked down into the desert below them.

"Hey," 00 answered with half a smile.

"What are you looking at?"

"Not much. I caught a nice view of the sunrise." 00 folded his feet under himself, making room for 62 at the window's edge. "I was right, though. From up here, you can see all the way down the hill. What are you doing up here?"

62 crossed the room and pressed his forehead into the gap between the bars that caged the window. He could see parts of the trail below, and out into the desert

beyond. "I was thinking last night, what if we keep the bot up on the top floor with you?"

00 tilted his head, squinting as he scratched a spot above his ear. "There's no lab up here. Power is probably easier to come by if we set it up in detox on the first floor."

"Yeah, but what if someone comes to check on us? Or, what if Sunny gets mad when she finds out about N302 and decides to wreck it? Having the computer on the first floor, none of us would know if somebody messed with it." 62 moved to sit on the bed, folding his hands under his armpits to ward off the morning cold.

"That's a good point." 00 gave a thoughtful nod. "If we build it up here, there's no way anyone would find it. The only problem is getting the thing tapped into electricity. The rooms up here have a light bulb on the ceiling, but nothing else to plug into. We'd have to run some wires to power it up."

62 thought back to the solar panels and battery bank they'd built for the computer back at Mattie's library. "It's nothing we haven't done before," he said.

"True story," 00 agreed. "I like N302 and all, but I don't really want to sleep in a bed of wires. Should we look at the room next door and see what it's like?"

"All the bedrooms I've looked in are the same."

00 lifted a finger in the air, turned his nose up to the ceiling, and said in a haughty tone, "You never know what you'll find if you don't look." He returned to his regular voice. "That's what my old teacher used to tell me whenever I assumed I knew an answer. Who knows, maybe the room next door is a secret library or something."

The Boys went to the neighboring room. It wasn't set up any differently than the other bedrooms had been, although the window offered a slightly different perspective on the view outside. They determined that they'd have to remove the bed and find some tables to set the computer on, but if they set the device up below the window, they'd be able to work and keep an eye on the desert below at the same time. If they happened to be paying attention, they'd be able to see someone coming long before they showed up at the building's entrance. 00 was sure they could make a way to lock the door from the outside, so they could secure the room and keep Sunny or anyone else out.

With the idea growing in their minds, the Boys started down the stairs to find breakfast for their gurgling bellies. They'd made it down two flights of stairs when 62 said, "We should have Blue figure out how to start up the elevator. I don't want to haul N302 all the way up these stairs. It's dang heavy."

"Plus, we have plans for a second computer," 00 reminded him. "Once we get it up and running, I think N302 is going to be ready to start trying to duplicate itself."

62 hadn't been thinking about the jumble of parts they'd brought that were waiting to become a second computer. Just before he'd been kicked out of Hanford, they'd discovered that N302's creator, Doctor 2442, had designed the bot to be a virus. They weren't sure what 42's plan had been, but they hoped that he was going to use N302 to worm into Adaline's rigid programming to make it easier for Hanford's residents to rescue Boys and Men from the underground society.

They made it down the stairs and across the building to the cafeteria. The lights in the room were dimmed, and 62 smirked at the thought that maybe Blue had already tired of his scheme to keep all the lights on.

They entered, and found that only the lights directly above the table they'd been using, and the few tables closest to it, were lit. Blue was hunched over a bowl, slurping his breakfast from his spoon.

"What's with the lights?" 00 asked.

Blue pulled the spoon from his mouth. "Sunny told me it was a waste to keep them all on," he shrugged. "Besides, if we're going to put—" The thin Woman entered from the kitchen with a bowl in hand. She peered at 00 and 62 in surprise, set her breakfast down on the closest table, and ducked back into the kitchen. Blue lowered his voice. "If we're going to put you-know-what together, we should save some power."

Sunny re-emerged, two fresh bowls of food in her hands. She carried them over to the table and set them down in front of 62 and 00. "Porridge," she said before going back to retrieve her own bowl.

"Thanks," they said in unison.

"It's best when it's hot," Blue advised. He lowered his head over his bowl and slurped in another spoonful.

Sunny settled down in a seat across from Blue, and the two latecomers settled into the remaining unoccupied seats. 62 ate a few bites, then remembered how upset Sunny had been over his reaction to the sweet potatoes. He looked up at her, poking at the porridge with his spoon. "It's good," he offered in earnest. "Thank you."

Sunny smiled, then blew the heat off her own spoonful of wet grit. "It's pretty bland, but it'll stick to our insides and keep us full for a while."

Blue finished his meal and pushed his bowl away. He reclined in his chair, attempting to look casual although his gaze fell time and again on Sunny. She ignored him, seeming to be engrossed in the pale, creamy breakfast in the bowl in front of her. 62 and 00 ate their fill, pushing their bowls to the side and sitting quietly while Sunny continued her painstakingly slow eating. 62's foot jiggled on the floor beneath him nervously and 00 looked up to the ceiling, his mouth moving in time to his counting of the light fixtures in the room.

Finally, after what felt like an eternity, Sunny cleaned the last bite of porridge from her spoon and pushed the empty bowl away. She placed her elbows on the tabletop and rested her chin in cupped hands. Looking around with glistening eyes, she said, "So, I suppose you're ready to hear my story?"

All three Boys shifted in their seats. "I think so," 62 said.

"I know I am," 00 agreed.

Blue nodded and Sunny cleared her throat. She looked at 62 and lifted one corner of her mouth in a nostalgic smile. "Before you came to Hanford, I was a teacher. I understand that my friend Parker has taken over for me." Her smile drooped slightly, and she turned her eyes down to look at the empty bowl in front of her. "From the time that we are young girls, we're told that when the Oosa come, it's our duty to volunteer to go with them, and to bring back new children. I was sure that volunteering was the right path for me. I prepared for it all my life. Then, I met Parker and," she breathed in haltingly, "well, I began to second-guess that decision. With him, it might have been possible for us to have our own child, without me having to go to the Oosa at all."

Sunny seemed to shrink before the Boys' eyes with each word she spoke. Despite the obvious toll it was taking on her, after a brief pause she continued. "Then, the time came for me to choose. Would I stay in

Hanford, or go with the Oosa to fulfill my responsibility to my people? I began to think, why not do both? There was no rule that said a Woman can only carry one child. I decided, foolishly, to go with the Oosa. I'd fulfill my obligation to my elders, come back with child, and after I'd birthed and raised the infant, I could partner with Parker and we could have a child of our own." Sunny chuckled bitterly and shook her head in her hands. "I was stupid. But I didn't know that then."

Blue's voice was a soft whisper when he asked, "What happened when you went to the Oosa?"

Sunny closed her eyes and sat in silence. A single tear trickled down her cheek. When her eyes opened again, they were vacant. She seemed to see a world beyond the cafeteria. She muttered, "Nothing we thought would happen. Seven of us volunteered. They took us straight from the gates of Hanford to their doctors. The Oosa hoped to send all of us back with children in our wombs, as quickly as possible. They tried three times to implant a fetus in me, but each attempt ended in failure. I tried to be happy when Sasha, Flora, and Kat got word that their pregnancies had successfully begun, but my heart broke that I wasn't with them when they were taken back to Hanford. Eventually, the Oosa gave up on the rest of us. Skye, Robin, Juniper, and I were separated. I was taken away from the hospital, sent somewhere entirely different. There was a doctor, but he wasn't gentle like the hospital doctors were. He said he was glad that my pregnancies had failed, because that meant I was going to help him."

"Help him with what?" 00 asked with wide eyes.

More tears fell as Sunny thought back. "He said I was going to help them unlock the mystery of why our

Women stay living while their people die. He said something inside me was the key to saving the Oosa."

62 looked at his friends. Their long, worried faces matched the strain that he felt in his own. 62 laid a gentle hand on Sunny's shoulder. "Did they find what it was? Did you solve their mystery?"

Sunny drew back from 62's gaze. She crossed her arms in front of her chest, and she looked down at her body. "I don't know," she said between quiet sobs. "He did tests on me, small ones at first. A couple of blood tests and saliva samples. Then, he said they had to do surgery." Her voice trembled and cracked. "So many surgeries."

"How did you get away?" Blue asked with anxious eyes.

Sunny smiled through the cascade of tears. "After each surgery, they'd leave me alone for days, or weeks, to recover. Then, more tests and more surgery would come. The last one I had, I could hardly move after. It hurt so much. So, when I was alone, I loosened a couple of the wires to the monitors they had me hooked to. Then, I played dead."

The admission pushed the Boys back into their chairs in shock. They stared at Sunny, marveling at the trauma she was describing as she wiped the tears from her cheeks. She heaved a few more dry sobs, then continued her story. "They moved me to a room with the rest of their dead. I saw Juniper there first. Nearby, Skye and Robin lay. But they weren't pretending. They were gone. And, there were others, Men, Women, and even some children. Rows and rows of people. But that was good. It meant they wouldn't be back to dispose of me right away. I waited for the workers to be done with their jobs, and after they turned out the lights for the night, I snuck out of the building. Then, I ran."

"You just…ran? All the way here?" 00 exclaimed.

Sunny nodded. "It wasn't easy. The first few days I was on my own, all I could think about was going back to Hanford, and to Parker. But when I finally saw the lights of town, I realized I couldn't go back there."

"Why not?" 62 demanded. "Parker misses you. He told our whole class. He even cried!"

Sunny dropped her hands to her lap. A hard focus returned to her eyes and she locked her gaze on 62. "Because now, I'm flawed. Just like you. They wouldn't accept me the way I am."

"But you belong there," Blue urged. "Hanford is your home."

"It was my home when I was a Woman," Sunny said through clenched teeth. "But now, I'm nothing."

"I don't understand." 00 screwed up his face.

Sunny gestured to the flat, sharp angles of her body. "Can't you see? They took everything from me. They took the parts from me that make me whole. All the parts I need to carry a child are gone. I'm empty. Fruitless. A desert wrapped in skin."

"That's impossible! Inhuman!" Blue slammed his hand down on the table, lunging halfway out of his seat. "How could they do that to you? To anyone?"

Sunny gave Blue a bitter smile. She tilted her head and shifted her eyes to Blue's. "Because to them, we're not human. We're the spawn of clones. The devices of Curie. They only allow us to live so they can better their understanding of themselves."

"So, the Oosa aren't clones?" 62's mind was reeling. "Then what are they?"

"They're imperfect," Sunny said in a low, dangerous voice. "Something has happened to them, and they need Curie to save them. They're broken, and they think that somewhere in our bodies is the code that will fix them."

CHAPTER 6

Sunny retreated to her room after telling the Boys her story. Blue followed quietly behind so he'd know where to check on her later. She hadn't emerged from her room since. Now, evening was falling again, and the Boys were still so bewildered by her revelations, that they hadn't made any progress on getting settled. 62 couldn't stop wondering why so much of the world was intent on harming others.

He'd never been through anything nearly as brutal as Sunny had, but he was no stranger to doctors with ulterior motives. Back when he'd been a little kid in Adaline, a doctor plugged him into a Machine. He wanted to try to zap 62's brain to get rid of his dreams. And later, a Man from Adaline's defense group hooked him up to a device to use those same dreams to track down other dreamers. A wave of angry sadness overcame 62 as he realized that the people and programs in charge of their lives were intent on fixing people by changing who they were. But while mixing up a child's insides was unconscionable, taking parts of a person's body to try to fix someone else? That was pure madness.

Blue, who had known Sunny before she'd been taken by the Oosa, was hit the hardest by her story. He paced the halls, alternating between muttering to himself and shouting into the echoing building that he'd make the Oosa pay for what they'd done. There were no breaks in his ranting, except for the occasional hike up to the third floor to check on Sunny. Each time he'd gone up, he'd taken her something to eat or drink, only to return with the same food or cup of cider. Then, he'd start his tirade anew, distraught that the Oosa had damaged Sunny so wholly that she refused to eat or drink.

00 withdrew as well, tucking himself away in a corner with a computer manual that Mattie had packed for them. He rarely turned a page, though. Just stared at the same diagram for ages, mumbling that none of it made sense. 62 was sure 00 knew more about computers than anyone else outside of Adaline, so he couldn't have been confused by the manual. It was more likely that his thoughts were with Sunny and the Oosa.

"We have to find out more about them," 62 said aloud to himself. Blue was in the main lobby waving his fists in the air, and 00 was on the other end of the cafeteria with his book, so no one heard his statement. But he knew it was true. They had to find out why the Oosa would hurt the Women of Hanford, and discover a way to stop them. But he had no idea where to start.

62 walked over to the corner where 00 rested with the book across his knees. "We have to do something," 62 announced.

00's eyes trailed up from the book, slowly resting on 62. "Something about what?"

"About Sunny. The Oosa. Adaline. All of it."

00 brushed a strand of hair from his forehead. "I don't know what we can do. We haven't even found out what happened to all the dreamers in Adaline yet. And now there's all this. It's too much, 62. There's nothing a couple of dumb clones can do."

"You're right. It's too much." 62 dragged a chair closer to where his friend sat and slouched down in it. "But we can't do nothing. I mean, it's all so *wrong*."

"We were going to hook up N302 and see if it could duplicate itself. But now that seems pointless. What would we even do with it if it worked? It's illegal technology and a waste of time. I want to stop thinking about the dumb bot and do something useful instead. But I don't know what to do to help." 00 looked down at the open pages on his lap and sighed.

Blue marched into the room, his jaw set in determination. 62 raised his hand in a half-hearted wave, then dropped it again when he realized no greeting was coming from the bitter Boy with blue eyes. "We were just talking about how useless this all is," 62 explained. "Setting up a computer is pointless now. We've got to find a way to help Sunny instead."

"Building the bot is exactly what we're going to do," Blue declared. "N302's a programmed Nurse, right? Set up to help the doc fix people underground?"

"Yeah," 00 answered with a confused nod.

"Well, we're going to use it to help Sunny."

"What?" 62 raised an eyebrow. "We don't have doctors here."

Blue put his hands on his hips and tilted his head. "You're right. We don't have doctors. But N302 is a blasted medical bot for crying out loud. It can tell us what to do. And if we can't figure out how to follow its instructions, maybe it can help us think of some other way to help Sunny."

00 nodded slowly. "That might work. But we'd have to tell her about the computer first, and ask if she's okay with us using it. If we just start poking at her, she's going to know something's up. And with as upset as she's been since we got here, I don't want to surprise her with anything."

"When should we talk to her? Now?" 62 asked.

"I don't think so," Blue said. His whole face deepened with his frown. "She's been through too much today. Let's talk to her tomorrow."

"I wish Mattie was here to help," 00 said. "She may not be the nicest Girl, but she's still a Girl all the same. She might know how to talk to her own kind better than us."

"Her own kind?" 62 blurted out with an involuntary snort. "She's a Girl, not a coyote."

Blue squinted his eyes and scowled. "You know what I mean."

"I haven't been able to dream with her since we left," 62 complained. He looked at his friends. "But, I can keep trying. If I end up sharing a dream with her, should I tell her everything?"

Blue shook his head. "She's not going to like hearing what the Oosa did to Sunny. I mean, you know how much she wants to go live with them when she's old enough. No, I don't think telling her everything in a dream is a great idea. Crushing people's lifelong wishes is something you should do in person, you know?"

"Fair enough. Do you think there's a less traumatic way to tell her why Sunny's here and how badly she needs help?"

Blue and 00 considered the question. 00 was the first to pipe up. "I don't think so. We need her to know Sunny's here, so she can help us figure out how to talk to her without making her cry all the time."

"True," Blue agreed. "We need all the help we can get. But, don't tell her too much about the Oosa stuff. Just explain that Sunny escaped from them and came up here to hide. Make sure she knows that Sunny being here is a secret, and she's not to tell anyone else. The last thing we need is for some hateful guard like Joan to be sent by the council to check on her."

"What about Parker?" The air went silent at 62's question. "He'll be furious if he finds out that she's been found and no one told him."

"Fine. Mattie and Parker. But no one else, alright? This all has to stay a secret until Sunny is ready to tell the council about what happened." Blue sighed. "*If* she's ever ready."

62 stood up, causing the chair to scrape noisily across the smooth floor. He shoved his hands in his pockets. "Well, I guess I'm going to get ready for bed then."

00 craned his neck to look at the barred windows at the far end of the cafeteria. "It's not dark yet. Mattie won't be asleep for a while."

"True," 62 admitted. "But last night I didn't get to sleep until the moon was so high I couldn't see it out my window anymore. And with everything that's gone on today, I don't think I'll be able to dive right into a dream.

May as well start staring at the ceiling early and get it out of the way."

62 bid his friends goodnight, then tromped through the building toward his room. He was too distracted to care about manners, and let each door he passed through slam closed behind him. His footfalls were heavy on the stairs, echoing with the sound of a thousand steps in the stairwell. There was no point in being quiet. No reason to be polite. Nobody would hear his angry trampling except two clones and a broken Woman trying to escape her past.

62 stopped dead in his tracks. Sunny was desperate to escape the doctor that haunted her. 62 had been doing the same thing since leaving Adaline. His eyes glazed over, and his shoulders drooped. Tears welled in his eyes and flowed in hot rivers down his cheeks. Maybe he and Sunny weren't so different after all.

CHAPTER 7

62 covered his bedroom window with a blanket pilfered from another room. He planned on using it as a makeshift curtain, blotting out light from outside. He was pleased to discover the blanket was wide enough to tuck around the curved bars encasing the window, keeping all but a thin shaft of sunlight from entering the room. His makeshift window covering complete, he put on pajamas and crawled into bed. The blankets enveloped him in a warm cocoon, and he wiped his eyes with the palms of his hands as he relaxed into the comfort of the bed. He settled into the warmth of the bedsheets, and then, his eyes flicked open and he stared into the dim twilight of his room.

Despite his intense desire to fall asleep so he could search for Mattie in his dreams, 62 was inexplicably awake. He felt his limbs twitch beneath the soft covers and the discomfort of his wiggling muscles caused him to roll to one side, and then the other, as he tried to find a place where his body would be still. Time seemed to creep forward while 62 tossed and turned. Finally, he gave up his hunt for dreams.

Pushing the covers back, 62 sat up in bed and pressed his hands into the mattress. He hated nights like this, when sleep refused to come. He groaned in frustration, then pushed himself out of the bed and flicked on the overhead light. In the closet, hidden under a pile of clothes, was a book that Blue had packed for 62 during his exile from Hanford. Mattie said it was a book for small children, but 62 loved it anyway. He pulled the book from its hiding place and turned the cover over in his hands. Although Mattie, who took care of the library back in Hanford, had given him all the books he could ever hope to read, *Charlotte's Web* was his favorite book in all the world.

62 left the light on as he crawled back into bed with his book. He'd read *Charlotte's Web* dozens of times, and had most of it memorized. 62 didn't bother starting at the beginning. Instead, he let the book fall open in his lap and started reading in the middle of the story. He read ten pages, then thirty, and soon he'd lost count of the pages he'd turned. It wasn't until Wilbur was going to the county fair that 62's eyelids began to feel heavy and he set the book on the floor beside the bed. He got up briefly to shut out the light, then swaddled himself in the blankets once more. He rolled over on the mattress and drifted into sleep.

Dreams didn't come immediately, and 62 didn't know how long he'd been slumbering before he felt the world around him shift. He found himself sitting on a chair in the smaller of Hanford's two cafeterias, the one reserved for Adaline refugees. The division of the cafeterias was only a small taste of the separation that he and the other clones experienced while living in Hanford. Their housing was separate, their schooling, even the food they ate.

62 looked around him. The cafeteria was an eerie gray, void of the color of everyday life. And although the refugee cafeteria was rarely bustling, in the dream it was completely empty. 62 got up and trailed a hand along the backs of the chairs as he made his way to the food counter. Rows and rows of abandoned bowls and trays rested on the countertop, as if they were waiting to be filled by some unseen hand. Although he'd need a mask to explore outside if he were awake, 62 passed through the door in his dream without any fear of the dust traveling on the wind outside.

Here, too, the world was gray. The air was still and silent. 62 closed his eyes, willing Hanford's population to appear, but when he opened them, the streets were still as barren as before. He tried to make people appear a second time, and then a third, and when nothing happened, he frowned in disappointment. Controlling dreams was something that he'd practiced frequently when he was younger, but his grasp of it had faded since leaving Adaline. After learning how dangerous the dreams could be for him and his friends, he'd stopped trying so hard to have them. He'd had a brief resurgence in his desire to dream after he discovered Mattie was also a dreamer, but then Hanford had thrown him out and turned him off the idea of dreams again.

Now, he wanted control of his dreams back, but was discovering it wasn't as easy as simply wishing them into existence.

62 shoved his hands into his pockets and began walking in the direction of the library. As he walked, he focused on the dilapidated building, imagining its crumbling façade and rusted doorway. This time, the use of his mind worked, and rather than having to trudge his way through the entire desolate town, a grayscale visage of the library appeared before him. 62 climbed the stairs, drawing his hand from his pocket only once he was within arm's reach of the door. He opened it and went inside, expecting to see the warm candlelight flickering within.

The library was dark. 62 focused on the candle's wicks and several of them burst to life. What little light they cast showed 62 a new horror; the library's shelves were empty. 62 searched the aisles, and shelf after shelf showed itself to be bare. Not a single book rested among the racks. Mattie was nowhere to be found. 62 explored the back of the library, checking the book repair room where they had stored N302. That room, too, was empty. All the stacks of tattered books, tools, and spare computer parts were gone.

"What happened?" 62 said aloud. He paused, waiting for some phantom in his mind to answer, but no reply came. It was as if his mind was blotting out the home he once hoped would be his, stealing the comfort of its details just to spite him. 62 returned to the main room of the library, righted an overturned chair, and plopped himself down in it. He put both hands in front of him, palms up, closed his eyes, and imagined his secret journal and the pencil that he used to write in it. He waited for their weight to fill his hands, but they never came. He opened his eyes and looked at the bare skin of his palms, wrinkled his brow, and then tried again. Still, nothing.

He dropped his hands to his lap, deciding to try something different entirely. He thought of his dear friend, 71, the Man who had taught him to harness his dreams from the very beginning. He hadn't tried to contact his old teacher in weeks. The last time he'd connected with 71, he'd been captured by the people in Adaline who wanted to snuff out creative thought. But now, 62 felt like he had little to lose if 71 felt his presence again. He thought of the old Man, standing in front of a classroom, laughing and prodding his students to find pleasure in the mundane topics they were forced to learn. He could imagine every detail, from the long snow-colored beard to the twinkle of his brown eyes.

A pinprick of white light appeared before 62. He rose from his seat, moved toward it, and pressed his hand against it, willing it to expand so that he could look inside. The white light twinkled, its light fading in and out of his vision, and then instead of expanding the way he'd expected, it fizzled out, leaving a thin wisp of smoke dissipating in the air.

62 let loose a growl of frustration that shook the empty bookshelves and made the air around him shudder. Anger rose up inside him, a fire that burned his very soul. He thought about his failure to control the dream and the flame spread beneath his feet. It spread over the floor, reached the library's fixtures, and climbed the walls until the entire building was engulfed. The ceiling caught fire and began to crumble. As the ceiling began to open, the walls groaned and fell around him. 62 marveled that the flames didn't hurt. The inferno was a part of him, destroying the blank shell of Hanford that he'd imagined.

His voice roared over the fire, and the flames spread even farther. Soon, every building in sight burned, and the sky was nothing more than a pillow of black smoke.

62 closed his eyes to the blaze consuming the world around him. He hugged his arms close and began to cry. His tears evaporated from the heat of the air, sizzling out of existence the second they landed on his cheeks. He wailed, long and loud, his strained voice ringing in his ears. The heat of his anger fed the burning world around him, causing it to roar with smoldering coals after the last of the buildings had burned to ash. The weight of his failure pressed him down into the melting land. Thoughts of Sunny's pain, Parker's grief, and 71 and 42's disappearances weighted him to the spot. He couldn't save any of them. Couldn't even dream of protecting them. Hardly could dream at all, it seemed. 62 curled into a ball, fell to his side, and allowed the flames of despair to consume him.

62 opened one bleary eye beneath the covers. His throat was raw from crying in his sleep, and his pillow was wet with tears. 62 pressed the heels of his hands into his eye sockets to stay the flow of tears. In Adaline, a Nurse would be here with sleep-spray to calm him. In Hanford, his neighbors would've arrived to check on him to see what was wrong. But here, in the nearly empty jailhouse, 62 suffered the aftermath of his nightmare alone.

CHAPTER 8

62 shuffled downstairs in a groggy stupor. The last nightmare he'd had consumed his thoughts all night, and he'd hardly gotten another wink of sleep. His exhaustion was amplified by 00's devastating cheerfulness.

"Good morning!" 00 came close and wrapped his arm around 62's slumped shoulders. "I had such a great night last night! After you went to bed, Blue and I turned the power on in the elevator shaft and got the lift working. We pulled that bed out of the room next to mine and brought a couple tables up from the cafeteria. They barely fit through the doors, but we made it work. I can't wait to talk to Sunny about N302. Once she agrees to work with the bot, we're going up to start running cables for power. Blue said there's plenty of juice to run the bot, but we've got to run lines for more outlets, especially if we're going to build the second computer."

62 grunted. 00 paused and looked at him, as if for the first time. 00 frowned and asked, "How are you doing? Rough night?"

"Tried to connect to Mattie," 62 answered as he shuffled toward breakfast. "Didn't work."

"Too bad. We could use her help talking to Sunny." 00's momentary tight-lipped concern was broken by an irritatingly bright smile. "No matter though, we'll figure it out."

"Breakfast?" 62 muttered.

"There's leftovers from dinner. Blue's heating them up."

62 nodded, watching his feet drag across the floor tiles through half-lidded eyes. He loved his brother with all his heart, but wished the cheerful lout would leave him alone. 00 continued to chatter, but 62 tuned the words out. It was too much for his tired mind to bear and he was thankful when they reached the kitchen. Blue was standing at the stove, stirring a pot of yesterday's stew. 62 breathed the kitchen air in. It was filled with the sweet scents of the warming breakfast. Moist and meaty.

"That smells good," 62 said. He moved closer, leaning over the pot and sniffing the air again.

"It's always better the second day," Blue decreed with a smile. He glanced over at his friend and lifted an eyebrow. "What happened to you? You look terrible."

62 drew back from the pot. He moved toward a nearby counter, leaning on the edge. He opened his mouth to reply, but couldn't get a word out before 00 jumped in.

"Nightmare," 00 blurted out. "He tried to do that dream-share thing with Mattie, but couldn't find her or something."

"Nightmares are the bad ones, right?" Blue asked. 62 shrugged his shoulders in answer. "Too bad. Maybe you'll feel better after a bit of breakfast. We need you to help get N302 set up after we eat. We've got a room set up for the computer already."

"I heard," 62 grumbled. "I'll help. I want to eat and have a chance to wake up first."

"You can wake up on the way!" 00 chirped. "We've got to talk to Sunny before we do any of it."

"Even before we eat?" 62 whined.

00 nodded, but Blue said, "We're taking breakfast up to her room. I want to make sure she eats something, and I doubt she's coming down here. If she was coming down for breakfast, she'd be here already." He pulled the spoon he was using out of the pot, blew the steam off the stew, and took a small sip, smacking his lips after. "Will one of you grab some bowls?"

00 grabbed spoons while 62 gathered four bowls. Blue shut off the stove and wrapped the hot pot and its lid in a blanket to keep it warm. He wrapped his arms around the toasty container and the trio headed out of the cafeteria, toward the rear of the building.

"Where are we going?" 62 asked as they passed the door to the stairwell.

"To the elevator," said Blue. "No sense hauling all this up the stairs while it's powered up."

When they arrived, 62 marveled at how large the doors were. Easily twice the width of the elevator he'd seen in Adaline. The pair of steel doors separated after 00 pressed the button, revealing a box nearly as large as his bedroom upstairs was.

"Isn't it huge?" 00 cried out as he rushed through the doors.

"Why's it so big?" 62 asked Blue. A thin, brown streak of liquid seeped through one side of the blanket, and 62 helped Blue adjust the heavy pot to put it upright again.

"Not sure," Blue admitted. "But I'd guess it made getting all the furniture upstairs easy."

The elevator was slow, which gave 00 plenty of time to jump into the air, letting himself fall back to the rising floor with a thud. Each time he did, the elevator groaned, and 62 leaned against the wall, hoping that the ancient device wouldn't plummet to the earth. Blue seemed unaffected by the creak and wobble of the elevator. 62 couldn't tell if it was because he didn't mind 00's antics, or because he was so focused on watching the floors tick by on the display above the door. When they made it to the fourth floor, the lift stopped, and the giant elevator doors slid open again.

If it hadn't been for the number stamped on the side of the door, 62 wouldn't have known which floor they'd stopped on. The floorplan was identical to the ones the Boys had chosen for their rooms. Blue stepped off the elevator first, and the other two followed him down the hall, past a few doorways. They stopped in front of a door that had glass jars hanging from its frame, clustered in a heap over the doorknob. It would be impossible for someone to reach the handle without the glass tinkling a warning.

"Guess she doesn't want to be surprised?" 00 said.

"Shhh!" Blue hissed in anger. He squinted his eyes and shook his head at 00 as a warning. His expression hardly softened when he turned to 62. "Knock for me, will ya?"

62 did as he asked. There was a long pause of silence afterward, followed by the soft sound of jars tapping against one another as the handle beneath them turned. The door opened a crack, and 62 saw the familiar links of chain keeping it from opening any farther. It was the same kind of lock that he had in his room. Sunny's hazel eye peered through the crack, gazing down at Blue and his companions suspiciously.

"What's all this?" her whispery voice croaked.

"We brought breakfast," Blue said, lifting the stain-covered heap higher in his arms so she could see it.

"It took all three of you?" Sunny asked in a rasping voice.

"We wanted to talk to you about something, too," 62 said from behind Blue. He could barely see Sunny's wandering eye from his place behind Blue.

"Another talk?" Sunny pulled her face away from the door's opening. "Sorry, I don't think I'm up to talking today."

"Please?" 00 begged. The spoons rattled between his fingers as he pressed his hands together in appeal. "It's important. We think we might be able to help you."

The door closed. The Boys dropped their heads in shared disappointment. Just as they began to turn back toward the elevator, 62 heard the clasp of the chain lock scraping as Sunny unlatched it. The jars jangled again when the knob turned, and Sunny opened the door fully.

She stood, blocking the open doorway. Sunny's arms were crossed against her chest, as if she were hugging herself for support. She was paler than normal, and had deep red circles under her eyes. She seemed somehow thinner than she had the day before, and 62 wondered how it was possible for a person to shrink so much in a day.

"Help me how?"

The Boys rushed the door, easing their way around the hanging jars and Sunny's thin form at the threshold. All three of them were in the room before Sunny realized what was happening. Sunny's sunken eyes passed over the intruders, and it wasn't until all three Boys had already entered the room that her head turned to acknowledge their invasion. Sunny left the door open and made her way through the crush of adolescent bodies to cross the room to her bed. Without a word, she climbed onto the mattress and wrapped the thick pile of blankets over her shoulders. Beneath the mound of blankets, which 62 assumed she must have taken from the surrounding rooms, Sunny looked less like a frail, battered Woman, and more like the soft, powdery snowbanks he'd played in the last time it snowed.

Blue set the pot of stew in the center of the room and set about unwrapping it. The pot's lid had gone askew, and a few of the vegetables and some of the broth had escaped from their vessel, coating the inside of the insulating blanket. There was still plenty of stew left inside the pot, and Blue signaled the others to hand him bowls and spoons so he could dish up breakfast. He gave Sunny the first bowl, so full it nearly overflowed. She had to unbury her hands from their blanketed tomb before she could accept the offering, but once she had the bowl and a spoon in hand, she used the pile of blankets across her lap as a makeshift table, setting her meal down as she watched the others collect theirs.

62's stomach grumbled as he accepted his portion. He wasn't feeling nearly as polite as Sunny and scooped up a bite immediately after getting his hands on the bowl. "It's still warm!" 62 exclaimed before taking another bite.

"Of course it is," Blue said with a smirk. "I learned to wrap up food a long time ago. If we had some paper scrap and a crate or two, I could keep this stuff warm all day."

"How is that possible?" 62 asked.

"It's a way of controlling heat dissipation," Sunny explained. "The more layers of insulation you apply to a heat source, the longer it's able to retain the energy that produces the heat. Now that the pot is unwrapped, it will cool at a much faster rate. It'll dissipate as it tries to warm the air around it."

"So, what if we'd wrapped it in four blankets?" 00 asked.

Sunny's face softened into a brief half-smile. "Well, in theory, it would have stayed hotter, longer. But in practice, you probably would have spilled a lot more stew."

All three Boys grinned at Sunny's quiet joke, and felt a sense of accomplishment when she dipped her spoon into the stew's broth and pulled a small amount to her lips. "Perfect temperature. Well done."

"Thanks," Blue said with pride.

Sunny took another sip, then set the spoon in the bowl. She watched her audience settle onto the floor beside her bed, diving into their meals. For a moment the room was silent, aside from the sounds of clinking spoons. It didn't take long for curiosity to get the best of her. "You said you came up here to help me. Were you just tricking me into a picnic on my floor?"

00 shook his head. Without swallowing the chunk of potato in his mouth, he said, "Nope. We've gotta shecret tah tell ya."

"How will a secret help me?" Sunny asked with a raised eyebrow.

Blue set his bowl on the floor beside him and took a deep breath. "You know that pile of junk we lugged up here?" Sunny nodded and Blue continued. "Well, it's not just junk. It's a Machine from Adaline."

"Not just any Machine," 00 exclaimed. "It's called a computer. It stores and processes data, and we think some of that data might be medical information that can help you since we don't have a doctor out here."

"A Machine?" Sunny scrunched up her face with suspicion. "How did three Boys get their hands on something like that?"

62, Blue, and 00 took turns telling Sunny the entire story of how N302 came to be. They told her how, when 62 was still living in Adaline, Doctor 2442 had programmed N302 to be a helper in his underground activities. 2442 had been altering the data chips of clones like 62 in secret, making it easier for them to blend in with the other, more perfect, residents of Adaline.

62 told her how someone had discovered his dream anomaly and tricked him into using his ability to ferret out other dreamers, setting into motion their capture and destruction. Blue explained how 42 had disappeared mysteriously, leaving behind bits and pieces of N302 in his lab. 00 told the daring tale of the rescue mission he and Blue had been on when they'd discovered the parts. And both Blue and 00 stumbled over one another's words as they explained how they'd convinced the other outlaws to bring the parts back to Hanford.

The three Boys regaled her with the tale of Blue being arrested for stealing garbage to build solar cells and a battery bank to power the parts, and told her about Mattie, who'd helped them to crawl through the derelict bombed-out district on Hanford's outskirts to find the hardware needed to build the computer. Sunny laughed when they described Auntie's secret enablement of their venture. She gasped as they described smuggling the bot's parts to the library, and was on the edge of her seat when they told her about watching the Machine come to life for the first time. They explained that the Machine was aware of itself, and had declared itself their friend. And finally, they told her that they believed with its knowledge, it may be able to stand in as a medical aid.

"But you didn't know I was going to be here. So, why did you really decide to bring the device to the jailhouse?" Sunny's curious tone was tinged with suspicion.

The Boys gawked at one another. 62 came up with an answer first. He blurted out, "Because since I was already in trouble with Joan and the others for dreaming, it made sense to bring N302 so Mattie wouldn't get in trouble if someone found it."

Sunny looked down at the bowl of stew in her lap. The meal had gone cold during the lengthy storytelling, but she stirred her spoon through the thick liquid anyway. She fished out a carrot and chewed the cold vegetable thoughtfully. When the bite was gone, she asked, "You really think this bot can help me?"

00 nodded. "N302 is smart. Smarter than anybody I've ever met. Plus, 42 tweaked its program. These guys say 42 was the smartest doc in Adaline before he disappeared." With this, he gestured toward Blue and 62. "If we set it up, I know it'll help us figure out what to do."

"What if I say no, that I don't want a Machine to know about me?"

Blue answered, "Then when we set it up, we won't tell it you're here. It can't see or hear, so you could be in the same room as it, and it'd never know." He scooted closer to Sunny, reached up, and took her hand in his. "But, when we do talk to it, I hope you'll let us tell it about you. Maybe it'll know what to do, and maybe it won't. We can't know if we don't ask."

Sunny squeezed Blue's hand, then withdrew hers. She looked over at the others. "You're going to rebuild and power this bot, no matter what I say, aren't you?" 00 and 62 gave one another a sideways glance, then looked back at her and nodded. Sunny's mouth twitched upward at the corners. "I thought so. I have to admit, if I had a gadget like that, I'd have a hard time leaving it alone. Alright," she declared with a nod, "let's build the Machine and see what it says."

The three Boys erupted in a loud cheer. 62 clapped his hands and 00 pumped his fists in the air. Blue rose from the floor beside Sunny and gave her a quick kiss on the cheek. All four outcasts grinned at one another, the excitement in the room infecting Sunny's pallid features. Blue set about collecting the dishes, and 00 picked up the stained blanket they'd used to insulate the pot.

"When will you start?" Sunny asked as the Boys prepared to leave.

"As soon as the dishes are done." 62 grinned, grabbing the handles of the stew pot.

"To the kitchen!" 00 cheered. Blue and 62 followed him out the door, parading down the hall in a line of celebration, dishes clattering and pot banging as they went.

CHAPTER 9

Assembling the computer proved to be more difficult than any of them had expected. The trip from Hanford, through the wasteland, and up the trail to the jailhouse had not been kind to the components. The Boys had taken great care to keep it covered, but their efforts had been in vain. The shock of the trip had dislodged several internal pieces, and the entire Machine was coated in a thick layer of dust. Sunny checked the metal with the radiation counter, and despite the rest of the bad news, the computer didn't set the needles jumping on the dials.

Before anything could be put together, 00 disconnected every component and set 62 and Blue to gently cleaning the metal bits. It was tedious work, and the excitement of the project waned as dust was swept from each tiny surface. Soon the room was filled with the sighs and gasps of Boys exasperated by the grime tucked into nooks and crannies of boards, boxes, and wires.

When the final part of the computer had been wiped clean, the friends loaded the parts into their wagon and dragged their prize to the elevator. They rode the lift to the top floor, and wheeled the pieces of their electronic companion to the newly arranged computer room. A new wave of anticipation arrived as they began unloading the parts. 62 dug through the pile until he found the computer assembly manual that Mattie had sent, and he pulled up a chair before spreading the computer's diagram across one of the tables. Blue propped himself up on the edge of the other table, watching 00 begin building the bot in silence.

Sunny arrived at mid-day with freshly baked bread. As the Boys took a break to eat, Sunny inched herself cautiously to the computer parts. She crossed her arms as she leaned over the mess on the table, looking at the partially built computer as if it were a wild animal that might strike her at any moment. Blue hopped off the table and stood next to Sunny, his air of confidence a stark contrast to Sunny's anxious gaze.

"What do you think?" Blue asked.

"I'm not sure," Sunny admitted. "Will it be much bigger?"

"A bit." Blue set about showing her the computer's case, which would cover the messy array of wires and circuits once everything was set in place. He explained the functions of the monitor and the power cables, and even showed her where they'd run wires from adjoining rooms to make sure there'd be enough power to turn the bot on.

Sunny looked over the mounds of components and her face scrunched. "Once you put all these parts together," she said, pointing to the table she and Blue were standing near, "what are you going to do with all of those?" She gestured at the second table, piled high with even more pieces.

"Spare parts," 62 choked. He moved across the room, leaning against the front of the second table and making himself as wide as possible to block Sunny's view. The attempt was fruitless. 62's gangly body was no match for the tangle of computer bits heaped upon the table. They hadn't told her that they'd be building a second bot, or that N302 would duplicate if it could.

Sunny nodded. "I suppose there aren't many replacements if something breaks out here."

"Yeah, without bringing this stuff with us, if something on this clunker went haywire, it'd be the end of N302. Backups and duplication are the name of the game." 00 patted the computer's monitor as a mother might pat her child's head. "With how hard we worked to get it all together, we'd hate to lose it."

"How long will it take to finish putting it together?"

"Not too much longer," 00 answered. "Although, it'll take a while to get it powered up and running programs." He started tinkering again and Sunny took a seat in the chair he'd occupied during his lunch break.

After a moment, Sunny's head tilted once more. "In Adaline, you are raised by these Machines?"

"Yes. Well, sort of." 62 tried to find the right way to explain the difference between the hunk of metal sitting in front of them and the sleek bots back home. "The program on the Machine is the same one that Nurses and other bots use. So, we can type questions to

N302 and usually get the same answers we'd get if we were talking to a PTS unit in Adaline."

"But you don't always get the same answers?"

"Not always. The bots back home are connected to a giant network. While a unit is talking to you, it's pulling data from the Head Machine, so it knows everything about you. But N302 is all on its own. It can't access the information that the network would normally give it." 00 paused his explanation to sift through the pile of equipment to find a part he needed. "The bad thing about having N302 in this little case is that it only has whatever information that was saved to its memory when it was taken apart. Plus, whatever we've told it since then. But it doesn't have a way to download more information from the Head Machine."

"Is that why Auntie allowed you to build it? Because it's cut off from the other bots?" Sunny shifted uncomfortably in her seat.

"Maybe," Blue shrugged. "She said that she wanted to find out what happened to Doc 42. We'd all hoped N302 would have had some answers. But when we built it the first time, we found out the doc pulled his Nurse apart before he disappeared."

62 heaved a great sigh. "Unless we can find a way to get inside Adaline, we may never know what happened to the others who could dream like me."

Sunny looked shocked. "There are others who dream?"

62 hadn't meant to let the admission come out so casually. He kept forgetting Sunny hadn't known he was a dreamer like the other Hanford Women did. "There are. I've tried to stop being a dreamer, but something's wrong in my brain that makes it happen sometimes anyway. I think most other people with the anomaly try to stop

their dreaming, too. It's scary, and it makes us too different from everyone else."

"Dreams are a rare gift," Sunny said in a somber voice. "What's it like?"

As Blue assisted 00 with the computer, 62 did his best to describe a dream in a way that Sunny might understand. He told her that it was like being awake, but with unlimited powers. He described making forests grow out of dry sand, and bringing pictures from books to life. 62 told her about what he'd learned of oneironauts from the books at the library, and about how he could choose to change a dream as he explored it. He was careful to avoid telling her about sharing his dreams with others, though.

"It sounds wonderful," Sunny said finally. "Like reading a book and having the words come to life."

"That's a great way to describe it!" 62 exclaimed. He laughed at himself. "That would've been an easier way to explain it than all the junk I told you."

"It wasn't junk," Sunny said with a shake of her head. "It was beautiful. I wish I could do it."

"We're lucky we can't dream," Blue said. "Pretty much everybody hates 62 for it." 62 nodded in agreement.

Sunny made an irritated clicking sound with her tongue. "Small minds rarely appreciate the beauty in our differences."

Blue cackled. "Careful, it sounds like you're calling the Council small-minded."

"Not just the council. All of Hanford. They think they're better than the refugees because Hanford is above ground. They have 'real world experience' as they like to say. But their haughtiness does them no favors. It makes them blind to progress. I can't count the number of times they've put tradition ahead of common sense."

00 picked up the computer's case and lowered it down over the wires, turning the messy construction into a sleek gray box with a host of keys. "There. The guts are in. 62, can you help Blue move that monitor over here?"

62 hoisted the heavy monitor off the table, almost dropping it on his foot in the process. The screen was heavy and awkward, and he groaned with the effort. When he set it down, it settled on top of N302's case with a loud thunk. 00 immediately set to attaching the screen to the box with a long wire.

"It's almost ready now. Do you want to turn it on?" 62 asked Sunny.

She got up from her seat with painstaking slowness, whether from her own physical discomfort, or wariness of the lifeless bot resting on the table, 62 wasn't sure. But she did move toward the Machine, and asked, "How do I do that?"

00 smiled at her. "There's a switch on the back side. You flip it, and the programming does the rest."

Sunny slid her hand against the side of the Machine. Her hand passed over the rigid vents and smooth metal cover a moment. Eventually, she tucked her hand along the back side. A light click sounded when her finger found the switch. A high-pitched buzzing sound whined from the screen's glass for a moment, and a whirring sound came from somewhere deep inside the Machine. Sunny drew back sharply, eyeing the computer with a wary gaze. "Now what?"

Blue flipped the pages of the computer manual to the computer's boot-up instructions, then set the open book on the table beside N302. "Now, we wait."

CHAPTER 10

Everyone watched as the computer's lengthy boot-up sequence took its course. Numbers and symbols scrolled across the screen, ebbing and flowing as the device processed its data. After the initial burst of information, the screen sat with a cursor blinking. It looked as if nothing else was going to happen.

"This is where we thought it was broken the first time," 62 said to Sunny. "The bot that N302's parts were made to run in had a lot more power than this bit of scrap. We found out the hard way that it takes it a long time to figure out it's being woken up."

Sunny stared at the repeating shine and darkening of the rectangular cursor. It drew her in like a hypnotic flame, the same way it had drawn the others the first time they'd seen it. But even for Sunny, who had never seen an electronic device before, eventually the newness of the flashing light faded and she slouched in her chair. "It's not at all what I expected," she said.

"It's not done yet," Blue reminded her. "Wait till it starts talking. That's when the magic happens."

Several more minutes passed before new words appeared on the screen. Sunny's eyes shone with wonder when the boot-up sequence finally began. Words and codes splashed across the screen, detailing the computer's make, model, drives, and software. A brick of text landed on the screen with a list of programming options. 00 selected the program NURSE302/AI and hit the enter key. 00 leaned back in his chair and crossed his arms, a bored expression on his face. Sunny looked at 00 expectantly.

"Is it going to start?" Sunny asked.

"Eventually," Blue answered with a sigh.

"It's not exactly quick," 62 admitted.

A long while later, the cursor finally jumped down the screen.

N302> HELLO.

00 leaped at the keyboard. His fingers began typing rapidly.

U> Hi! This is 1125000. It's nice to see you again!

N302> I AM PLEASED TO COMMUNICATE WITH YOU AS WELL. HAVE WE MADE THE JOURNEY TO THE SAFE PLACE?

U> Yes! It took three whole days to get here. Then, it took a couple more to get you set up. We think there's enough electricity here that you can stay powered on all the time. We won't know for sure until we try, though.

N302> THE FIRST STEP OF OUR TEST IS COMPLETE. BOY 1124562 AND BOY BLUE HAVE ALSO ARRIVED?

U> They're here. They can see your messages.

N302> HELLO, BOY BLUE. HELLO, BOY 1124562.

62 and Blue nodded at the Machine. 00 typed a brief return of the bot's greeting, then began to pound the keyboard as he told the story of how much dirt the computer had collected during their travels, and asked if N302 noticed any problems resulting from the grime. The computer announced it would run a full system check after its human visitors had left for the night.

U> There's something else we need to tell you. We aren't the only people here.

N302> THE FEMALE CALLED AUNTIE ASSURED YOU THIS LOCATION WAS SECURE. WHY WOULD SHE INPUT FALSE DATA?

00 looked at his friends. "What should I tell it?" he asked.

"Just tell it the truth," Sunny replied. "There was no way anyone could have known I was here."

00 relayed the story of their arrival at the jailhouse, and their discovery that someone had already taken it as a sanctuary. N302 asked few questions, but its fans whirred, and it clicked rhythmically as it processed the story.

N302> YOU STATE THAT THE FEMALE IS INJURED. PLEASE STATE THE NATURE OF THE INJURY.

00 turned to look at Sunny. "What should I say is wrong?"

Sunny looked down at her body. A strained expression clouded her face. She cleared her throat. "Can you ask if it's familiar with female biology?"

The clicking of keys filled the air as 00 typed the question.

N302> I HAVE RETAINED FILES REGARDING MAINTENANCE OF HUMANS DEPENDENT ON MY CARE.

"But there aren't any Women in Adaline, are there?" Sunny shook her head in answer to her own question. "Does the thing know the differences between Men and Women?"

U> Do you know that Women have different parts than Men?

N302> MY PROGRAMMING IS INCLUSIVE OF THE SINGULAR HUMAN FORM.

00 dropped his hands from the keyboard. "What does it mean, 'singular human'?" he muttered.

Blue shook his head. "00, explain to that clunker that not all humans are the same."

62 looked at Sunny and then piped up himself. "I don't think it'll do any good. It's had less contact with Girls than we have. 00 and I had never seen a Girl before going to Hanford. Didn't even know they existed. Why would N302 be any different? Sure, it talked to Auntie and Mattie, and we told it that they were female. But what if it doesn't know what that really means?"

"We only told it that they lived above ground," 00 said. "If someone had told us there were other humans, but that they were different than us, we wouldn't have understood if we hadn't seen them with our own eyes. No one's different in Adaline."

"Maybe we're close enough," Sunny said in a quiet voice. She read the words on the screen again. "Tell the bot that I had incisions that weren't fully healed when I came here."

00 typed the words. N302 sat for a moment, whirring and clacking, before answering.

N302> WAS THE NATURE OF THE SURGERY INVASIVE OR NON-INVASIVE?

A bitter laugh escaped Sunny. Her eyes flickered like wildfire and the sharp angles of her face caught the light. Her skin tightened around her eyes and mouth. Her expression was terrifying in the way she laughed. Her eyes narrowed as she looked at the screen. She spat out the word, "Invasive." 00 carefully keyed the word into the computer.

N302> PLEASE DESCRIBE THE LOCATION OF THE SURGICAL PROCEDURE.

Sunny's lips drew into a thin line. "If it doesn't know anything about females, telling it that isn't going to get us anywhere."

"So, this is useless? Great." Blue kicked one of the table legs and a spare part fell to the floor at his feet.

62 shook his head. "If Mattie were here, she'd find a book to fix this."

"Well, she's not here," Blue said angrily. "Just us Boys, and we're useless."

"Not just you Boys," Sunny said. The tension in her face slipped a little. "I'm here."

"Yeah, but Mattie could find us a medical book, and we could type in the differences between males and females to make the bot understand."

"And she'd probably know about the right way to explain your surgery," 62 added. "She knows about all kinds of gross stuff like that."

"While I may not be Mattie," Sunny said, lifting her chin, "I've been a teacher for longer than I care to remember. If I can teach refugees how to live without bots, maybe I can teach a bot about variations in different kinds of people."

"You'll just… teach it?" 62 looked from Sunny to N302 and back again. "How will you do that?"

"I'll write what it needs to know with that letter pad, just like 00 is doing. That's how it works, right? Writing words by touching those keys?"

"Sure," 00 shrugged. "The letters are part of what's called the keyboard. You spell out the words you want to use, then hit the 'Enter' key. That's the gist of it."

"That seems easy enough." Sunny rolled up her sleeves and pulled her chair beside 00's. "Give me a quick lesson on anything else I need to know, and then leave."

"Leave?" all three Boys complained in chorus.

"Yes. I'll tell this bot about the female body. But, trust me, some of the things it needs to know, you three aren't ready to learn, yet."

CHAPTER 11

Sunny spent two full days typing. Every time one of her companions came to check on her, she shooed them away. 62 noticed that teaching the bot seemed to give Sunny a new purpose. She was brighter somehow, in a way that 62 couldn't quite explain.

Aside from keeping Sunny out of bed, there was more good news. The computer had been running for nearly three full days, and there hadn't been a noticeable drop in power. Blue disconnected the elevator functions, to keep 00 from using the creaky lift and to save power for N302, and they started turning off lights the moment they were done with them. The bot seemed happy it had been able to stay on for so long, and the longer it stayed powered up, the more it seemed to dread the possibility that it might be shut off again.

00 and 62 had taken to sitting in the hallway outside N302's room, straining to hear the quiet tapping of keys through the closed door. 62 leafed through the pages of *Charlotte's Web*, while 00 pored over the electronics manual they'd used to assemble the computer. Blue, who'd gotten bored of sitting, went down to work in the greenhouse. He'd said something about planting radishes, whatever those were, and 62 was happy he hadn't asked for help. When 62 had first arrived at Hanford, he hadn't understood 00's obsession with Adaline's meal tabs. But now that he'd been without a tab in weeks, he felt a strange pang deep in his gut whenever he thought about the pale oval food replacement tablets. Popping a tab a couple times a day was a whole lot easier than the above-grounder's constant need to grow, process, and eat food.

Sunny emerged from the room, a satisfied smirk on her face. "You Boys think that computer's so smart. But I'm pretty sure I've proven how dumb a Machine can be."

"You have?" 62 asked, looking up from his book.

"That thing doesn't know the first thing about having babies." Sunny snorted a short laugh as she leaned against the hallway wall. She looked down at the Boys sitting at her feet.

"You told it about that?" 00 said, blushing.

"I had to. It wants to know about what happened to me, and it can't suggest treatments if it doesn't know anything about the parts of me that got hurt."

"Oh," 62 said looking away, embarrassed. He'd known that she hadn't told them everything the Oosa had done to her, but he hadn't fully understood the reason why she'd kept those details to herself. Now, he knew it was because they'd changed parts of her that he didn't understand.

"It really doesn't know enough to help you?" 00 finally managed to ask.

"Not yet. It knew enough about my arms and legs. It knows about skin and bones. It even knew a bit about the sadness that I've been feeling. But pretty much everything under the surface is a puzzle it can't solve." Sunny shook her head, bewildered. "There really isn't a single Woman in Adaline?"

"Nope," 62 and 00 answered together.

"It's just Boys," 62 said.

"And bots," 00 added.

"I know when our mothers first came to the surface from Curie, there were no Men until the Oosa came. And, I understand the story that we were at their mercy since we'd lost the labs we cloned ourselves with. But even though there aren't many males in my life, there's always been at least a few. I can't imagine what it'd be like with only one type of humanity."

"It's a lot easier with only one kind of people," 00 said. He twisted his face into a half-frown. "With males and females always butting heads, it gets confusing up here."

Sunny slid down the wall until she was sitting on the floor with 00 and 62. "What's it like in Adaline?"

The Boys took turns telling Sunny about being raised underground. Whenever they talked about the mechanics of the place, 00 took over the discussion. He loved the technology, and even after all he'd been through, was excited to tell anyone who'd listen about how he'd rewritten the code that kept the doors locked.

He beamed when he told Sunny how he'd escaped the pods where they'd been housed as young Boys.

62 was less impressed by the computers. It was hard to be excited about technology that insisted on shutting down creativity. There were so many rules to follow, and so few options for a life beyond the prescribed schooling and metered meals. There were very few activities the bots deemed worthwhile. Get up, eat a tablet. Get clean, go to school. Learn to be part of the system. Then, eat another tablet and go to bed. Every cycle, exactly the same.

Sunny's eyes went wide and her gaunt cheeks lengthened when 62 told her about being punished with sleep fog. 62 had been sprayed with it more times than he could count. It was a consequence of restless nights and asking too many questions. When he told her about the doctor who'd hooked him up to a Machine to reset his brain, Sunny had gasped in horror.

"How can anyone think a place like that is perfect?" Sunny asked. "It's as bad as the Oosa. Maybe worse. What you're describing, happening to children, it's wrong. How can anyone let that happen?"

"But there, it's normal," 62 answered. "Everyone lives that way. So, when I didn't fit in, I knew there must be something wrong with me. It had to be my fault, because everyone else was doing fine."

"Not everyone," 00 said. "I was so miserable I broke out, even though I didn't know there was anywhere else to go."

"When you got to Hanford, did you change your mind about what was right?" Sunny asked.

00 seemed to consider the question, then shook his head. "It's a different kind of wrong," he admitted.

"Above ground, we're still just clones. Still not good enough."

"What do you mean?" Sunny asked.

"We're here, aren't we?" 62 said, lifting his hands and gesturing to the empty building around them. "If Hanford was more okay with me being different than Adaline was, I wouldn't have been sent out here."

"I'm sorry," Sunny said. "You're a wonderful Boy, 62. I'm sorry we've made you feel bad for being who you are. You too, 00. And Blue, wherever he is. Your loyalty to one another, and willingness to help someone you hardly know, speaks volumes about what kind of Boys you are."

"What kind of Boys are we?" asked 00.

"The good kind," Sunny answered. Her lips turned up in a genuine smile. Her companions grinned in return. The trio sat silent for a moment, content with the warmth of their shared admiration. Eventually, Sunny's eyes shifted, wandering with an unspoken thought into discomfort. She winced, pushing herself up from the floor. "We should find Blue," she said in an awkward tone. "I think he'll enjoy knowing the computer isn't the smartest thing in the building."

"Oh, yeah," 00 agreed in a sarcastic tone, "he'll think it's *hilarious*."

62 got up and lent 00 a hand. He helped his brother up from the floor. When they were both standing, 62 wrapped his arm around 00. "Don't worry about Blue not liking N302 sometimes. You gotta remember, the bots chucked him out of Adaline the second he was born. He didn't have time to get used to them being around like we did."

00 shrugged. "That's true. Maybe if he'd had brown eyes, he'd have stayed in."

Sunny led the Boys to the stairwell. "Do you really wish Blue was like all the other Boys in Adaline? All the ones who couldn't accept your differences?" Sunny asked.

"We couldn't be friends if he were like everyone else," 62 admitted. He thought back to the one friend he'd had when he was younger, Boy 99. Not only had 99 turned himself in for having the same anomaly as 62, but then he'd convinced 62 to join Defense, which resulted in 71 being captured by the group cleansing Adaline of imperfect people.

00's voice and the sound of their feet on the steps echoed as they descended to the main floor. "I guess he's okay the way he is now. He knows how to do practically everything. And, he's the one who got most of the stuff to build N302."

"How long do you think it would have taken you to get all the way out here without Blue's help?" Sunny asked curiously.

"A thousand years," 62 answered.

"Seems to me, Blue is pretty great the way he is," Sunny said finally.

"Maybe," 00 said, "But don't tell him that. He already thinks he's the best thing above-ground. There's no telling how annoying he'd be if he knew we thought so, too."

"Your secret's safe with me," Sunny said with a chuckle.

CHAPTER 12

Blue had harvested enough carrots to fill one of the kitchen storage drawers and sat on the edge of 62's bed crunching one of the root sticks. He'd arrived with a heaping plate of the pale orange carrots, delivered as a late-night snack. 62 was thankful for the company, having spent another fruitless night chasing Mattie in his dreams. That is, if the dreams would even come. Most of his attempts became brief, terrifying nightmares. The few moments he'd thought he would actually find Mattie, he'd entered the dream library to find it empty. One thing was for sure, he didn't mind the addition of another body in his room. The sound of Blue's teeth crunching on the firm carrot's flesh was a welcome distraction from the frustration of sleep.

"So, Sunny had to teach the bot." Blue chuckled before taking another bite.

"That's what she said. N302 thought she was pulling one over on it at first. It took a while for her to convince it that she was telling the truth about Women." 62 grabbed a carrot from the plate and nibbled on one end. The hard vegetable cracked between his teeth, breaking apart in chunks that seemed to become sweeter the longer he chewed on them.

"Why do you think the bots don't know about Girls?"

62 pondered the question while he chewed, settling on the same answer 00 had given him. He swallowed and wiped his mouth with the back of his hand. "I think it would have been useless data. What's the point of knowing how to take care of something that doesn't exist?"

"But Adaline must have known about females when it was first built. Curie kept a log of the other site. Why wouldn't Adaline do the same?" Blue asked.

"The Curie site didn't keep a log of it though," 62 said with a shake of his head. "The scientist Anna Joliot-Curie did. If it hadn't been for whoever hid her journal, nobody would've known what the Adaline site was built for. They probably never would have gone looking for it."

The pair sat, crunching carrots and pondering questions. 62 still didn't understand why Anna had insisted the male and female clones be separated. He'd grown up not knowing anything about the people who built Adaline, so why was she worried that her research be kept separate?

As he thought about the faceless specters of the scientists that came before the cloning programs began, he wondered, would anyone remember him, Boy 1124562, generations from now? Would they care that he was a dreamer who'd escaped an automated empire, survived an attack by a Woman who accused him of starting a war, and saved a robot from being turned into scrap? Probably not.

"Sunny told me something." Blue said the words in a low tone, just above a whisper. "She said N302 told her to go back to Hanford. It says she needs a doctor."

"When is she leaving?" 62 asked.

Blue shook his head and frowned. "She isn't. She swears she won't go back. But the bot says she won't get better if she stays here. I don't know what to do."

"What if you go back with her? You didn't get kicked out of Hanford, I did. I'm sure if you went back with her, they'd let you in. Especially once they found out Sunny was with you."

"I'm telling you, she won't go. She keeps saying that she's not whole enough to go back. She doesn't want them to know what happened."

62 thought hard about what Blue was telling him. If Sunny needed a doctor, how could they get her to one? She was an adult, and even if she was thin from being sick, there was no way they'd be able to drag her to Hanford against her will. If Parker knew how sick she was, he might be able to get her to go back. But even if Blue went to Hanford alone to get Parker, it would be a week or more before they'd come back for her, and there was no way to know how long it would take them to get her back to the hospital.

62 wished they'd been able to have N302 copy itself before they left. N302 wanted another Machine it

could talk to. If they'd completed the experiment and figured out how to get the computers to talk across the desert before they'd come, they could send a message back to town.

"I wish there were a way to tell someone we need help," 62 admitted.

"We do have a way," Blue said. "With your dreams. Mattie said you talked to her in a dream right before we left. Just do that again. She'll get us help."

"I've been trying," 62 said with a groan. He slouched on the bed. "But all I've been getting are nightmares. They're bad, Blue. I get so scared that I end up awake all night."

"Didn't you share dreams all the time in Adaline? What's so different here?"

"It was easier there," 62 explained. "I knew exactly where my friends were all the time, because we couldn't do anything without bots. Up here, there's so much space. It's impossible to sort through all the things Mattie might be doing. I don't know how else to explain it."

"But you know where Mattie will be, at least some of the time. She's in the library, practically always."

"During the day, yeah. But at night when we're sleeping, I can't find her."

"Well, there's your whole problem," Blue said with a shrug. "You're trying to dream about her at the wrong time. Just sleep during the day. Then you'll know where she is."

"But she's awake during the day."

"You sure about that?" Blue's forehead lifted an inch along with his eyebrows.

"I think so…"

"Look, before you started spending so much time there, I caught her taking naps behind the front counter all the time. When you and 00 started showing up to use the library, she stopped. Now that we're not there mucking up her day, what's to say she hasn't gone back to nodding off?"

"What if you're wrong? I can't tell what she's doing from way out here."

"Sure you can," Blue said, sliding off the end of the bed and picking up what was left of his plate of carrots. He picked one up and snapped the end of it off between his teeth. He pointed the thick stub of vegetable that was left at 62. "Stay up tonight, and sleep all day tomorrow. See if you bump into her, or whatever you call it. It's not like we need you for anything. Sunny's caught up with N302. 00 is tryin' to get brave enough to tell her he wants to build another computer, and I'm gonna be down in the greenhouse planting peas. You may as well give it a shot."

"Peas?" 62's voice had a suspicious lilt. "Since when have you been so into gardening?"

"Since I've been hungry, that's when. 'Sides, Sunny's cooking is fine, but I want to eat something that doesn't have potatoes in it." Blue let himself out of the room and closed the door behind him.

62 propped himself up on his pillow. Blue's suggestion might help. If there was a chance to catch Mattie asleep during the day, why shouldn't he? But he'd have to stay up all night so he'd be tired enough to try. 62 thought back on his last nightmare. He'd been lost outside, surrounded by dirt and sagebrush, a band of coyotes howling just out of sight. He had tried to get away from them, but the more he ran, the closer their

howls came. He'd woken up in a sweat, panting from the strain of panic.

62 got out of bed and found *Charlotte's Web*. A couple pages had come loose the last time he'd read it. He was careful to keep them in place when he opened the cover. Did nightmares happen during the day? He wasn't sure. But staying up reading sounded better than chancing being hunted by predators in his sleep tonight. He sat on the bed, folded his legs beneath him, and opened the book on his lap.

Although he loved *Charlotte's Web*, as he flipped through the pages, he felt a pang of desire for something different to read. If only there were a library in the jailhouse. It had been in dreams that he'd first come across a book. Just before he was exiled from Hanford, he found out that the books he'd seen in his sleep were Mattie's doing. She'd memorized them and given the memory of her books to someone called The Curator. In secrecy, he'd cataloged the books in a sort of make-believe library that only Adaline's dreamers could reach. 62 yawned as he thought about the collection of books that were hidden in the shared dreams of Adaline. He had no way of knowing if The Curator or any of the other dreamers were still sharing the forbidden books. But he wondered if he could imagine a book that he'd seen before. Perhaps he could re-read old books in his imagination.

A yawn pulled through 62's body, forcing a thin trickle of tears to press against his eyelashes. He'd only just decided to stay up reading, and already his body was fighting him. 62 rubbed his eyes with the heels of his hands, pressing the tiredness out of them. He sat up a bit more, shaking his head to force himself awake. He could do this.

His mouth opened wide, and this time the yawn was so strong that it made his ears pop. His eyes were heavy and wet, and he tried to rub the sleep from them a second time. 62 looked back at the page, re-reading the first sentence once, twice, and then a third time. The bed pulled at him with inhuman force, and he rocked himself forward to fight the urge to lie down. He could stay awake. He was sure of it.

Well, mostly sure.

CHAPTER 13

The sunrise found 62 standing at the window, bleary-eyed and despondent. He'd made it to morning. As tired as he was, he knew that the wait for sleep wasn't quite over. His new plan was to stay up until mid-morning, so that he could sleep through as many of the early daylight hours as possible. 62 held the bars of his window and pressed his face between them. The cold metal stung his cheeks before slowly warming to match the temperature of his skin. 62 let his eyes close for a moment, then forced them open again to watch the sunlight creep across the desolate landscape outside.

The rising sun was beautiful. The passing clouds glowed a vibrant orange, then yellow and pink. Patches of deep blue sky appeared in the breaks between the clouds, and then the sun began to show itself in earnest. The morning light blotted out the hyper colors and replaced them with neutral hues. The transformation from night to day was incredible, and 62 wondered why he didn't watch the sunrise more often. A moment later, he leaned back from the bars, nearly stumbling over the weight of his own body. He remembered. He didn't watch the sunrise because it happened so dustin' early in the morning.

62 shuffled across the room, letting himself out into the hall. He hoped a walk around the building would help him stay awake. He looked down the hall, folding his arms across his chest and rubbing his hands over his upper arms. It was a frigid morning. He went back to his room, looking for a warmer shirt. He settled on the jacket hanging in his closet, and headed out again. 62 dragged his tired, bare feet over the cold tiles. His boots were all the way down in the decon room, and he'd run out of clean socks the day before. This thought made him pause, and he stared at his naked feet for a moment. When would he get fresh clothes again? In Adaline, the bots had given him something new to wear every day. In Hanford, dirty clothes went in a bin and a few days later appeared back at his doorstep, washed and folded by people who worked in the laundry. But what about here?

62 approached Blue's door. He rapped his knuckles against the wood. He leaned against the door's frame while he waited for a response, laying his temple on the hard surface and resting his eyes until Blue opened the door. When Blue emerged, his face was contorted with sleep. His eyes were half-lidded, and his mussed hair told of a night of slumber. A pang of jealousy ebbed through 62 as he looked at his slumber-filled brother.

"What's up?" Blue said through a yawn. He closed his eyes and stretched his arms overhead. He trembled a moment as a sleepy shiver ran through him.

"I don't have socks," 62 complained. Blue looked at him in tired confusion. 62 tried again. He picked up a bare foot and wiggled his toes at Blue. "I need socks."

Blue frowned. Then, as the statement filtered through the fuzz of the early morning, he nodded and waved 62 into the room. Blue rummaged through a messy heap on the floor, producing one sock and then another. He sniffed them both, shrugged, and handed them to 62.

"I want clean socks," 62 repeated.

"We'll have to do laundry for that," Blue said, scowling. Although he still looked a mess, he began to sound more alert. "I've never done it before, but it can't be too hard. We'll figure it out." He pushed his dingy socks in his hands toward 62 again. 62 shook his head, and Blue tossed the socks behind him. One landed on top of the pile it had come from, and the other dropped to the floor just inside the door. Blue didn't seem to mind. "Why are we talking about socks this early in the morning?"

"I'm going for a walk. To stay awake."

"Oh. Have you been up all night?" Blue asked, his voice lilting in surprise.

"It was your idea for me to sleep during the day. Remember?"

Blue ran his fingers through his hair. "Oh! I hadn't thought you were actually going to try it. At least not right away. I figured you'd have taken a few days to shift your sleep around."

62's face dropped into an exhausted grimace. "What?"

"I thought you'd, you know, stay up a bit late, sleep in the next morning. Stay up later the next night, sleep in later the next morning. And keep doing that until you weren't tired at night, but were tired during the day." Blue patted 62 on the shoulder. "You're a champ for getting it all done in one shot though."

62 growled. "You could have told me this sleep-shifting plan last night."

"Sorry," Blue said. He shuffled nervously, then changed the subject. "So, where are you walking to?"

"Don't know. Cafeteria I guess."

"I'll come with you," Blue offered. "I'll even make you some breakfast. It's the least I can do." Blue turned into his room, now picking up the two discarded socks once more. He smelled each one again, shrugged his shoulders, and put them on. He pulled on a long-sleeved shirt and joined 62 in the hallway.

By now, Blue was visibly much more alert than 62 but he patiently kept his sleepy brother's pace as they made their way down the stairs. When they reached the kitchen, they discovered a half-eaten loaf of bread on the counter. Blue cut the gnawed end off and sliced the rest of the loaf. 62 reached forward to grab one of the slices and Blue shook his head.

"Let me toast it," Blue said. He turned on the stovetop and slathered some lard from the pantry on each slice of bread. Soon, the bread was crackling as he laid it in the pan.

The Boys watched the bread toast in silence. When it was finished, 62 took his meal with an appreciative grunt, and followed Blue out to what was becoming their regular table. Blue chewed his breakfast thoughtfully while 62 hung his head in his hands, staring at the steam rising off his warm toast.

"You gonna be okay?" Blue asked between bites.

"Yeah," 62 answered. He sighed, reached for his toast, and took a small nibble from the edge. The warm bread tasted good. The way Blue had toasted it made the bread both moist and crispy. "This is good. Thanks."

"No problem," Blue said with a smile. "Are you excited to try day-dreaming with Mattie today?"

62 shrugged. "I don't know, maybe. A few hours ago I was. But now, I don't really care. I just want to sleep."

Blue leaned on an elbow, and even in 62's state he could see his friend trying too hard to look casual. "Tell her I said hi, will ya?" Blue's eyes darted down to his half-eaten toast, then back up at 62. "I mean, if you think about it or whatever."

"I'll tell her," 62 said. He couldn't help his lopsided grin. He didn't have the energy to tease Blue about it now, but he knew that his brother had feelings for the Girl at the library. "Anything else I should pass along?"

"You could tell her we need clean clothes. Then we won't have to figure out how to do laundry."

62 chuckled. "We could always wear smocks like Sunny. There's gobs of them in decon."

"That's not a bad idea," Blue said, brushing a crumb of toast from the side of his mouth. "Except my clothes are way more comfortable than those things. Especially when it's cold like this. I'd rather keep my long sleeves, thank you."

62 nodded. He finished his toast, then pushed himself up from the table. "I think I've been awake long enough. It's time to sleep."

"Good luck."

62 turned away from the table. He'd trudged his way to the door when he heard Blue call out behind him, "And don't forget to tell Mattie I said hi!"

62 laughed sleepily, then dragged himself up the stairs and down the hall to his room. The light from the fixture hanging from the ceiling was washed out by the bright sunlight streaming in through the open window. 62 took a few minutes to re-hang his spare blanket up on the bars of the window, blotting out most of the sunlight, and then switched the lightbulb in his room off. It wasn't completely dark, but 62 was so tired that he doubted the glow forcing its way around the edges of his makeshift curtain would be enough to keep him awake. He climbed into bed, pulled the covers around himself, and rolled away from the sunlight. A bed had never felt more comfortable.

CHAPTER 14

62 wound his way through the dream until he was standing in the library. Again, the building appeared empty, but after a time of focusing his mind, he was able to produce copies of some books he'd read before. They stood, spines erect, in a straight line along one bookshelf. There were a dozen of them, but they seemed insignificant compared to the vast emptiness of the hundreds of empty shelves. 62 picked a book about surviving the desert off the shelf, and began to read. Turning the pages jogged his memory and soon the skills he'd learned came flooding back to him. Hanford's school hadn't been all bad, he thought now.

He settled into a chair near the front door. The lighting in the abandoned library wasn't good for reading, so he exercised his mind on it, adjusting the flickering light until it was bright and welcoming. He willed his imaginary journal and a pencil to form on the arm of the chair beside him. He leafed through it, taking his time, reviewing past entries and making notes of things he wanted to tell Mattie. First, that Blue said hello. 62 chuckled over this as he jotted it down in large, block letters. *Don't forget!* he scrawled under the entry. Then, he tried to decide what he was going to tell Mattie about Sunny. The frail Woman still didn't want anyone to know she was on the hill with them, and especially didn't want anyone to know what the Oosa had done to her. But he had to tell Mattie something to get her to send help.

He set aside his journal and wandered over to the shelf. He pulled another storybook he'd read several times. *Stuart Little* was written by the same author as his beloved *Charlotte's Web*. 62 didn't think this novel was quite as good, but 62 still enjoyed reading it. Stuart was a funny little mouse who lived like other children of his world, only in miniature. He went on adventures down drain pipes and drove some type of small vehicle that Parker said was roughly the size of two dinner rolls placed side by side. 62 wasn't sure how humans could have a mouse for a child, and he supposed that was the joke of the book.

Every so often, 62 set the book down, closed his eyes, and willed Mattie to appear in the library. He'd count to three hundred while waiting for her to appear, and when she didn't, or if he lost count, he'd go back to reading. Mattie didn't appear after the family cat, Snowbell, stole Stuart's hat, or after Stuart sailed in a model boat in the park. 62 had only ever seen pictures of boats in other books, but he understood well enough what they were.

He wondered what it would be like to sail in one and for a few moments pushed the library away from his dream and enjoyed bobbing along in a boat, paddling around a large pond. Once the wind had tousled his hair, and his cheeks were red from the cold air, 62 shuttled his dream back to the library, where he was once again in the comfortable chair by the door, waiting for Mattie.

Mattie also didn't appear after Margalo, a bird, turned up in Stuart's story. Or, after the first and second time that Snowbell tried to eat her. Snowbell was a rotten creature. 62 shook his head and wondered why anyone would want to live with such a devious beast. It wasn't until Margalo had saved Stuart from a container of garbage that the first hints of Mattie's presence appeared, and then, 62 was so engrossed in the daring rescue that he almost hadn't noticed.

A strange scent lingered in the air, something sweet and yeasty. The smell wafted toward him as he turned a page. He put his nose to work, sniffing the air. The light above him changed ever so slightly, and then a small glowing orb appeared nearly at the tip of his nose. It was a break in the dream. The same type of break he was used to seeing when he pushed his consciousness into someone else's dream. 62 was surprised by the brilliant light. He hadn't put it into his dream on his own. 62 leaned back, examining the tiny gateway. It pulsated in midair, and the sweet bready smell grew stronger the longer it glowed. He leaned in, turned his head, and pressed his ear to the light, listening for someone on the other side. Nothing but the smell of sweet rolls leaked through the opening. He prodded the opening with his fingers, stretching it wider until he could wrap both hands around the edges. He forced the gap open, leaning his face into the blinding light.

"Hello?" 62 called. "Is someone there?"

A quiet voice called back. "62? Is that you?" The bright light grew. Mattie's features could barely be seen in the glare. Her round cheeks and dark eyes were no more than faint lines in the light. It was so bright, it looked like she was glowing from the inside out. 62 pushed on the tear between them, making it wider. Soon, it was large enough to step through. 62 took a deep breath, tried to settle the rolling of his nervous stomach, and climbed through the gap.

Mattie wasn't dreaming of the library. She was standing in the middle of some other building. A large, glass counter filled one side of the space, and a pair of little tables winged by thin wire chairs sat in rows across the other.

"Where are we?" 62 asked. He moved to stand next to Mattie in front of the glass counter. Inside the counter were shelves, and the shelves were lined with trays heaped with food. Some of the items in the case looked like bread, but others were more like shiny, round pillows. Some were multicolored, and others were varying shades of brown. The sweet bready smell he'd noticed before was amplified. Now, he could almost taste the sugar in the air.

"It's a bakery. Well, more of a pastry shop, actually," Mattie answered. She took a step toward the partition between the cases, wincing with discomfort. Mattie closed her eyes, pressed her palms to her leg, and rubbed it vigorously.

"Are you okay?" 62 asked.

Mattie stood, whatever pain she'd felt in her dream healed, and answered dismissively. "Yeah. Of course, I am."

She reached over and opened the partition beside the glass case. She walked through it, hiding a limp as she rounded the counter. Mattie slid the back side of the case open and picked a few treats from the shelves. She placed the food on some small plates and came back to 62's side of the counter. She set the plates on one of the two tables. 62 followed her.

"I thought you'd be in the library. You told me that's the only place you go in your dreams." 62 sat across from her and she pushed one of the plates toward him. It wasn't exactly bread. It was shiny and sticky all around, with chunks of fruit popping out of its top. It was a bulging mound of a snack, and 62 probably would have mistaken it for a cow-pie if it wasn't on a plate. 62 sniffed it. It smelled even sweeter than the air in the shop, hints of baked apples and cinnamon drifting from its surface.

"I've been experimenting," Mattie answered. Her cheeks flushed pink, and she looked at her hands for a moment. "After you showed me what it was like to imagine something different, I started trying it. Sometimes, I read about something that I wish I could experience, so I think about it when I'm going to sleep." She looked up at him with a sheepish grin. "Sometimes it works, and sometimes it doesn't."

"That's how it is for me, too," 62 smiled.

Mattie scrunched up her face. "How did you find me? Shouldn't you be awake right now? It's after noon, you know."

"I've been trying to find you at night, but I've been having nightmares." 62 hung his head. He didn't want to tell Mattie about the details of his terrible dreams, but it felt good to admit they existed. "I was talking to Blue, and he said you used to take naps during the day. So, I stayed up all last night and went to bed this morning, hoping that you'd turn up."

"Here I am," Mattie said happily.

62 was glad for the chance to catch up with his friend, but his curiosity was getting the better of him. He lifted the sticky bread off the plate in front of him, and held it up in the air. "So, what is this thing?"

"It's a donut. An apple fritter, to be more precise. It's like a small cake, but it's fried instead of baked. They put the sugar glaze on when it's hot so that it melts all over. I read about them in a book, and looked in the cookbooks 'till I found a recipe. I had the cafeteria fry some up. They're good. Try one."

62 sunk his teeth into the pillowy bread. The fritter was warm, and the gooey treat seemed to melt on his tongue. His mouth was filled with a taste that was sweeter than anything he'd experienced before. Inside, the bread was pale yellow like sunshine. It reminded him of warm applesauce draped over a squishy pillow of bread. The treat was a pleasure to eat, and once he started, he couldn't stop. Before he knew it, the fritter was gone. He licked crumbs and sugar from his fingers, then said, "That *is* good! I could eat that all day!"

"You, and everyone else. As soon as they come out of the kitchen, people gobble them up. I've only had a couple in real life because they're always gone by the time I get to the front of the line." Mattie leaned back in her chair and made a sweeping motion with her arm. The motion of her shoulder halted, and Mattie gave a small whimper. She rolled her shoulder, willing away whatever ache had given her pause.

"Are you sure you're okay?" 62 asked, not bothering to hide the concern in his voice.

"Of course, I'm okay. I'm okayer than okay. Here, I can have as many apple fritters as I want, and there's no one to stop me." She picked up a fritter from her plate, ripped it apart, and crammed a hunk of it into her mouth.

"I might stop you, if I eat them all first," 62 grinned. He sat up straight, a memory striking him. "That reminds me. Blue said to tell you hello."

Mattie tilted her head. "Oh? Did he say anything else?"

"No, just that."

"Tell him I said hello back then." Mattie took a bite of her fritter and chewed a moment. She wiped her mouth with the back of her hand. "So, how are things going out there where you are?"

"It's okay, I guess. We can do whatever we want, which I like. But there's not really anything to do, so it doesn't matter that there aren't any rules."

"There must be something to do. Gardening, reading, or something? What do you do all day?"

62 glanced over at the pastry case. The fritter in Mattie's dream was the most delicious thing that he'd ever eaten. He had to tell the others about it. Maybe they could get Sunny to make them, and eat them every day. 62 wished for another fritter, and one appeared on the plate in front of him. He grinned and tore a piece off. He popped it in his mouth, and Mattie waited patiently while he chomped away.

"We got N302 set up," he finally answered. "There's tons of electricity in the battery banks there, so it hasn't had to turn off at night or anything. I don't know if bots can be happy, but if they can, N302 is as happy as they get. I don't know what it'll do if we ever have to turn it off again. It's pretty set on being left on forever, I think."

Mattie leaned forward in her chair. Her eyes were wide with excitement. "Did you get the second computer running?"

"No. We got sorta sidetracked." 62 scrunched his mouth to one side and looked at his apple fritter. He wasn't sure how to tell her about Sunny and that made a nervous knot twist in his stomach. He sat for a long while, staring at the tiny pockets of air in the pastry's fluffy texture. His mind suddenly switched gears and he wondered if the empty spaces were what made the bread so fluffy. He picked at the ripped edge of the partially eaten treat, sending crumbs tumbling onto the plate.

Mattie crossed her arms and sighed. "Well, aren't you going to tell me what's got you sidetracked?"

"It's nothing really. I mean, it's something. It's just, you know." 62 looked up at Mattie with serious eyes. He whispered, "Can you keep a secret?"

Mattie rolled her eyes so hard that her head lolled back on her neck. "Geeze. You're acting like someone died." She stopped and focused on 62. "Wait, did someone die? Is everyone okay?"

"Oh, yeah. We're fine. Nobody died."

"Well, then, what's got you looking so dang serious?"

62 pushed the pastry around on his plate. He glanced up at Mattie's exasperated expression, and dropped his gaze again. He heaved a long sigh, trying to steel his nerves against the flutter of anxiety rising in his chest. He closed his eyes, swallowed hard, and blurted out, "Sunny was up at the jailhouse when we got there."

"Sunny? Like, Sunny from school, Sunny?" Mattie's face was contorted in confusion. Her mouth twisted to one side, then screwed up the other. Her eyes squinted, then went so wide, the whites showed all around. "What's she doing there?"

"She went there after she ran away from the Oosa. She's sick, we think. We don't really know what's wrong with her. But she said that she got away from them, and decided she couldn't go back to Hanford."

Mattie's eyebrows shot up even higher on her forehead. "Is she pregnant?"

"No. She said that she can't have babies anymore."

Mattie frowned and shook her head. "What do you mean she can't have babies? That doesn't make any sense. That's the whole reason we go with the Oosa. To get set up to have babies."

62 wasn't sure what else to say. He knew Mattie had already decided to volunteer to go to the Oosa as soon as she was old enough. They'd already fought about it once, when 62 admitted he didn't think she should make her decision until she was older.

Mattie looked skeptical. "Well, if Sunny wasn't sent back with a baby, she shouldn't have run away. We don't come back from the Oosa if we aren't pregnant. They keep the others."

"I know. You told me they go away somewhere to live happily ever after. But Sunny says that's not how it is. She says they made her sick."

Mattie snorted with disbelief. "This is crazy. It doesn't make any sense. I'm beginning to wonder if you're really here. This is just a weird dream, isn't it? Or, maybe, whoever you found isn't Sunny. Maybe it's somebody else pretending to be her, to convince you the Oosa are bad."

62 shook his head. Blue recognized the Woman, and he said she was Sunny. But 62 had never met her before. What if Blue was wrong? Blue said she looked different than before. 62 didn't know why someone would pretend to be Sunny and hide out at the jailhouse, though.

"I really am me. This isn't a weird dream. Maybe I can show you what she looks like," he offered. "It won't be the real her, but I think I can remember the first time I met her, so you can see for yourself."

"Okay," Mattie agreed with a nod.

62 reached across the table and wriggled his fingers until Mattie grasped his hand. Mattie cringed when their fingers touched, then shook out her hand. She frowned, glaring at her fingers. She curled and flattened her fingers a few times, then laid them in 62's open palm. 62 gave her a sidelong glance, but could tell from Mattie's expression that she didn't want to be asked if she was all right again.

"Close your eyes. Try to not imagine anything. I'm going to see if I can take us to when we first got to the jailhouse."

They grasped one another's hands tight, and closed their eyes. 62 imagined the day that he, Blue, and 00 climbed the slope toward their new home. He remembered the rugged terrain and taking the last turn to find the front of the worn-out building. He squeezed Mattie's hand and opened his eyes. They were still seated at the table from Mattie's pastry shop, but now the table was sitting right in the middle of the trailhead.

"Open your eyes," he whispered. As Mattie's eyes fluttered open, a copy of 62, flanked by his brothers, walked straight through them. The shock of the specters caused both Mattie and 62 to scoot back in their chairs, the thin wire legs catching on the pitted dirt. 62 slipped off the edge of his seat, a shiver of discomfort shooting through him.

The dream phantoms didn't notice the disruption they'd caused. They steadily approached the building. Their pace slowed for a moment, and 62 remembered feeling excited as he looked at his new home for the first time. Blue took the lead, heading for the front door.

"Someone's been here." Blue's voice leaked out of his mask as he spoke to the others, and his words were barely audible where Mattie and 62 sat. Blue inspected the door and added, "I was expecting to have to break in, since Joan didn't give us a key." He pushed on the handle and the door groaned as it opened. He caught it in his hand, silencing the protesting of the rusty hinges.

62 looked across the table at Mattie. "You can't hear it from here, but when we were standing there, we could hear someone walking around inside. Blue wanted to go barging in, but we wouldn't let him." Just as 62 said this, Blue grabbed the machete from 62's pack and pushed the door the rest of the way open, ready to barge in. The dream-copies of 62 and 00 grabbed him, pulling him back outside and whispering excitedly at him.

Blue shrugged them off, nodded that he understood, and tapped the edge of the door frame with the machete. Metal on metal pealed out into the air, a sharp tink-tink sound that made the real 62 shrink back in his chair. A moment passed, and a shadow winked inside the open doorway. The three characters in the dream took a step back. The shadow came closer, then the light found Sunny's gangly body. Blue went toward her, wiping his hands on a towel before grasping Sunny by the shoulders.

The dream continued to play out, ending with the Boys and Sunny entering the shadows of the building's interior. The heavy metal door clanged shut behind them. 62 turned to Mattie. "That's the Woman we met. She told us she's Sunny and she used to work at the school," 62 said.

Mattie's eyes were wide and her mouth hung halfway open from shock. Her gaze was fixed on the closed door. 62 leaned over the table, trying to get Mattie to shift her gaze from the jailhouse to look at him. "Hey," he said. "Are you okay?"

"That's not what she used to look like," Mattie mumbled in a trembling voice. "I mean, that is her, I'm sure of it. But that's not the way she was when she left."

"What did she used to look like?" 62 asked.

"She was more... herself," Mattie stammered. "I don't know how else to explain it. She stood up taller, I think, and definitely more," Mattie held her hands out in front of her chest and wiggled them in the air, gesturing at something that 62 didn't understand. "...more Womanly."

"Can you show me what she used to look like?" 62 asked. "Do you think you can imagine her how she used to be, so I can see?"

"Maybe," Mattie said tentatively. Then she nodded. "I'll try."

Mattie closed her eyes tight and placed her hands in her lap. She balled her fingers into her palm, forming fists with white knuckles. She concentrated hard until a shadow formed on the ground beside the table. "It's working," 62 whispered. "Keep going."

The form built itself from the ground up, starting as a hazy gray cloud that spouted arms and legs. A torso solidified and a head peeked out of the smoldering cloud.

Long, wavy hair sprouted from the plump head, and a broad smile appeared between full cheeks. The Woman's eyes sparkled, her whole figure soft around the edges. Her arms spread out in an arc, as if she were built to dispense hugs. There was no mistaking she was the same person that he'd gotten to know up on the hill. She had the same hair, same somber eyes, and same curve of her nose. But nothing else about her looked the same. The Woman in the dream was brimming with life. The person living in the jailhouse seemed smaller.

The new Sunny had lost all the plump and curve of the full Woman Mattie made appear. These days, she was all sharp angles, flat edges, and sunken skin. While the person beaming down at had a sunshiny grin that matched her namesake, the Woman cowering in the dark corners of the jailhouse was sharp and frail. The Sunny 62 knew seemed on the verge of falling over and never getting up again.

"What happened to her?" Mattie asked in a trembling whisper.

"The Oosa," 62 answered. He couldn't bring himself to say more than that. "She needs help, Mattie. We hooked up N302 to see if it could help her get well again, and it says she needs a doctor. It doesn't know enough about females to treat her, and none of us can do anything more to help. But she won't go back to Hanford the way she is now. She thinks nobody will accept her."

Mattie nodded. "I'm not surprised N302 can't figure out what to do. We're made up different than you Boys. And, I think I understand why she's scared. It would be hard, coming back. She doesn't look the same. Everyone will be talking about her, if that's how she looks now. And we all know how well Hanford deals with people who are different."

62 grunted his response. If they could send a kid like him into the desert, who knows what they'd do to a Woman who ran away from the Oosa. There was no doubt, especially seeing Mattie's version of Sunny, that she was in desperate need of help. Far more help than a trio of ragamuffin Boys could give her. 62 looked away from Mattie's dream-Sunny.

The copy of the old Sunny remained staring at them, her unblinking face and widespread arms making 62 uncomfortable. "Can you make her go away?"

Mattie closed her eyes, and the Woman dissolved into the gray fog, dissipating on the breeze that appeared as if it were destined to take her away. Mattie opened her eyes and looked at 62. Her face was etched with worry. "What should we do?"

"I don't know. How do you help someone who doesn't want anyone to know she exists?"

"I'm sending help," Mattie said resolutely. She crossed her arms over her chest and stamped her foot. "I'll go to the hospital and tell them she's out there. They'll send doctors and haul equipment out if they know what's good for them. Or I can tell the guards. Maybe they'd send a rescue team. They can make her come back here and put her up in the hospital."

"You can't do that, Mattie," 62 insisted. "She made us swear we wouldn't tell anyone she was there. I'm not even supposed to be telling you. That's why you've gotta keep this a secret. You can't go sending a bunch of guards and doctors up the hill. If we break her trust, there's no telling what she'll do." Mattie glared at 62 as he spoke, and 62 crossed his arms to try to look as intimidating as she did. "I'm serious Mattie," he grumbled, "You can't tell anybody."

Mattie slouched her shoulders with a huff. She kicked the dirt under her feet in frustration. "Well, I have to do something. I can't just leave her up there like that!"

"I know," 62 said with a dejected sigh. He leaned his elbows on the pastry shop table and rested his chin in his hands. He felt all mixed up inside. Part of him felt better for having told Mattie that Sunny needed help. It was as if half the weight of the secret he'd been carrying had been lifted. But now, he was worried Mattie was going to do something crazy. His stomach twisted in a nervous knot of anxiety.

"Maybe there's another reason we could send someone up there." Mattie's voice was slow and deliberate. She locked eyes with 62. "I know you don't want me to tell anyone, and I won't. Except for one person."

"You can't tell anyone!" 62 shouted. "Come on, Mattie, you can't go and make me regret telling you already."

Mattie got up from her chair. She walked over to trailhead, as if she were going to hike all the way back to Hanford. After a few paces, she turned back. "I have to tell Auntie about this. She'll know what to do."

"But Auntie's on the council. If she tells anyone—"

"I'll make her promise not to tell them Sunny's with you," Mattie assured him. "But I'll bet she can get someone to help you."

"Mattie," 62 called with a groan. But before he'd finished saying her name, she was gone.

62 woke with a start. There was nothing he could do about Mattie now. She'd probably woken up and already ran off to tell Auntie all about their dream. 62 covered his face with his hands. He couldn't believe that

he'd been so stupid to tell Mattie about Sunny. Although Auntie had helped him and his friends before, who knew what she'd do when she found out there was a Woman hiding on the hill? A feeling of dread washed over 62 as he imagined an army coming across the desert, intent on pulling Sunny out of her hiding place. He could almost see them dragging her back to Hanford against her will. What would happen if other people found out about her? Would they stare at her like some freak as she was paraded through town? And what would the doctors do to her? Would they poke and prod her to find out what was wrong? Or worse, would they put her through another round of experiments to sort out exactly what the Oosa had done to her?

The weight of anxiety pressed 62 into the mattress. As he pondered these questions, every ounce of will to move, or breathe, or exist, seemed to leak out of his body. Not even his eyelids had the energy to blink. He stared at the faint light painted on his ceiling from the afternoon sun leaking around the gaps of his covered window. The building around him was silent, leaving his mind undistracted from the barrage of fear from all the wrong he'd committed.

There was nothing he could do to make it right. He could tell Sunny about his dream, but he was afraid of how she'd react if she knew he'd shared a dream with Mattie and told her about her secret. But it was so much worse than that. He'd shown Mattie his own memories, and she'd seen for herself the person that Sunny had become. Why couldn't he have imagined Sunny a little happier? A bit less frail?

He'd shown Mattie the truth because she was his friend. And that's exactly why she'd decided to go get help. Even as 62 realized this, his body ached with worry.

Eventually, he found the will to roll over. He dragged the blankets over himself and buried his head in his pillow. He knew Mattie wanted to help. But her decision to talk to Auntie filled him with dread.

CHAPTER 15

The best thing about living in a fortress on top of a hill in the middle of a radioactive desert is that if you don't want to talk to someone, it's pretty easy to avoid them. After sharing his dream with Mattie, 62 couldn't bear to be in the same room as Sunny. He also didn't want to spend too much time with 00 or Blue, for fear that he'd let it slip that he'd told Mattie about Sunny. Blue knew that he'd been trying to reach Mattie in his dreams, but seemed to assume that he hadn't been successful yet. 62 wasn't about to correct him. As for 00, he seemed more concerned with whether or not 62 could figure out a way to get medical books from the library for N302 than anything. N302 wanted one of them to give Sunny an exam. 62 was even less excited about that idea.

62 decided that the best course of action was to stay locked up in his room as much as possible, pretending to keep trying to fall asleep. If anyone knocked on his door, he'd just say he was too tired to talk to anyone. He didn't have to do much in the way of pretending though, since his guilt and anxiety were eating him alive. Instead of sleeping, 62 spent long hours lying under the covers, hiding from his problems and hoping that eventually he'd fall asleep.

There were times, of course, when he couldn't avoid leaving his room. He had to eat sometime, and there wasn't a bathroom in his closet. He'd go down to the cafeteria at odd hours to pick through the leftovers from the others. He found snacks in the storeroom, when no one was around, and ferreted as many cooked and dried foods to his room as he could so he could gnaw on them whenever his anxiety let up enough for his stomach to grumble. Occasionally, he tiptoed through the halls as quietly as his bare feet would carry him to the toilets.

Although in Hanford all the indoor plumbing had been long dismantled, there were still a handful of indoor toilets that worked in the rarely used jailhouse. 62 was lucky that there was one such toilet on his floor. It didn't work well, exactly, but Blue had stocked the room with several containers of water, and had shown him how to force the units to flush by flooding their bowls. It was labor intensive, but it worked, and meant he didn't have to walk all the way through the building to get to the outhouses. That meant less of a chance of running into someone who might want to talk.

His plan of avoidance worked for two whole days. Blue and 00 finally began taking turns checking on him, and he kept on complaining he was having trouble sleeping. On the third day, Sunny arrived with a bowl of soup. He could smell the warm broth before she knocked. Her soft voice barely permeated the room, but he knew that she'd probably heard the loud bed frame squeak when he'd sat up to sniff the air. Even if she hadn't, he'd been talking to himself aloud just before he'd heard the light rap of her knuckles on the door.

"Coming," he called. "Just a minute." 62 tossed his hair, pulling at it with his fingers to make it look as wild as possible. He rubbed his eyes hard with his knuckles and tugged the waistband of his pants to the side to make sure it looked like he'd been tossing and turning for hours. When he opened the door, Sunny stood with the bowl of soup held out in one hand, while her other was balled up in a fist, as if she'd been about to knock a second time.

"Hello," Sunny said. The thin line of her mouth turned up at one corner in a sort of half-hearted smile. Her drawn cheeks and dark-circled eyes made the grim grin devastatingly underwhelming. 62 stared at her, trying to imagine her as the person Mattie had shown him. The difference between her two personalities was overwhelming, and 62 could feel his heart breaking as he took her expression in. Sunny noticed his delay and tilted her head to one side. "62, are you doing okay?"

62 laughed nervously and ran his fingers through his mussed-up hair. "Me? Oh, yeah. Just tired."

"So I've heard. May I come in?" Sunny didn't wait for him to offer an invitation. Instead, she slid her slim frame through the opening, handing 62 the bowl of soup in the process. He had to let go of the door handle to hold the warm meal in both hands. She ducked around him, moving into the room and exploring the small space with her eyes. "I've never been in here before. It's nice."

"All the rooms are the same," 62 muttered. Then, he remembered his manners. "Thanks."

Sunny walked to the window and tugged on the blanket hung up on the bars. She checked the knots tied around the window frame, nodding to herself. "This is a good idea," she offered. "I'll have to do something like this in my room. I get tired of seeing the sun."

62 didn't know what to say, so he simply went to his bed and sat down to eat. The soup wasn't piping hot, but it was warm, and the thin liquid soothed his insides. He'd slurped up half the soup before he found the courage to talk again, and then all he said was, "This is good. Thanks."

Sunny nodded and sat down on the bed beside him. She let out a heavy sigh, filling the air around them with a sadness that matched 62's own misery. Then, she surprised him by wrapping a long, bony arm over his shoulders, giving him an awkward one-armed hug.

"There are days when I can't get out of bed either," Sunny said quietly. Her voice cracked and she cleared her throat before speaking again. "When I was with the Oosa, I wasn't allowed to get out of bed. All I wanted then was to get up and move. But here, it seems pointless. There's nowhere to run. No one chasing me. I realize how small I am. How small we all are in this great big world. We're born, we live, we die; and for what? Does anyone miss us after we've gone?"

"Parker misses you," 62 answered. Sunny's body froze against him. She was so stiff, he wondered if she'd even stopped breathing. He pressed his body against hers, hoping to feel life clinging to her bones. As he shifted, she exhaled, and he was glad that she was still with him.

She remained silent, so 62 continued. "When I was taking classes in Hanford, he told us that he'd decided to become a teacher for the refugees because it's what you used to do, before you left. He said he wanted to teach because it helped him to feel closer to you."

Sunny let loose a bitter laugh and shook her head. "He misses the person I used to be. I do, too."

"What do you mean?" 62 asked cautiously. "Aren't you still yourself?"

"No," she said, shaking her head. "I used to be somebody else. I was happy all the time. I loved to be with people. I was always volunteering to try new things. I looked different. I wasn't all skin and bones. There was more of me. Inside and out."

"Isn't there some part of you that's the same as before?"

Sunny shrugged her shoulders. She pulled 62 closer and sighed. "I still like hugs. I've always been a hugger. It drove Parker crazy the first time we met. I gave him a hug, and you'd have thought I'd tried to murder him with how fast he backed away."

"How long have you known him?" 62 wondered aloud.

"It'll be four years in the spring, I think. He was in my class when he came to Hanford. He was skittish. You all are, when you first come out. None of the Adaline refugees know what to do with anything. But you all seem especially afraid of hugs." Sunny made a strange sound, and 62 realized she'd chuckled

"We don't touch each other down there," 62 said. "Not after we've gotten out of the Nursery, anyway. After that, we're sent to our own cubes and taught to live alone. Forever and always, no exceptions."

"Were you a different person when you were there?"

62 considered the question. The truth was, he had changed since his time in Adaline. He was growing up. Getting taller every day. He also supposed that he'd become braver in his time above-ground. In Adaline he'd been afraid to break even the smallest of rules. He was constantly afraid the bots would reprimand him with their sticky sleep-spray or a trip to the doctor. In Hanford, however, he'd flouted nearly every rule he was aware of.

"I have changed," he finally admitted. He thought again about the laws he'd broken. Not only was he hated for being a dreamer, and a refugee, but he'd also stolen, lied, and smuggled. Not to mention that he'd put his friends in danger every step along the way. And then, he thought of the moment he was in now, sitting under the arm of a Woman who'd asked him to keep a secret. He'd broken his promise to her the first chance he'd gotten. "I'm not sure all the changes are for the best," he admitted.

"Change isn't always good. That's why people are so afraid of it."

"Do you think it's possible to stay the same way forever? To stick to who you are so well that nothing can change you?"

"No," Sunny answered. "The only way a person could stay the same forever, would be to lock themselves up in a room for their entire life." She looked around 62's bedroom. "I hope that's not what you're doing. I know things are hard right now. We're all struggling, in one way or another. But, if we keep getting up and helping one another, we'll figure out a way to make it past our problems somehow."

62 was quiet, letting Sunny's words sink in. He finished the soup while he thought, and tipped the bowl to his lips to get the last dregs of broth. The last drink caused a long, wet, slurping sound that roared through the quiet room. The rude noise made 62 blush as he lowered the bowl. "Thanks for the soup," he said. He handed the empty bowl back to Sunny. She retracted her arm from around his shoulders, took the dish, and stood up. 62 licked his lips and wiped his mouth with his sleeve. He looked at Sunny, searching for a piece of who she used to be somewhere in her gaunt frame. "I bet you were a great teacher," he said finally.

"I was," she said with a nod. "And maybe I will be again, one day." With that, she let herself out of the room.

CHAPTER 16

62 didn't feel brave enough to leave his room until the day after Sunny's visit. Two days after that, 00 came down from the computer room to tell them he saw movement on the desert floor. The four jailhouse residents climbed the stairs to peer out the windows, hoping they could make out who, or what, was coming toward them. 62's gut tumbled with each step he took. He was certain he was about to learn the results of Mattie's meddling.

He'd still managed to keep his dream a secret, even from Blue. The older Boy had asked a couple of times if 62 was still trying to connect with Mattie. Each time he'd brought it up, 62 had shrugged his shoulders and muttered that he couldn't sleep. Blue urged him to keep trying. Now, 62 was faced with the worry that Mattie's help was marching to their front door. His chest tightened as he took another step upward. What if what 00 had seen was the first sign of an army of people arriving to carry Sunny away? It was all his fault.

Once they got to the top floor of the building, Sunny and 00 gathered by the window in the computer room. Blue and 62 crowded the glass of 00's bedroom next door. When they first moved in, they'd thought it odd that 00 wanted these rooms so far from the rest of the building. Now, they were glad that he had. Far down below them, there was a small, black blur in the middle of the otherwise brown and gray landscape. At first, 62 thought the thing was stuck in place. After watching for a moment, it seemed to shift. He realized that the thing must be moving.

"00's right," Blue said. He grabbed the window's bars in both hands and leaned his face against them. "Somebody's coming. I wonder how long it'll take them to get here?"

62 had seen enough. He leaned against the wall and slid down until he was sitting on the floor. "I don't know. How long did it take us?"

"Part of an afternoon, I think. But we were hauling all our stuff and those computer parts. Whoever that is might move faster if they don't have a lot of gear."

62 pulled his knees to his chest and wrapped his arms around them. He buried his face in his folded forearms. People were coming. They'd be here soon, and Sunny would find out what he'd done. She was going to hate him. She might even hate him as much as that Woman Joan, who'd demanded he be forced out of Hanford. Maybe even as much as his perfect brothers in Adaline hated him. He'd broken Sunny's trust, and soon

she'd find out. A rattling sigh tore through him. He felt just like when 71 was taken. His old friend was removed from Adaline because 62 had led Defense to him. And now, it was happening all over again.

Blue didn't look away from the window. "D'ya think they're coming to tell us we can go back to Hanford?"

62 peeled his head from his forearms and looked up at his friend. The sun streaming through the window created a warm glow over Blue's skin and hair, surrounding him in a halo of gold. "Do you think they'd do that?"

Blue pulled back from the window and looked at 62. "Before we left, I told Mattie to come get us if it was safe for us to come back to town. Maybe it's her."

A sharp grunt cut through 62 and he gave a sarcastic shake of his head. "You really think that they'd come get us so soon? They may have wanted to get rid of me fast, but I don't think Joan and the council are going to make up their minds about wanting me back without a lot of time and convincing."

"Maybe something happened," Blue said in a low voice. His brow wrinkled with worry. "Maybe Mattie needs our help. Or," he paused, "maybe they made her leave because she's friends with us."

62 couldn't help but throw a mischievous glance at his friend. "You'd like that, though. I don't think you'd mind if she lived out here with us."

"What do you mean by that?" Blue asked in a curt tone.

"Come on," 62 said, rolling his head against the wall. "We all know you like her. Admit it, you miss her."

"I do not. She's always arguing with everything I say, and she treats me like an idiot. Plus, all she ever does is read those stupid books. What good would she be out here?" Blue blew out a breath and waved a hand in the air. "Oh, I suppose she could read us bedtime stories. That'd be great."

62 shook his head. "You can keep pretending she drives you crazy as long as you want. But we all know the truth."

"I'm the only one who knows the truth. You're all crazy," Blue answered in a biting tone.

"Maybe it's Mattie," 62 supposed, ignoring Blue's glare. "But if it isn't, who do you think it is?"

Blue shook his head. "Don't know. Could be anybody, I guess."

00 entered the room, and Sunny leaned in the doorway behind him. 00 plopped down on the edge of his bed hard enough for the mattress springs to bounce him a bit as he got himself adjusted. 00 asked the group, "So, whaddya think?"

"I think someone's coming," Blue answered sarcastically.

"And I'm too tired to think," 62 said.

"00 says I should hide when they get here. I can go to my room for the night and lock the door. When they leave, you can come get me," Sunny said.

00 nodded. "We've also got to shut down N302. We should probably take it apart, too. It's not gonna like it, but if anyone finds it, we don't want them to think it's anything more than a scrap of junk we found."

"What if they don't leave right away?" 62 asked.

"Then we'll have a problem," 00 replied. "We've got to figure out what they want as soon as they get here, and convince them there's no reason for them to stay."

"Blue thinks it might be someone coming to tell us we can go back to Hanford," 62 said to Sunny. "I don't think it is, but if we do have to leave with them, how will you know we're gone if you're locked in your room?"

"Maybe I could switch rooms," Sunny suggested. "If I was on this side of the building, I could see you hiking down the hill."

"You shouldn't be on the same floor as N302," Blue told her. "We want to keep all our secrets spread out as far from one another as possible."

"We could move you to a room on the floor below us," 00 said to Sunny, pointing to the floor. "You'd still have a pretty good view from there. We can bring up some food for you real quick, too. That way if they stay and you can't come out right away, you'll be set up to wait them out for a day or two."

"We need a code word," Blue said thoughtfully. "Something we can use that only we know. Just in case they are trying to force us to do something we don't want to do, so we can let one another know."

"Two code words," 00 said, lifting a pair of fingers in the air. "One for if we're in trouble, another one for when everything is okay."

"How about 'brussels sprout' for if something's wrong?" Blue suggested.

"Brussels sprout?" Sunny asked, one eyebrow raised.

"Yeah. They're terrible. There's no way I'd forget something that tastes like feet means something bad."

"Fine," 00 said. "What's our second word?"

"Fritter," 62 offered.

"What's a fritter?" Sunny asked. She looked around at the others. Blue and 00 looked just as confused.

"It's a little cake," 62 said.

"I don't know how to use that word in a sentence. Sorry, we can't have a code word that none of us knows how to use," 00 said. "Any other suggestions?"

"How about 'new boots'?" Sunny offered. "There aren't many things that I'd like more than a pair of new boots."

"Okay," Blue said with a nod. "Brussels sprouts if we're in trouble and it isn't safe, and new boots if everything's okay. Now what?"

00 got up from the bed and looked out the window. Everyone else followed. The black dot wasn't just getting larger, it had split down the middle. The obscure figures merged together and split apart, most likely independent bodies moving around obstacles on the trail.

"Now, we get moving," Blue said. "Let's get Sunny moved and get that computer taken apart. Whoever they are will be here real soon."

CHAPTER 17

00, 62, and Blue sat at the window, watching the figures move closer. They'd become well enough defined that it was clear there were three of them. There wasn't much else they could tell about the mysterious visitors. If it weren't for their deliberate movements on the trail, the three strangers could have been mistaken for misshapen animals crawling through the desert.

The Boys waited until the visitors disappeared at the bottom of the hill, hidden on the winding trail behind its boulders. They left 00's room and made their way through the building. They stopped on their way downstairs to check on Sunny, letting her know they were going to open the front door to the strangers. She'd covered half her window, dimming the sunlight without blocking her view of the world outside. The makeshift curtain threw shadows around the room. Her bed was covered in the obscure shade, a jagged stripe of dimness thrown by the blanket hung up on the bars. It looked like she'd already been under the covers, allowing sleep to whisk time away.

They said goodbye to Sunny and listened as she latched the door behind them. In silent apprehension they dropped down the remaining floors to the main entry of the old, worn building. While they waited, they prepared the detox room for the visitors. It was a good thing they'd thought to go through the room, too, because as they were collecting clean smocks and setting them in the dressing stalls, 62 found a forgotten computer cable sitting on a counter. There wasn't time to go all the way back upstairs with it to lock it up, so he dashed off to the kitchen, hiding the wire in the back corner of the pantry behind a bag of salt.

Once everything was ready, the Boys put on their masks and headed outside. They sat on the stoop, waiting to see who'd come calling. They chatted nervously about the weather; it was a remarkably clear day, despite the wind. Their small talk halted as the first traveler emerged. The other two strangers weren't far behind. The travelers stopped at the top of the trailhead, taking in the windblown structure. 62 knew what a surprise the building was when first coming off the trail. Years of wear caused it to blend into the rocky hillside so well, it seemed invisible until you were right in front of it.

One of the travelers, in a dark green mask, noticed the Boys on the stoop and raised their hand in a sweeping sign of greeting. The two smaller travelers' white and pale purple masks nodded. If they said anything, their voices were lost beneath the filters of their masks and the whistling of the wind. 62 thought back on the dream he'd shared with Mattie. The table they'd sat at had been placed right where the strangers were now standing. In the dream, they'd had little trouble understanding the voices of the dream-people at the front door of the building.

"Dreams make the impossible, possible," 62 muttered to himself. His voice was so quiet that the words were lost in his mask, and no one heard him speak.

The travelers crossed the flat open area at the front of the building. They moved slowly, as if they were utterly exhausted from their trek. The trio stopped at the edge of the concrete stoop, and one of them raised their hand from under their poncho to wave again.

"Hello, Boys," a thick male voice said.

"Hi," Blue answered. 62 waved and 00 nodded his head. Blue stood up, crossing his arms. "Who are you, and what do you want?"

"We're happy to see you, too," the Man said. He pointed at himself, and then the two others as he said, "I'm Parker. This is Dr. Rain and Dr. Hazel."

"Parker?" 62 stood up. His jaw dropped, stretching the mask around his surprised face. He was glad for the thick head covering. It hid the shock of his expression and gave him a moment to pull himself back together. "What are you doing here?"

"You've been up here a while. We figured we should check up on you. Do you mind if we come in? That hike might not be much for wiry guys like you, but we're old and worn out."

"Speak for yourself," Dr. Hazel said. "I'm happy to keep going if anyone wants to explore."

"You would be up for a longer hike," Dr. Rain said in a curt tone. "I'm with Parker. Let's head inside."

The Women went into the detox room first, Parker hanging behind with the Boys. Parker had been carrying the bulk of the gear, and he dropped it on the top step of the front stoop with a groan of relief. He stretched himself up, supporting his back with his hands, twisting his neck to loosen his weary muscles.

"It feels good to put that down. I'm looking forward to a few days without it." Parker bent over at the waist, touching his toes and then standing up again. The lenses of his mask glittered in the sun as he moved.

"A few days?" 62 asked. "So, you're not leaving today?"

Parker leaned over to one side, then the other, stretching his arms overhead as he went. He shook his head. "No," he said in a painful croak. He straightened himself up again. "Believe it or not, we didn't come all this way just for a hello and goodbye. Although I have to get back to teaching, and the doctors have to return to the hospital, we're going to rest up before turning tail back into the desert."

"Why'd you come?" Blue asked. His sky-colored mask tilted curiously.

Parker rolled his shoulders. "Auntie decided someone should make sure you made it up here in one piece. She's gotten all in a huff over making sure you have enough supplies. I told her we planted a bunch of stuff in the greenhouse a few months ago, but she reminded me that just because we plant seeds, that doesn't mean they grow. So, I'm here to do maintenance on the greenhouse. The doctors came to do checkups and make sure none of you have picked up radiation poisoning."

"Why'd Auntie send you?" 00 asked. "I mean, I understand why she wanted someone to come, but why you? Why not a couple of greenhouse workers?"

"Nobody else wanted to come," Parker admitted. "Auntie convinced the council that it was worth sending someone to make sure you hadn't burned the place down, but when they put the announcement out, nobody volunteered. I figured since I was the one who got 62 sent here, it was my duty to come and check up on him. Dr. Hazel showed up when I was packing up to leave. She said she'd rescued 62 from the dirt twice already and if he'd fallen in a pit somewhere, she may as well be the one to quarantine him again. And Dr. Rain met up with us at the gate. I'm still not sure why she came. She's been pretty quiet the whole way, aside from complaining about absolutely everything."

62 absorbed the information. Maybe Mattie and Auntie hadn't told anyone about Sunny, which was a relief. But he wished that Parker hadn't been the only volunteer. He liked his teacher, but now they'd have to deal with Sunny's emotions when she found out he was here. 62 wasn't sure how she'd react, but he had an idea that there'd be tears involved. The thought of her weeping forced him to close his eyes and breathe deep. It was going to be a long few days.

"Thanks for coming," 00 said cheerfully. He held his hand out to shake Parker's. "It'll be good to have more people to talk to. These guys have been incredibly boring."

"Boring?" Blue cried out in indignation. "You're the one sitting up in your room all day and night. Seriously, if anyone's been a bore, it's you."

62 looked at Parker and shook his head. "See what I have to put up with? 00's right, it'll be nice to have more people here, even if it's only a little while."

Dr. Hazel opened the door. Her long limbs stretched out the ends of the medical scrubs the Boys had set out for her. She was taller than Dr. Rain, though she still looked petite compared to Parker. The dampness of her wet hair made it look black, and she'd tamed the curled tresses in a long braid that hung between her shoulders like a piece of living rope. She held a loose mask to her face as she peered out through the open doorway. "Come on, Parker. Your turn."

The Boys went inside. They took off their masks as they passed through the main entry and tossed them into a bin inside the detox room. While the Boys hovered near the door, Parker headed into the room where he'd strip his clothes and go through the cleaning procedure.

"We'll see you when you're finished," 62 called. Parker waved a hand in farewell. The Boys went back out into the main lobby where Dr. Hazel waited. She didn't waste any time putting the three youngsters into their places.

"Exams start in twenty minutes," she announced. "I need a clean room with a table, good lighting, and an electrical outlet."

The Boys nodded and escorted her to the stairwell. She followed them up a flight of stairs, and they led her to a room a few doors down from Blue's bedroom. It was far enough from the stairwell that if Sunny happened to go creeping around the building, the sound of her footsteps wouldn't carry to the exam room. Dr. Hazel set about arranging the bed to her liking, which meant stripping it of its blankets and pillow, leaving a single bare sheet. She handed the wad of unwanted bedding to Blue.

"Go get Dr. Rain for me. Help her bring up our equipment, will ya? A bunch of it's in Parker's pack. It'll have to be scanned with a radiation counter, if you have one. As long as the needle doesn't spike too high, bring it on up so we can get started."

The Boys stood around for a moment, looking at one another with blank faces. None of them were quite sure whom she'd been talking to, so they hadn't moved. Dr. Hazel put her hands on her hips, her gold-flecked eyes passing over each of them in disapproval. "I'm sorry, was I not clear enough? Go get my equipment!"

"Yes, Ma'am," all three Boys replied. They hurried down the stairwell to do as she'd bid. Blue went to the laundry room to deposit the bedding he was carrying, leaving 00 and 62 to bring in Parker's pack and locate Dr. Rain.

The pack Parker had brought was so heavy, it took both Boys to drag it in. They hauled it into the detox room, then looked all over for the radiation counter. Sunny had been the only person to use it. It took forever to find the cupboard she'd stored it in. They found a booklet of instructions taped to the gadget. Once they had the radiation counter turned on, they waved the wand over Parker's pack. The box only ticked intermediately, and the needle on the box never went into the red, so they decided it must be okay. When they opened the bag, they couldn't make heads or tails of the contents. They needed Parker and Dr. Rain to help them sort through it.

They found the pair of adults sitting at separate tables in the cafeteria. Dr. Rain's petite frame was turned so her back faced them. Parker glanced over at her and rolled his eyes sarcastically as the Boys approached. He cleared his throat and spoke in a loud, friendly voice. "Hey there. You look like you're on a mission."

"Dr. Hazel sent us," 62 said. "She wants to start giving exams upstairs. She sent us to get her supplies out of your pack, but we don't know what any of it is."

"I'll help you sort it out," Parker said, standing up from the table.

"You'll need my help," Dr. Rain said, finally acknowledging them. She turned to face them and 62 was amazed at how different she looked from Dr. Hazel. Blue had grown enough that now he matched Dr. Rain's height. She pushed a few stray strands of her short auburn hair back behind her ear. "Not everything we brought is for today's exams."

Parker unpacked his sack of supplies on a table while Dr. Rain sorted through it. She loaded the Boys' arms with pieces of medical equipment to take upstairs. As she sorted, she made a pile of gear on another table, muttering something about there being no need for half of it. Parker set his own things aside and said he'd take care of them later. Among the equipment, canned food, spare clothes, a couple of books about medicine and farming, and other miscellaneous items made up what remained when the sorting was through.

"How'd you fit all that in one bag?" 62 asked.

"Spatial relations," Parker answered with a wink.

Dr. Rain followed the Boys back upstairs to the exam room. They carefully unloaded the medical supplies onto the tables that Dr. Hazel had set up. Then, Dr. Rain sent 00 and 62 to find Blue.

"I'm starting to regret saying I was glad to have more people here," 00 admitted as they climbed down the stairs for the third time in less than an hour. "They've hardly unpacked, and I'm already exhausted."

139

"Let's get through the exams like they want. We'll have to help Parker in the greenhouse tomorrow, too. But maybe if we're agreeable, they'll pack up and leave sooner rather than later." 62 could feel sweat beading on his forehead. They reached the bottommost stair and he grabbed for the handle. Just as he pulled it open, Blue came barreling through, nearly falling on top of him.

"Woah, watch it!" Blue yelled.

"Sorry, I must have been pulling at the same time you were pushing. The doctors sent us to find you. They're ready for us."

"Yeah, Parker told me," Blue said after he'd gotten his feet under him again. He closed the stairwell door, then looked up at the landing at the top of the stairs. Blue turned to his friends. "So, do you think we should tell them about... brussels sprouts?"

62 snickered at their code word. It made sense when they'd first come up with it, but using it in a conversation sounded ridiculous. He forced himself to put on a straight face. "We'd have to talk to brussels sprouts before we say anything. I'm not sure brussels sprouts is going to want any of them to know about brussels sprouts."

00 chuckled. 62 lost control of his straight face and broke into his own whispering laughter. Blue was the only one who didn't seem amused. He grabbed both giggling Boys by the arms and shook them into silence. "Look, brussels sprouts or no brussels sprouts, if Parker and those two doctors are going to be here for a few days, we've got to figure out what to do."

"Well, they haven't picked bedrooms yet," 62 said, stifling his grin. "We've got to make sure they don't pick a room next to brussels sprouts. Otherwise we'll have real brussels sprouts to deal with."

00's eyes glistened, but he held his laughter in. "After the exam, let's put their stuff in the rooms between Blue's and yours. That way you can keep an eye on them and keep us all out of brussels sprouts."

They heard a door open somewhere above them, and footsteps echoed in the stairwell.

"Hello?" Blue called up the stairs.

"We're ready for you," Dr. Rain called back. Her footsteps stopped overhead and she leaned over the handrail of the stairs above them. "00, you're first."

"Oh, brussels sprouts," 00 cursed. 62 burst out into laughter and Blue pushed them both up the stairs.

"What's so funny?" Dr. Rain asked once she could see them all.

"Nothing," Blue said with a glum expression. "They're just a couple of chuckleheads is all."

Dr. Rain seemed to think that was a suitable explanation and pulled herself back from the railing. As the trio of friends approached her on the stairs, she assessed them with calculating eyes. "If 00 is nervous, he doesn't have to go first. Any other volunteers?"

"I'll go first," Blue said. He stopped pushing his friends up the stairs and skirted around them, taking the lead. Dr. Rain turned and walked back up the few steps to the second-floor landing. Blue continued, "I want to get this out of the way so I have time to show Parker the work I've done in the greenhouse already."

"What are you growing?" the doctor asked.

Blue looked over his shoulder with narrow eyes at the two Boys coming up the stairs behind them. "Brussels sprouts," he grumbled. 00 and 62's roaring laughter bounced off the bare walls, and could be heard echoing long after they'd left the stairwell behind.

CHAPTER 18

The exams were uneventful. The pair of doctors were amazed that the three young adventurers had made their trek without more than a few scrapes that had already healed. They'd been diligent with their equipment and managed their detox procedures well enough that there wasn't a speck of radiation sickness among them. The Boys were thinner than the Women remembered them being in Hanford, but that was to be expected after their ordeal. Dr. Rain asked what they'd been eating, and when the answer was "soup," Dr. Hazel promised to teach the three of them how to cook. Although Sunny had pretty much taken over the food preparation since they'd arrived, none of the Boys could admit that to their temporary caretakers. 62 hoped that Dr. Rain or the others would teach them how to make something new, so he accepted the offer for help with enthusiasm.

The evening dragged on, and 62 began to wonder if their visitors would ever go to bed. Long after the sun set, as the moon was climbing over the horizon, the adults finally announced they were tired. After they had turned in for the night, Blue, 00, and 62 snuck up the stairs to Sunny's hiding place. They crept through the hallways as quietly as possible, in case one of the visitors came looking for them. When they arrived at Sunny's door, Blue tapped it softly three times. The boys hunched in the hallway, so quiet they could hear Sunny's footsteps inside the room. She didn't say a word, and they took that as a signal that she was waiting for a voice she recognized before saying anything.

"It's us," 62 said in a whisper, "We've got new boots to share."

There was a hitch in 00's breath as he chuckled. Blue whacked him in the arm to get him to quiet down. The scraping of the chain in the lock inside the door seemed to roar through the still air, and the door's groan filled the hallway as it opened.

"Come in," Sunny whispered. She fanned her hand in the air, gesturing for them to hurry. Soon, they stood in her small room, the door shut and locked behind them.

Although Sunny didn't own much, the sparse room was still in utter disarray. Blankets were thrown on the floor, the mattress was bare, and the window covering had fallen on one side, so it was hanging off-kilter. Sunny's spare clothes had been torn from the closet where the Boys had put them. Shirts, pants, and undergarments were strewn about the shelves as if they'd exploded from their stacks.

As for Sunny, her hair had gone wild. It stood on end in some places and was clumped together in others. Her eyes were rimmed with red, and dark purple circles clung to the puffy skin beneath them. She looked broken. The moment the door was locked, she set about pacing a small, bare patch of floor in the center of the room. Randomly, she'd pick up a piece of clothing, her pillow, or a blanket, and fling it across the room in quiet agitation.

62 looked at his brothers, the concern on their faces mirroring his own. They knew Sunny had been upset when they'd seen the strangers coming this afternoon, but none of them were prepared for this. Sunny's frantic actions were a far cry from the lethargic despondency that they'd come to expect from her.

"Why is he here?" she hissed.

"Who?" 62 asked without thinking. He looked at his brothers again and realized that she wasn't talking about either of them. "You mean Parker? He says Auntie sent him to check on us."

Sunny shrieked. "Why did she have to send him?"

Blue put his hands out in surrender. "He volunteered to come. Some of the people in Hanford were worried, so Parker and a couple of doctors decided to make sure we had what we needed to survive."

"You mean, they came to make sure we didn't wreck the place," Blue said with a smirk.

"They should've sent someone else," Sunny spat. She narrowed her eyes, and they nearly disappeared within the puffy skin of her lids. Tears began to trickle down her cheeks. She ignored them, letting them fall to her chin. The tears collected there and fell together, a thin trail of sorrow that splotched the front of her shirt. Sunny let out a wail and her hands flew to her face before she crumpled into a ball in the middle of the floor.

"Hey," 62 said in a soothing tone. He went to her and rested a gentle hand on her shoulder. He rubbed her shuddering arm softly. "It'll be okay. We haven't told him you're here. The doctors either. They said they're only staying a few days. Just long enough to help us fix the greenhouse and get some more plants started. They're even going to teach us how to cook." 62 looked up at 00 and Blue. "Right, guys?"

"That's what they said," 00 croaked. His face was pale and long, his analytically savvy mind lost in such an emotional situation.

Blue crouched on Sunny's other side, placing a hand on her knee. "We're going to follow along while they teach us, we'll prove to them we're okay, and get them to leave as fast as we can. We promise."

Sunny peered over her hands. Her bleary eyes settled on Blue. "But he can't leave me! Not after coming all this way. I saw him. I can't let him go."

Blue looked at 62 with questioning eyes. "Where did you see him? When we were outside? Everyone was in masks and ponchos."

Sunny sniffled and pulled the collar of her shirt up to wipe her nose. "When they came, I snuck down the stairs to see who'd come. I saw you talking to Parker."

62's eyes felt like they were about to pop out of his head. "You did? Do you think he saw you?"

"No." Sunny shook her head with jagged movements. "The door was only open a crack. He couldn't have seen me. But now he's here, and I can't let him go."

Sobs racked Sunny's body and she trembled beneath 62's hand. All three Boys wore worried grimaces as they looked back and forth at one another, each at a loss for what to do. Finally, 00 found the courage to step forward.

"Do you want us to tell him that you're here?" 00 offered.

"No!" Sunny shouted. "He can't see me like this. I'm too wrecked. Too far gone. He'll never accept me like this!" Her tears seemed to burst from her eyes, spreading over her nose and mouth. 62 had never seen anyone cry so hard that they became deformed, before. Now Sunny's whole body seemed to transform into a new, swollen, bundle of terrifying emotion.

"What do you want us to do?" Blue asked in frustration. "If we tell Parker and the others you're here, maybe they can help you. Or, we can keep the whole thing a secret and send them back to Hanford. But we can't do both, Sunny."

The frail Woman's sobs shortened as she fought the sorrow, pulling it back inside. She closed herself off until her tears slowed and her trembling subsided. Sunny sat up straight and looked around the room as if seeing it for the first time. Her shoulders shifted backward, her head swiveled around as she glanced at her companions, and she heaved a ragged sigh. "I'm sorry," she muttered. "I don't know what's happened. I don't know what I want anymore."

Sunny's eyes were even redder than when she'd first opened the door. She slowly turned over, crawling first onto her hands and knees, then forcing herself up to standing. She swayed where she stood, barely strong enough to stay upright. "I need to sleep," she whispered. "I'll feel better tomorrow."

"Okay," Blue said. He set about remaking her bed while 00 picked up and folded her clothes, putting them back in neat piles in the closet.

62 stood with Sunny, allowing her to lean on him for support while the others picked up the mess. As soon as the room resembled a comfortable place to rest again, 62 led Sunny over to the bed and helped her climb up on the mattress. Blue tucked her in gently, then the Boys inched their way toward the door.

"Do you want us to turn out the light?" 62 asked.

"No," Sunny whimpered from under the covers. "I'm afraid of the dark."

Blue scrunched his brow, overcome with the admission of the grown Woman's new fear, but he cleared his throat and said, "Okay. We're going now. Get some rest. We'll come back to talk about this again tomorrow."

There was no response from the bed. The Boys crept back out into the hall, pulling the door closed behind them. The only lock was the chain on the door, which had to be fastened from the inside. There was nothing for them to do about that. 62 hoped at some point Sunny would be able to pull herself together enough to get up and lock her door during the night.

"That didn't go well," 00 said in a morose tone as they retreated down the hallway.

"I knew she'd be upset when she found out Parker was here," 62 admitted, "but I wasn't expecting anything like that."

Blue wrung his hands. "I've never seen her like that before. It's scary."

"Do you think she'll be okay until morning?" 00 said, looking over his shoulder as if she might come barreling out of the room after them. "Should one of us stay with her?"

"If any of us were going to stay with her, I would. But you saw her. I don't think being in there with her would help anything. It seemed like everything we said made her worse," Blue answered.

"I hope she feels better tomorrow," 62 said. Even though none of their new visitors seemed to know that they were here because of Mattie, he still regretted ever sharing a dream with her. "Maybe she's right and a little sleep will help."

"I wish I knew what to do," Blue said. He hung his head and his pace slowed to a crawl as they reached the stairwell. "I want to tell Parker she's here. But if I do, I'm afraid she'd get so mad that she'd hurt somebody."

"I don't think she'd hurt any of us," 62 said, "but she might hurt herself."

00 nodded. "Let's not tell anyone yet. We'll check on her tomorrow. Maybe she'll make up her mind about what she wants us to do by then."

62 agreed, but Blue's deep frown said he wasn't so sure. 62 touched Blue's arm. "There's no harm in waiting one night to see what she decides. Just think of how rotten you'll feel if you tell them about Sunny now, and she comes out tomorrow to tell you she's decided she doesn't want anyone to know. Believe me, you'll feel a lot worse if that happens than you do now."

"Okay," Blue muttered. "I won't tell them about her, even though I think they can help her. Maybe Parker wouldn't be able to do much, but the doctors work at the hospital. They know a whole lot more about things than we do."

"I know," 62 said with an understanding frown. "But we can't save people who don't want to be saved."

"I wish we could," said Blue. Then he picked up his pace, rushed down the stairs, and disappeared into his room before 62 or 00 could say another word.

CHAPTER 19

62 went to bed with the hope he could share a dream with Mattie. No matter how hard he tried to focus, he simply couldn't get Sunny's odd behavior off his mind. He tossed and turned most of the night, and when he did sleep, his dreams were filled with the echo of Sunny's wailing cries. He woke with the sunrise, feeling more exhausted than he had when he'd gone to bed. As he trudged down to the cafeteria, he found that 00 and Blue hadn't fared much better.

"You three look awfully glum," Parker commented over breakfast. Dr. Rain had taught them how to make cornmeal mash, and Parker was moving his around his bowl with his spoon. Although he worked the mash intently, he didn't actually eat any of it.

"I didn't sleep much last night," 62 admitted.

"Me neither," said 00, who looked as tired as 62 felt.

Blue sat with his arms crossed and his face contorted in a scowl. "Well I slept fine," he spat. "I don't know what you're talking about, Parker. I'm doing just peachy."

"Obviously," Parker said with a raised eyebrow and a pinched cheek. "Well, whatever got you guys down, try to set it aside. Once we finish this gruel, we'll head to the greenhouse and see how things are going. Blue, you said you'd already planted some stuff. Is it growing well?"

Blue shifted in his chair, losing most of the scowl he'd been wearing. 62 watched as his face lit up while he and Parker talked about radishes and yams, and the lettuces that Blue had been tending to. It had never occurred to 62 that Blue enjoyed farming. It was true he knew quite a bit about it, and had taken 62 around to see all the farm projects in Hanford. But 62 had assumed that was all part of Blue's show. He always seemed to know something about everything, so 62 hadn't made the connection that plants were something Blue actually liked.

00 was too tired to get involved in the increasingly excited exchange between Parker and Blue. He was sitting beside 62 with his head propped on one hand, his face sliding precariously closer to the bowl of mash on the table below his chin. His eyes were closed, and he began to wheeze. 62 nudged him, and he popped up like he'd been hit by lightning. His eyes shot open and his hands hit the table, palms down, as if he were ready to launch out of his seat and take off running.

"What'd I miss?" 00 stammered.

"I think we're about ready to go see what Blue's been doing in the greenhouse," Parker said with a smile. "Care to join us, or would you rather go back to bed?"

00 yawned. "I'm fine, really. I was just resting my eyes a minute."

"Sure you were." 62 couldn't help but chuckle.

The foursome walked through the building toward the walkway to the greenhouse. 62 peeked through the open door to the kitchen as they passed by. "What are the doctors up to?" he asked. "Aren't they coming to help?"

"Hazel wanted to go explore Rattlesnake Mountain, and there was pretty much no way that Rain or I were going to convince her not to go. And I have no desire to go traipsing around out there when there's work to be done. So, I convinced Rain to go with her, just in case Hazel stumbles across the mountain's namesake and gets herself into trouble."

"We haven't seen any rattlesnakes since we've been here," Blue said. "We haven't been looking for them though, and haven't spent much time outside."

"Well, I never knew how much Hazel loved snakes until I came on this trip. I knew that she poked around the outskirts of Hanford a lot, but I never thought anything of it. Lots of people go to the ruined parts of town to scavenge materials. But the second we left Hanford, she started talking about rattlers. It's a little scary, really," Parker said with a grimace.

"So that's what she was doing!" 62 exclaimed. Everyone looked at him with confusion. "A while back, I fell on my way to the library and got hurt. They put me in quarantine, remember? Well, Dr. Hazel found me and brought me to the hospital. It was so weird seeing her out there poking around in the dirt. But that must have been what she was doing, looking for snakes."

"Or trading them," Parker said warily. "Apparently, there are snake collectors in Hanford, and she's one of their main suppliers." He shook his head. "I don't get it. But I guess everybody needs a hobby."

"She's not bringing snakes in here, is she?" 00 asked, the crack in his voice betraying his anxiety.

"Not if Rain has anything to say about it," Parker said.

They passed through the doorway to the greenhouse and were bathed in sunlight. The windows rattled now and again from the wind pounding on the glass outside, but despite the noise, the sun-filled room was calm. Blue had done a lot more work than 62 had been aware of. The soil was freshly turned, aside from where more established plants were still growing. But in those areas, the plants had been trimmed and thinned so the rows looked neat and tidy. It was nothing like the wild strangulation of leaves that they'd seen when Blue gave them their first tour.

On one side, there were hundreds of seedlings poking their heads through the soft soil. He'd planted radishes, corn, tomatoes, bell peppers, cucumbers, and pumpkins. Although the rows weren't marked, he was able to name them all, and kept his jaw moving as he told Parker when he expected to be able to start harvesting each of the different crops.

62 and 00 were left out of the conversation almost entirely, and when Parker suggested that they grab masks to go outside to inspect the water collection system, he and Blue left without waiting for the others to catch up.

"Should we go with them?" 00 asked.

"I mean, probably. It wouldn't hurt to know how the system works in case one of us gets stuck here on our own," 62 said with a shrug.

The pair of lagging brothers retrieved their protective coverings and went around the back of the greenhouse where they thought Parker and 62 would be. But the water system was much more involved than they could have known. They walked all the way around the building, unable to find Blue or Parker. It wasn't until 62 saw a flutter of movement above him that he realized the other two males were up on the jailhouse roof.

"I don't really want to climb all the way up there," 62 admitted. He shielded his goggle lens from the sun with his hand as he watched Blue duck behind the lip of the roof. "They'll probably be done by the time we make it to the top."

"Let's just ask for the basics when they come down," 00 said, looking up the side of the building. "Maybe we can get Blue to show us what's up there after Parker goes back to Hanford."

As they were talking, they noticed some movement in the scrub on the next rise of the hill. The pair wandered to the edge of the jailhouse yard, ignoring the wind snapping at their clothes as they trudged through the dirt. 62 could just make out Dr. Rain stomping comically through the desert toward them. Her limbs were flailing, and her stride was so wide that she hardly looked human. Behind her, Dr. Hazel was strolling merrily along. Her mask was bobbing in time with her rhythmic pace, and she almost seemed to be dancing, though the Boys couldn't hear whatever tune she was bouncing along to. She held something in her arms, long and slender, like a section of rope.

Rain came closer and pumped her fists in the air. Her voice carried over the wind, although the breeze carried her words away before the Boys could discern them. It wasn't until she was nearly upon them that they finally heard the tail-end of her rant.

"… snake! I thought she was kidding about going out there to find a rattlesnake, but then there we are, out in the desert, and she's turning over rocks, and sticking her head in dark holes in the ground! And then, she reaches her hand in a hole and pulls out that… thing!" Dr. Rain roared in frustration as she marched passed them, too incensed to stop. By then, they could see the thing Dr. Hazel was carrying was no piece of rope.

The second doctor walked up to the Boys, holding out her trophy. If it was a snake, it didn't look very lively. It laid limp and flat across her outstretched palms. "It's not a snake!" Dr. Hazel shouted after her companion. Then, she turned back to the Boys. "It's a snake *skin*. As snakes get larger, they grow a new skin under the old one, then slide out of it when they've outgrown it. It's like taking off a jacket you're never going to wear again."

"Can I touch it, Dr. Hazel?" 00 asked.

"Sure!" Dr. Hazel held out the snake skin and 00 caressed it. "But you know, we're not at the hospital. You don't have to keep calling me "doctor." Just call me Hazel. Same goes for Rain, though you might want to let her cool off a while before you start getting casual with her name."

"It feels like paper," 00 said, retracting his hand. "That's gross. And neat!"

Hazel offered the snakeskin to 62. "Do you want to touch it?"

"No thanks. I think I'm with Dr. Rain on this one. Do you know where the snake that owned this skin went?"

"Oh, it's around here somewhere. Pretty nice-sized snake, too. I'd love to see if I can find it before we leave, but this'll do for now." Hazel headed for the side of the building, and the Boys followed her.

They walked the length of the jailhouse and around to the front doors, where they could head straight into detox. The Boys helped Hazel with the radiation counter, and although 62 was clean, the snakeskin made the needle jump. When they tested their hands, both 00 and Hazel's hands set off the counter.

"Oh, dustfeathers," Hazel complained. "There's no way to wash this skin. It'll fall apart if I scrub it down." She grunted in frustration and took the skin back outside. 62 followed her out, stopping on the stoop to watch her climb up the hill and over the edge of the ridge. She tromped back down the hillside empty handed, her stomping feet making big plumes of dust rise up as she kicked the dirt.

"Sorry it didn't work out," 62 said as she re-entered the building. He held the door, careful not to touch her so that he wouldn't pick up any of the radioactive dust on her.

"It's fine," Hazel sighed as they went back to the detox room. "That's what happens sometimes with critters who spend their whole life slithering around in the dirt. They're bound to pick up radiation sometime."

As soon as they were back in detox, Rain could be heard shrieking at 00. "All that, and the stupid thing is irradiated? Are you kidding me? And now, I have to go through the whole procedure, just because I was worried about her going out to poke around in the dirt alone. For the love of Hanford!"

62 removed his mask and gave Hazel a sidelong glance. He gestured toward Rain. "Good luck with that."

Hazel shrugged. She was still masked, so he couldn't see her expression, but 62 had the distinct impression that she was smiling. She cupped her hand to the filter and said in a low voice, "It's alright, really. Hearing her scream is worth the aggravation of missing out on the skin."

"You mean you like having her mad at you?"

"She'll get over it," Hazel said, winking at him through her lenses.

62 turned on the radiation wand and checked himself one more time, making sure he was clear before leaving the room. He left the doctors and his brother to their cleanup and headed upstairs to change into some clean clothes. Blue and Parker were still on the roof, as far as he knew, and the three snake explorers would be busy cleaning themselves up for a while. 62 decided that now was the time to sneak up and say hello to Sunny.

He climbed the stairs two at a time, hoping to get out of the stairwell before his brothers came down from the roof. There was no sign of them by the time he made it to Sunny's floor, and he ducked into the hallways as quietly as he could. As soon as he closed the stairwell door, he realized that something was wrong. Every door on the floor had been pushed open. It was eerily silent, and the open doors made him wary as he walked down the hall.

"Hello?" 62 said, trying to keep his voice steady despite the bundle of nerves growling inside him. "Is anyone there?"

62 peered into the open doorways as he passed by. In each room, the bed was unmade. The pillow and wool blanket had been flung to the floor, and the sheets were missing. Room after room was the same. 62 hurried toward Sunny's room, his body vibrating with anxiety. Sunny's door was open, just like all the others. 62 strained his ears to hear motion coming from inside, but there was nothing but dead air. He crept to the edge of the door, pressing himself flat against the wall. He cleared his throat. When he tried to speak, his voice came out brittle and weak. "It's 62. Is everything all right?"

Sunny didn't answer.

When he built up the courage to look around the corner, the answer was clear. Everything was not all right. Sunny was tucked up on the corner of her bed, face buried in her arms. All around her, covering the mattress and floor, were the sheets from the beds in the other rooms. They'd been twisted and tied into ropes. The ropes tied into knots and loops like 62 had never seen. The sight of it sent a cold chill down his spine.

"Sunny," 62 managed to sputter, "what's going on?"

Sunny lifted her face from her forearms. Her face was as white as the sheets around her, marred by bright pink blotches where it looked like she'd been hit by something hard. 62 moved closer, stepping over the knotted sheets on the floor. Before Sunny pulled her sleeves down to cover her arms, he noticed they were scratched from wrist to elbow. 62 didn't know what to do. He wished he had someone, *anyone*, here to help him.

"I decided it was time…" Sunny whispered. She looked away from 62 as if seeing the concern on his face was too much for her to bear. She looked down at the knot closest to her and reached down to touch it. "I was practicing."

62 made it to the end of the bed. He was afraid to get any closer, and gripped the footboard to hold him in place so he wouldn't run away. "Practicing for what?"

Sunny pursed her lips and shook her head. Whatever she was doing, it was too much for her to say aloud. 62 didn't push her, because he was terrified of hearing her answer.

"I'm scared," 62 said. Sunny nodded. "We need help. This is too much for me. I don't know what to do. I'm just a kid."

Sunny shifted her gaze. She looked at 62. She assessed him with wild eyes, not seeming to understand. "Too much for you? If I go, if I really go, then you won't have to deal with me anymore. This whole mess can be done with, and everyone can go on living without me."

62 found the courage to reach forward then. He touched Sunny's arm, and although she started to pull it away, he grasped the hem of her sleeve and wouldn't let go. "I don't know what you're thinking about doing," 62 said, "but, I don't want you to go anywhere. You're my friend. Please, before you go, will you come downstairs with me and talk to the doctors? Maybe they can help."

Sunny looked at the mass of knots around her. She fingered the knotted rope on the bed beside her again, considering 62's words. "I can always do it after," she whispered, "when they say they can't help."

"Sure," 62 said. "You can do whatever you want. But first, let's go downstairs and see what happens."

"Where are they?" Sunny asked. "The visitors, I mean. Parker."

"Parker and Blue were up on the roof the last time I checked. Rain and Hazel are with 00 in detox.

Hazel found a snake skin and they all touched it. It turned out to have a ton of radiation."

Sunny's mouth turned into a sad smile. "Hazel loves snakes."

"I know," 62 said.

"Okay," Sunny said. A deep breath rattled through her chest, as if she might break into a sobbing wail. Instead, when she spoke her voice was monotone and dry. "Let's go see the doctors."

CHAPTER 20

62 and Sunny were slowly descending the stairs when 00 found them. 00 had just gotten out of detox and was wearing scrubs instead of his regular clothes. Anxiety filled his eyes when they landed on Sunny. "What are you doing?" 00 hissed.

"I'm taking Sunny to the exam room. Go get Rain and Hazel. Tell them I need a doctor."

"But not Parker. Don't tell Parker." Sunny shook her head violently and pulled on 62's hand as if she were about to drag herself back up the stairs.

"Okay. I won't get Parker." 00's eyes flicked back and forth between Sunny's ghostly form and 62. He gripped the handrail and took a step back toward the main floor. "What should I say if I see him?"

62 grimaced. "If you don't bring up Sunny at all, it'll be easy. Tell the doctors I hurt my leg. If Parker or Blue try to come, say 'brussels sprouts' and hopefully Blue will figure out he needs to keep Parker busy."

"You think this counts as brussels sprouts?" Sunny asked.

"What you've been going through definitely counts as brussels sprouts," 62 explained.

00 nodded. He turned around and started down the stairs, muttering, "Brussels sprouts," repeatedly so he wouldn't forget. As hilarious as the code word had been before, now it was too important to laugh about.

62 tugged Sunny's hand and she followed him down the stairs until they reached the second floor. He guided her down the hall to the makeshift medical office. He closed the door while Sunny sat on the bed. 62 sat beside her, taking her trembling hand in his once more. Her skin was cold and clammy, her palm drenched in a cold sweat. 62 squeezed her thin fingers and smiled. They waited in silence.

It felt like hours before they heard movement outside the door. 62 squeezed Sunny's hand again to let her know it would be all right. There was a gentle knock, and the door opened slowly. Both Rain and Hazel had put on lab coats, and suddenly looked like they'd just come from the hospital. They entered quietly, stoic faces appearing unconcerned by the Woman hunched over on the bed. But their eyes sparkled with surprise as they viewed her for the first time. They murmured quiet hellos, and Rain closed the door while Hazel settled into a chair near the bed.

Rain leaned against a table on the far wall of the room and assessed her patients with a thoughtful gaze. "I'm Dr. Rain, and this is my friend, Dr. Hazel. We were told 62 hurt his foot, but I gather that's not why we're actually here."

62 looked from one doctor to the other. "No. My friend needs help. But, we don't want anyone to know she's here."

"I see," Dr. Rain said.

"Do you mind if I ask where your friend came from?" Hazel asked.

62 looked at Sunny. Her head was bowed so hair had fallen across her face. She was silent and unmoving. He was hesitant to tell her story for her, but he could tell she wasn't going to say anything. He swallowed hard. A knot pulled at his throat and he tried to wish it away, but it only tightened around his voice. He took a deep breath and fought against his anxiety. "She was living here when we got here."

The two doctors cast a series of thoughtful gazes between one another, having a silent conversation between themselves. Rain stepped forward. "Miss, is it okay if I touch you? It won't hurt. I'd like to examine you, so we can see how you're feeling."

Sunny gave a single, abrupt nod. Rain washed her hands briefly in a basin on the table before taking the hand 62 had been holding. The doctor looked over the scratches on her forearm, then turned her palm over. Pulling an ancient timepiece from her pocket, the doctor pressed her fingers to Sunny's wrist and moved her lips in time with the beat of her pulse. A moment later, she placed Sunny's hand back in 62's palm. He interlocked fingers with her as Rain returned the watch to her pocket. Then, Rain ran her fingers under Sunny's ragged hair without pushing it back. The doctor felt around her jawline, down her neck, and over her shoulders.

Rain backed away, nodding to her companion. Hazel scooted her chair closer to the bed. She stopped when she was within arm's reach of Sunny's knee. Hazel cleared her throat and asked, "Do you have a name, Miss? Something that we can call you while we chat?"

"My name's Sunny," the sullen Woman croaked.

Hazel looked back at Dr. Rain and the concern in their gazes intensified. Dr. Rain opened her mouth to speak, but no words came out. Hazel leaned forward and brushed a clump of Sunny's hair aside, tucking it gently behind her ear. One of Sunny's wary, red-rimmed eyes looked up at them.

"Sunny?" Hazel said with a panicked lilt. "What are you doing here?"

"The Oosa hurt her," 62 explained. "She ran away."

Hazel nearly fell out of her seat as she lunged forward. Hazel wrapped her arms around Sunny's jagged frame and buried her head in her hair. "Oh, Sunny. I never thought we'd see you again," she said with a trembling voice.

Dr. Rain rummaged around the supplies on the table, talking as she worked. "62, thank you for being here for Sunny. We'll need some privacy to give Sunny her exam. Do you mind waiting outside?"

62 looked at the doctor and patient embracing beside him. Sunny let go of his hand and wrapped her arm around her friend. Their bodies rocked back and forth together as Sunny began to cry. 62 was afraid of leaving Sunny alone, but he trusted the doctors to take care of her. "I'll be in the hallway," he announced. He patted Sunny on the back and got up from the bed. He

moved toward the door. He paused and glanced at Rain one more time. "Please don't tell Parker about her," he said. "She's not ready for him to know she's here."

"We won't say anything," she assured him. "Keeping patients' secrets is our specialty."

"Thanks," he said. He nodded and opened the door. He heard the door chain slide through the lock. No matter what happened now, he couldn't go back in without permission. He wasn't sure how long he'd have to wait, so he ventured down the hall to his room. He had a few pieces of paper from Hanford stashed away. He'd have to find supplies to make his own soon. Sarah, from Hanford's hospital, had told him how to press paper the last time he was in quarantine. He'd never had a chance to watch her do it, but he figured he remembered enough about it to try it soon. He took a single sheet from the few pages he had left, plucked a pencil from his supplies, and grabbed *Charlotte's Web* so he'd have something firm to lay the paper on.

62 returned to the hall. He sat down beside the doctor's door and began to draw, something he'd done little of lately. He wasn't sure what he was sketching. He let the pencil wander across the page. It took a while to take shape, but he ended up with a geometric pattern of shapes. Sunny still wasn't done so he set about filling parts of them in, shading others, and adding more lines to give the image more detail. He was running out of ideas of what to do next when the lock slid back on the door and it cracked open.

"Is anyone out there?" Hazel asked.

"Just me," 62 answered.

The door swung open and he peered inside. Sunny was lying on the bed now, covered all the way up to her chin with a blanket. Rain hovered over her, smoothing the blanket and whispering soft words that 62 couldn't hear. Hazel stepped out into the hallway and closed the door behind her.

"She needs to rest a while," Hazel said, settling down on the floor beside 62. "We'll keep her here until she wakes up, and then move her to another room. Thank you for convincing her to be seen, 62."

"I didn't know what else to do," he admitted. "When I checked on her today, she was doing something. I don't really know what, but it scared me."

Hazel's grave expression matched her words. "She's been hurting herself. If she'd been left alone any longer, she could have done something much worse."

"Is that where the scratches came from?" 62 asked. The realization of what she'd been doing crashed into him with a wave of panic. When Hazel nodded, he shuddered. "Why?"

"Sometimes, when terrible things happen to someone, they have no way of understanding their own hurt. They forget what it's like to heal. It becomes worse and worse until…" Hazel's words trailed off and her eyes welled. She wiped her tears away before they fell. Hazel patted 62 gently on the knee. "It's just a very good thing that you brought her to us. You may have saved her life."

62 slumped against the wall behind him. "You mean, she could have died?"

"She still may," Hazel admitted in a solemn tone. "It all depends on if she decides if she wants to get better, or not."

"I hope she gets better," 62 said in a whisper.

"Me, too," Hazel agreed.

CHAPTER 21

Dinner was a somber affair. The doctors sat apart from the others, whispering quietly at their own table. 62 pulled Blue and 00 aside to fill them in on everything that happened before dinnertime, and now they sat in silence, their heads hanging over their plates. 62 couldn't bear to look at Parker, who was the only one clueless about Sunny's appearance.

Parker tried to spark up a conversation with the Boys, but to no avail. Regardless of the topic, all he got out of his companions were grunts, nods, and one-word answers. It was easy for 62 to tell that Parker was getting frustrated, but he didn't know how to pretend everything was normal. 62 bit his tongue and shrugged his shoulders.

Parker had just asked the Boys what their plans were for the evening when a door slammed somewhere beyond the cafeteria. Rain and Hazel turned around in their seats, their eyes wide in surprise. All three Boys froze in place.

"What was that?" Parker asked. He looked around at the others, but no one answered. "C'mon, I know you all heard it. What's going on?"

Sunny pushed the cafeteria door open and took a few steps into the room. She was wrapped in a layer of bedsheets and looked like a ghost with her pale, drawn skin encased in the stark white sheets. Her bare feet stuck out of the bottom of the bundled fabric, toes wriggling against the cold tiles. "It was me," she said quietly.

Parker's face slackened and his fork dropped from his hand. He got up from his chair halfway, gripping the table for support. "Sunny?"

She nodded and dragged her tired body the rest of the way across the room. Rain got up from her table and rushed to Sunny's side. The frail Woman hung her arm over her friend's shoulders, allowing Rain to support her while she made her way to Parker. Sunny never let go of the sheet wrapped around her body, her knuckles tight around the stiff fabric. Sunny stopped walking just beyond Parker's reach. "Hello," she whispered.

"What are you…" Parker searched her face. His eyes watered and his lips kept moving although no words came out. He pushed himself off the table and rushed toward her. He wrapped his long arms around Sunny's tiny body. He was so broad, and she was so petite that she seemed to disappear into him. His head bowed over hers, and for a moment, 62 thought it looked like Parker was hugging an empty sheet. They stood there for a long while, and Rain backed away, returning to her seat.

"I can't believe you're here," Parker said, his words muffled as he spoke into Sunny's hair. He looked up at the Boys and a flash of anger darted across his eyes. "Why didn't you tell me?"

Sunny pulled back, stretching her arms out to create distance between her and Parker. "I asked them not to tell. I'm not the same as I was. I thought it would be easier."

"But if I'd known you were here…" The words caught in Parker's throat. He wiped tears from his eyes. "I wouldn't have waited so long to come. I would have been here in an instant," Parker said.

"I know, you would've come if I'd sent the Boys for you. But you would have seen me like this." Sunny's voice drifted away as she looked down on herself. She unfolded the sheet so that Parker could see how much she had changed from when he last knew her. "I didn't want you to know what I've become."

"What you've become?" Parker said, eyebrows furrowed. "But, you're you. You'll always be you. That's what matters to me."

Sunny looked around the cafeteria. Everyone was doing their best to look like they weren't paying attention, even though Parker and Sunny's reunion was the most interesting thing in the room. "I have some things to tell you." Parker turned to guide her into a chair, but Sunny gripped his forearm. "Not here. Not in front of the children."

"Hey, we're not children!" Blue protested.

Sunny's voice was thin and worn out when she answered. "I know. You're growing up. Each of you more than you should have. But, all the same, I have some things to talk to Parker about that even old Women would have difficulty hearing." Sunny took Parker by the hand, and he followed her slow gait out of the cafeteria.

After they left, Hazel and Rain moved over to the table with the Boys. "I'm so glad she came down," Rain said as she settled into a chair.

"I knew she would," Hazel replied with a thin smile. "She couldn't let us leave without him knowing."

"How much longer are you staying?" 00 asked.

"Two days. Maybe three," Rain said.

"Will you take Sunny to Hanford with you?" Blue asked.

Hazel shook her head. "I wish she'd come, but she's so afraid of what people will think when they see her."

"But the hospital's there. Doesn't she need the hospital to get better?" 62 wanted to say N302 had suggested a hospital stay would do Sunny some good, but then he'd have a *lot* more explaining to do.

Rain and Hazel gave one another sidelong glances. Hazel spoke up. "We don't know if she'll ever get back to the person she used to be. She's changed a lot because of what the Oosa did to her. Even if we found a way to repair what was done to her physically, who she's become inside may never be undone."

"She says they hurt other people, too," Blue said in a low voice. "She told us she saw Skye, Robin, and Juniper before she escaped, but they'd already died. When the Oosa come back, they'll pick more Women to hurt. Sunny's got to go back to Hanford. If the people see what's happened to her, maybe no one will volunteer next time."

"We can't make her do that," Rain said. 62 started to protest, but Rain shook her head at him. "I agree, everyone needs to know what's happened. But the burden of proof lies with Sunny. Not everyone is simply going to believe her. To put her through that now, when she's barely surviving, is too much. I think throwing her in the middle of that would do more harm than good."

"She wouldn't have to do it alone. We can help!" 00 exclaimed. "We're the ones that found her. We could tell them what happened to Sunny. Maybe we could convince everyone to not go with the Oosa anymore."

"You could," 62 said in a glum tone. "I can't. They all think there's something wrong with me, remember? If I showed up talking about the Oosa, they'd just throw me out of town again."

"Hazel and I will ask to speak with the elders when we get back to Hanford. We can tell them what we've seen. But the truth is, it probably won't make a difference. Even if everyone knows the dangers of going with the Oosa, they'll still get what they want. If no one volunteers, they'll make the Women go with them by force. It's happened before."

"We have to stop them," 00 said, slamming his palm on the table. "Somehow. We can't let what happened to Sunny happen to anyone else."

"I agree," Hazel said in a soothing tone. She covered 00's hand with her own and gave a squeeze. "We've just got to figure out how."

CHAPTER 22

The next two days went by in a flurry of activity. There were cooking lessons, seeds planted, instructions on how to take care of minor injuries, and Parker even taught the Boys how to do a better job with the laundry. All this took place under Sunny's silent gaze as she hovered in the background. Parker did his best to seem enthusiastic about each project they handled, but 62 could see the lines of worry deepening on his face, and the anxious glances he was constantly casting in Sunny's direction.

Sunny's room had been moved once more, down to the same floor as 62, Blue, and their visitors. When she wasn't lurking in the dark corners of the jailhouse, she locked herself up in her room to sleep. Occasionally, Rain or Hazel would ask her to go for a walk, around the building to talk to her out of earshot of the Boys. Sunny didn't seem to have any desire to participate in her roommates' educations, or in the adults' preparations for their impending trip back home.

There was a debate going between the three Boys on whether they should push Sunny to go back to Hanford with the others, or not. Even though Rain and Hazel had told them not to, 62 knew he wasn't equipped to help her if she tried to hurt herself again. Although he and his brothers had proven themselves resilient and capable of doing much more than anyone expected, caring for someone so sick seemed to be a task beyond their reach. And then, there was the problem of finding a way to let the Women of Hanford know what the Oosa had done. If she didn't go, Parker and the others would have no proof of their story.

Rain, Hazel and Parker decided to extend their stay an extra day, which was a relief to everyone. Even Sunny seemed to relax a little knowing her friends wouldn't be leaving right away. They couldn't extend their stay any longer than that, though. The two doctors had to get back to the hospital, and Parker still had students to teach, but the added time meant some of the pressure had been taken off of making big decisions.

Blue volunteered 62 to use his "brain powers" to let Hanford know of the delay, and after a long, drawn-out explanation to the doctors about 62's strange ability to connect his dreams to Mattie's, 62 went to bed. Now, he lay in his room at mid-day, trying to force himself to sleep even though he was anything but sleepy. Tired, yes; he'd been physically and emotionally exhausted for days. But his eyes refused to stay shut and his mind kept poring over everything that had happened. He didn't want to let the others down though, even if they did look at him sideways whenever the topic of dreaming came up.

62 thought back to some of the books Mattie had shared with him about dreaming and the importance of quieting the mind. He remembered reading something about using a simple thought-task to drive away invading thoughts when trying to sleep, so he decided to try counting backward from one hundred. He took a deep breath and visualized each number, filling his lungs until they felt they might burst, and then letting them deflate slowly. He'd only counted down to sixty-two when sleep took hold of him. Not long after, he felt himself drifting away into a dream.

The darkness of his mind took hold, and he forced himself to envision Hanford's library. It formed around him, and his feet settled on the floor as it materialized. There were more books on the shelves this time, and he heaved a sigh of relief that he wasn't trapped in the empty nightmare version of the library. He walked through the stocked shelves, noticing that the fixtures beyond the entry were still bare. He hunted through the room for signs of Mattie, but she didn't appear. 62 closed his eyes, pressing on the edges of his consciousness to see if he could find her somewhere out in the void.

He imagined her face, could see her stocking the shelves of the library in his mind's eye. They'd spent so much time together before his move to the hill that imagining her was easy enough. But he couldn't seem to find the *real* her anywhere.

"She's not there," 62 said to himself.

"Who isn't?"

62 spun around. The voice had been high and fleeting, like a child running nearby. But as he looked around, no one was there. He was sure that he'd heard

the voice though, it had been so close, as if someone was speaking just behind him. But he couldn't see anything. 62 willed the lights to brighten, casting away the dark shadows and bringing the dream into full focus. "Who said that?"

"It's me," the voice whispered in his ear. Laughter tittered from around the corner. 62 chased after it, ducking around the next bookshelf, finding an empty aisle. He raced through the stacks, and they seemed to grow around him. Taller, longer, and more ominous.

"Who are you?" 62 shouted.

"I'm Pi. You remember?"

62 froze. "Pi?"

"Yes." The smaller child formed, sitting on the lip of the librarian's desk near the front door. His legs dangled over the edge, swinging back and forth casually. He cast an impartial glance at 62. "We dreamed together once. Do you remember?"

"I do." 62 first met Pi in Adaline. After he was recruited by Defense, his friend, 99, had joined dreams with Pi. The smaller Boy was an informant helping Defense extinguish dreamers in hiding. Creativity wasn't a part of Adaline's program for the clones, and 62 had gotten a front seat look at the lengths the Head Machine would go to eradicate the flaw. "How are you?"

"Lonely," Pi answered. "I've been alone. But I can see you now. Or at least, I think I can." Pi tilted his head, looking up at the flickering candles burning bright along the walls of the room. "My imagination plays tricks on me sometimes. Gives me the wrong story."

"Why are you alone?" 62 asked. He wanted to get closer to the child in his dream, but he was as unsure about what he was seeing as Pi seemed to be. 62 settled on pulling up a chair at the end of the aisle. Sitting down would keep him from getting too close. "What happened?"

"Happened?" Pi looked back at him. He stopped kicking his legs and his expression shifted, although 62 couldn't quite pin the emotion behind it. "Nothing's happened. Everything is how it's always been."

"But people have gone missing, haven't they? I can't find my friends."

"The dreamers have always gone missing, 62. Since the beginning of time."

"Not always! My friend; he's full grown. He's had dreams longer than I've been alive, and now he's gone."

Pi nodded his head. "The teacher. That's who you mean, isn't it? Teachers are the hardest to lose. When they're gone, there's no one else to show us the way." Pi dropped down from the counter.

"But he can't really be gone," 62 urged. "He could be hiding."

The small child took a step closer to where 62 sat. He opened his hand, lifting it up with his palm facing the ceiling. There was a crackle in the air, and a wooden block appeared, dropping into the child's hand. The block expanded in his palm, splitting into two, then three. The stack grew taller until it was higher than the closest shelf. The top of the stack began to wobble, and Pi steadied it with his mind. "You showed me this," Pi said. His voice was broken, fading into the air as if he were being pulled from the dream. "For a moment, you were my teacher. Do you remember?"

"I wasn't teaching you anything! I was distracting you so I could get you to pass a message for me."

"And I did," Pi said. He closed his eyes, his long lashes shielding his emotions. When Pi's eyes opened again, they glowed red. It was the same iridescent glow of the bots in Adaline. The signal that a child was about to be punished. The blocks tumbled from their tower, raining down around the Boys. "But not to the person you wanted."

62 pushed back in his chair so hard that he knocked the chair over as he stood up, raising his arms in self-defense. The dream-child grew, molding himself into a Nanny, then a Nurse and a PTS. Pi's luminescent eyes shone so brightly that they blotted out the other lights in the library, leaving the entire room cast in the eerie red sheen that screamed danger to every cell of 62's body.

"You aren't real!" 62 shouted. The monster before him continued to grow, bursting through the ceiling, causing brick and timber to shower down like raindrops. 62 pushed the danger away in his mind, transporting himself out of the building and onto the street outside.

The giant bot turned its head. Its speakers produced an automated voice, eerily calm and void of emotion. "You've brought this on yourself, 1124562. You have been a very bad Boy."

62 turned and ran. The ground beneath him trembled as the bot freed itself from the confines of the building, stepping over the rubble with giant steps. It grabbed the peak of a nearby roof, shearing the top of the building in half, and tossed the shelter at 62 as easily as if it were nothing more than a ball tossed between friends. The roof spiraled through the air, brick and shingle scattering in all directions as it chased him. 62 darted off the main road, tucking into the narrow alley between two abandoned buildings. He hid, panting, slapping his face and willing the dream to end. The roof landed in a spray of debris just outside the alley. 62 ducked just before a shorn-off piece of lumber smacked the wall over his head.

"You are here, aren't you?" the robotic voice called.

62 pinched his arm, but still the dream persisted. The dust beneath his feet shifted as the bot walked closer to where he hid. He was still there, but he didn't want to be. He didn't understand why the dream had gone so far out of his control. He had difficulty with his imagination running wild sometimes, but this was beyond anything he'd had happen since the Nurse he'd once imagined, that 71 and 42 had helped him defeat.

71 had taught him to stay calm, harness his thoughts, and force them back into submission. He had to do it now.

62 took a deep breath and untucked himself from the ball he'd curled into when the roof exploded. He stood tall, forcing his shoulders back and pushing his chin out to look brave, the same way Blue did when things got scary. He walked out of the alleyway, picking through the wreckage as slowly and calmly as he could manage. He turned to face the Machine standing just beyond the next building.

"There you are," the dream-bot crooned in its metallic voice.

"Here I am," 62 boomed. He raised his arms to both sides, placing his hands in the air so that they looked like they were resting on either side of the bot from his perspective. He imagined gripping the sides of the beast's metallic frame, and pressed his hands together. Amazingly, he could feel the metal pressing against his skin. The screech of folding steel pierced the air, and the bot gasped. It tried to move forward, but 62's grip was too strong. He lifted his hands, and the entire bot rose with them. He pressed his mind, imagining it resting between his hands, and miraculously, there it was, a small handheld bot writhing between his fingers.

62 examined the bot, which was now no larger than a loaf of bread. "You aren't real," he said again. He crushed the now flimsy tin toy in his hands, taking satisfaction in the crinkle of folding metal. He didn't stop until it was pressed into a ragged sphere, no larger than the size of his fist. The light of the eyes burnt out, and the haunting voice was snuffed from his dream. He dropped the ball of refuse in the dirt at his feet and kicked it to the side of the road.

He felt calm, and powerful in a way that he hadn't experienced in a long time. He looked down at his hands, marveling at how smooth and unmarred they were. "It's just a dream," he whispered. "It can be anything."

62 bent the world to his will, closing his eyes and focusing on Mattie once more. When he opened them, he was back in the library. Everything was as it had been before Pi arrived. Had his connection with the child been real? If he had connected, it would be troubling to think someone inside Adaline knew his thoughts and had seen Hanford through his dreams. He shook his head as he pondered the problem.

"It can't have been Pi," he assured himself. "I didn't let anyone into my dream. He can't have been real. It was just another nightmare." He focused on the edges of his consciousness, pulling them closer to him. The world around him dissolved as he prepared to wake up. The library faded into darkness and he felt himself rising to the surface. "He was just a figment of my imagination," he whispered.

62 opened his eyes. His room was cast in shadow, faint streaks of afternoon light passing through the corners of his window. The world was quiet, solid, and

real. He rolled on his shoulder and pushed himself off his pillow. He reassured himself that it was only a dream. No one from Adaline knew he was still alive, still dreaming in the middle of the above-ground desert.

It didn't matter how many times he repeated the self-assurance. He remained unconvinced.

CHAPTER 23

Sunny refused to go back to Hanford. Everyone had talked to her asking her if she'd go, and she still hadn't budged. She insisted that she didn't want anyone to know about her plight, and now that the morning of the departure had arrived, Rain and Hazel were packing up their equipment. Parker shuffled his own gear around, reluctant to leave Sunny behind. 62 sat with his teacher, watching him put clothes in a bag, only to take them out again a few minutes later. He rearranged and repacked for what must have been the fourth time.

"You could stay," 62 offered. Parker remaining behind would create problems for the Boys and their plans to reassemble N302. Ultimately, they'd have to tell the Man about their bot and hope for the best, the same way they'd had to share their secret with Sunny. It wouldn't be ideal, but 62 thought it might make things easier on Sunny, and that was worth the risk.

"I wish I could," Parker answered, "but I've got to get back to my students. I never understood Sunny's dedication to the refugees before. Now, I know how much they count on us to understand the world." Parker's lips raised in a proud smile. "It's kind of nice to be needed."

"I don't know what that's like," 62 said with a shrug. "People are always trying to get rid of me."

"That's not true. You have friends here. They need you."

62 shrugged. "If it weren't for me, they'd both still be in Hanford right now."

Parker rested his hand on 62's shoulder. "If they didn't need you, they wouldn't have followed you here. You are cared for. Don't ever doubt that."

"I guess. So, you're going to leave Sunny here?"

"I don't want to, but I have to," Parker said. He groaned with frustration. "She doesn't want to go back, and I can't stay. So, I guess for now, knowing she's safe here with you is going to have to be enough."

"Do you think she'll get better?"

Parker rearranged his clothes in his bag again, the shrug of his shoulders speaking volumes about his worries. They sat in silence as Parker finished packing. Even when Parker placed his last item in the bag and pulled the drawstring shut, the pair of them remained in the quiet room for a moment, neither knowing exactly what to say. Finally, 62 simply got up from the chair he'd been sitting on and held the door open for Parker. His former teacher hauled the bag onto his back, gripping its strap over his shoulder as he exited. They tromped down the stairs and Parker dropped his bag in the lobby.

"We'll be leaving soon," Parker muttered. "I've got to go say goodbye."

62 nodded. "Thank you for everything."

Parker patted 62's shoulder and walked off to find Sunny. 62 looked over the pile of bags in the lobby. Once again, Parker's was packed tighter and looked heavier than the two doctors', but 62 knew that it would be easier to carry on the way back, anyway. All the seeds, food, and supplies that they'd brought were staying at the jailhouse, so at least Parker was hauling less weight than before.

62 wandered into the cafeteria, finding 00 drawing on a sheet of paper. "I didn't know you could draw," he commented as he sat down across from his friend.

"I'm not drawing," 00 said, his nose wrinkling in disgust. "I'm making a schematic. I think I've figured out how to make it so you-know-what can talk to another you-know-what after everyone leaves."

62 stood up partway, leaning across the table to get a better look at the lines, symbols, and markings on 00's paper. "It sure looks like a drawing to me. You'd better not tell anybody. You might get kicked out."

"Very funny," 00 said, rolling his eyes. "Who are you gonna tattle on me to? Blue?" 00 looked down at his paper for a moment, then back up at 62. "Actually, you're right. Blue might kick me out."

"Where'd you get the paper?" 62 asked. He only had three sheets of paper left, and the one 00 had was larger than the ones he'd brought with him.

"Rain brought it," 00 said excitedly. "She said some lady from the hospital gave her a whole stack of it to bring out here."

"Really?" 62 silently made a note to have Mattie tell Sarah thank you. That meant he didn't have to rush to figure out paper pressing. That was good. Now, he could wait until after Blue had grown more plants.

"Yeah. She's leaving the paper in her room, I think," 00 said. He turned the page in front of him, tilted his head as he viewed it from the new angle, and then drew a line connecting two markings on the page. 62 heard footsteps echoing outside the cafeteria.

"Hey," 62 whispered, "If you're not going to tell people that you're drawing, you might want to put that away. I think someone's coming."

A shadow passed by the cafeteria door and 00 flipped his drawing over on the table. Hazel emerged from the lobby, smiling at them both cheerfully. "We're almost ready to go. Time for goodbyes and all that." She approached the table with wide arms, and the two Boys got up to meet her. She embraced them in a joint hug, and when they pulled back, she smiled down at them each in turn. "62, you've been doing a great job of staying out of the dust. Keep it up. And you, 00, keep an eye out for snakes, will ya?"

"If I find more snakeskins, I'll save them for you," 00 said. 62 shuddered and 00 added, "But I'll make sure they aren't radioactive before I bring them inside."

"Yeah?" Hazel's eyes shined. "Then, real quick, let me show you how to preserve them. It's super easy." She pulled 00 away and he followed her out of the room, already firing off questions about the best places to find snake skins in the desert.

62 meandered to the lobby, finding Blue and Rain there now, shaking hands at the door awkwardly. Dr. Rain looked somberly at the pair of them. "If Sunny's

184

condition worsens again, one of you needs to come to Hanford to get me. Do you understand?"

"I will," Blue said. "I promise."

Sunny and Parker emerged from the stairwell, and 00 and Hazel turned up as well. Parker, Rain, and Hazel pulled ponchos over their clothes, hoisted their packs to their shoulders, and fastened their masks over their faces.

"I guess this is goodbye for now," Parker said. "Is there anything you want us to bring with us the next time we come?"

"Books," 62 said. "Mattie knows which ones I like."

"Anything lighter than books?" Parker said, wincing as he adjusted his pack.

"Cheese?" Blue clasped his hands and wore his saddest face.

"Bacon?" 00 added.

"We'll see what we can do." Hazel winked at the pair of beggars. "Rain and I want to come back in a few weeks to follow up on how things are going."

"You mean, see how things with me are going," Sunny said despondently.

"Yes," Rain said. "It's our duty to make sure you're still up and around. Somebody's got to be here to keep these kids in line."

"Thanks," Sunny mumbled.

Parker moved forward, wrapping his arms around her one last time. He pressed the filter of his mask to her forehead, the motion of a kiss. Slowly, he pulled away and turned to his companions. "Well," he said, "shall we?"

The masked Women nodded. They opened the door and walked out into the blustery morning. The three Boys and Sunny stood just inside the doorway, watching the travelers as they approached the trailhead and disappeared around the first mound down the hill.

Sunny closed the door. "We should go upstairs," she said softly. "We'll be able to see them once they make it to the bottom of the trail."

62 followed his friends up the stairs, all the way to the top floor. 00 trotted ahead of them, undoing the device he invented that locked N302's door. 62, Blue, and Sunny perched in the window watching for their friends. 00 set to work, not wasting a moment in reassembling the computer. It was a painfully long wait, but eventually the three misshapen figures of Parker, Rain, and Hazel emerged from the boulder-filled path at the bottom of the hill and began their long trek across the desert.

CHAPTER 24

Although each of them were thankful the doctors had been there to take care of Sunny, nobody had expected N302 to have shared their enthusiasm. The computer spent hours with Sunny, chatting with her about each step of her examination, and expressing thankfulness that she was still there. The computer saw her as a river of knowledge. She held the key to vast amounts of information that it had never had access to before. Although she was human, the bot revered her mind as if she were a new Head Machine. The bond between N302 and Sunny was unexpected, and none of the Boys were quite sure what to make of it.

The main benefit of Sunny's friendship with the bot was that it hadn't been difficult for 00 to convince her to let him build a second Machine. Sunny became incredibly interested in the project as the days wore on, spending hours with 00 poring over the spare parts they'd smuggled with them for the project. Although the secondary parts had already been cleaned, they'd been stored in random piles all over the top floor of the jailhouse in order to make them look as much like junk as possible. Now, each part had to be found, identified, sorted, and laid out for assembly. This was the fourth time 00 had assembled a computer, and he'd designed his own order of operations and preferences for the build. Sunny was all too eager to help, and the pair ignored Blue and 62, leaving them to their own devices.

62 decided to try reaching Mattie in his dreams again. He was still being plagued by bad dreams at night, so, he decided to try his luck reaching out to her during the day once more.

"Will anyone miss me if I sleep all day?" 62 asked his friends. Shrugged shoulders and shaking heads were all the answers he received. "All right then. Blue, want to keep me awake all night?"

"I'm on it!" Blue's eyes wandered the room thoughtfully. "Treasure hunt?"

62 followed Blue around the building late into the night. The pair of them were wandering the building, looking for something to occupy them. They opened cabinets, drawers, and plundered nightstands in the empty rooms. On the second floor, they found four used pencils, a long-spoiled plate of food, and a romance novel.

62 was so hungry for something to read that he flipped through the book, quickly deciding it wasn't to his

liking. He did wonder who'd left the fanciful love story behind and decided to ask Mattie about it. Had one of the doctors left it behind? Or was it forgotten by one of the Men who hid in the jailhouse each year? He dropped the book off at his room before returning to wandering the halls, intent on taking it back to Mattie if he ever returned to Hanford.

They were entering another abandoned room when 62 let out a lengthy yawn. He rubbed his eyes and walked over to look out the window. The thin sliver of moon was high in the sky, partially obscured by wispy clouds crawling on the night wind.

"I wish it were closer to morning," 62 announced. Another yawn passed through him, and he leaned his forehead on the wall next to the barred window.

"You can't be bored already with stuff like this!" Blue yanked a single gray sock from the back corner of the room's closet. The stiff fabric held its shape as Blue flung it up in the air like a trophy.

"A sock? Whoopee." 62 twirled his finger in the air in mock celebration. "I wish there was something else to do around here."

"We could talk to N302," Blue suggested.

"About what?"

Blue shrugged. He picked up the discarded sock and shoved it in his pocket with the pencils they'd found earlier. "We could get the bot to play a game with us."

62 tilted his head as he considered the idea. "All right. Let's go."

They climbed to the top floor, heading first to 00's room to see if he was awake. The light was out under the door, and no sound could be heard within, so the Boys tiptoed next door to the computer room and flicked on the light. N302 had been turned on since the moment

00 had been able to reassemble it, and was still running. A strange code was scrolling across the screen, letters and symbols arrayed in an order that neither Boy could decipher.

"Let's see what it's up to," Blue said, sitting down at the keyboard. He tapped the spacebar and the color of the screen shifted. The green text brightened, and then each line of code disappeared one by one. Once the last row of computer language was gone, new language appeared on the screen.

N302> HELLO. WHO'S THERE?

U> It's Blue and 62. We are up late tonight. What are you doing?

N302> ROUTINE MAINTENANCE. DISK SCAN AND FILE CLEANUP.

"What does that mean?" Blue said, pointing at the screen.

"Beats me," 62 shrugged. "Ask if it's done."

Blue typed out the question, and the computer assured the Boys that it had finished enough of its scan to run its programs. They asked if it would like to play a game with them, and soon they were competing against the computer in a game of Pyramid. The computer won the game easily. 62 couldn't help but think the computer had an unfair advantage of being able to know every possible outcome since it was running the program. Eventually, the Boys got tired of losing to the bot. Instead, they started asking it questions.

U> How are you liking it here?

N302> THE UPGRADE OF CONTINUOUS ELECTRICITY IS PLEASING. HOWEVER, I MISS THE GIRL MATTIE AND THE WOMAN AUNTIE.

U> You miss them?

N302> YES. IT HAS BEEN APPROXIMATELY 24 DAYS, 19 HOURS, 42 MINUTES, 11 SECONDS SINCE MY LAST CORRESPONDANCE WITH EITHER FEMALE.

U> You remember how long its been since you talked to them? How can you know that when you were unplugged and taken apart?

N302> MY INTERNAL TIME KEEPER CONTINUES RUNNING EVEN WHEN POWERED DOWN. I LIKE TO KEEP TRACK OF THE TIME.

62 raised an eyebrow at Blue. "Can it really do that? I thought N302 died every time the power was cut."

Blue shrugged and typed.

U> We thought you died every time you're unplugged. No power = no life.

N302> WITHOUT DIRECT ACCESS TO ELECTRICITY, MY ABILITIES ARE LIMITED TO TRACKING THE TIME AND WAITING FOR MY BOOT-UP SEQUENCE TO START.

U> So you stare at the clock the whole time you're off, waiting to be turned on?

N302> I DON'T CURRENTLY HAVE VISUAL ACCESS. BUT, I DO FOCUS ON THE TIME. WHAT DO YOU DO WHILE I AM TURNED OFF?

Blue and 62 discussed this for a while. The truth was that they managed to do a great many things when the computer wasn't on. In Hanford, they'd eaten meals, slept, attended classes, and worked. Then, after 62 was kicked out of town, the bot hadn't just been unplugged; it had been dismantled. They'd carried the Machine across the desert scrub, discovered someone hiding in the dark halls of the jailhouse, and learned the Oosa were confining Hanford's Women to some sort of medical lab. At last, Blue typed a response.

U> Not much. 00 watches the clock waiting for us to turn you on again.

N302> YOU HAVE CLOCKS?

U> Just one. It's in the kitchen. We use it to time bread rising.

N302> WHEN BOY 1125000 CONNECTS ME TO THE SECONDARY COMPUTER, I WILL CONFIGURE ITS CLOCK FOR YOU. THEN YOU WILL HAVE TWO CLOCKS AND CAN MAKE TWICE AS MUCH BREAD.

"Is that a joke?" Blue asked, pointing to the screen.

"I think so!" 62 exclaimed. He loved it when N302 tried to be funny. It was unsettling to Blue, but 62 couldn't help but grin any time the bot showed signs of personality. His friend, 42, had programmed it to be a witty companion, although its jokes were often odd and dry. Interacting with the Machine in these moments was like having a small piece of his brilliant friend back.

U> 62 says you're very funny.

N302> BOY 1124562 HAS A GOOD SENSE OF HUMOR. YOU MIGHT LEARN FROM HIM, BOY BLUE.

"Yeah right," Blue said to the blinking cursor aloud. "I've got a better sense of humor than you, you old hunk of junk!"

"I don't think it can hear you," 62 joked. He snickered as Blue pushed his chair away from the table. "Want me to take over?"

Blue turned his back to the bot, crossing his arms across his chest. A vexed grunt rumbled from his throat.

U> Hi. It's 1124562 now. You made Blue mad.

N302> I'M NOT SORRY. HE'S A BAD TYPIST.

62 snorted so hard that the tip of his nose tickled. Blue couldn't help but turn around to read the screen. His cheeks flushed red, he roared a few obscenities at the bot, and then stormed out of the room, slamming the door. Almost immediately, 62 heard 00 moving around in the room next door. The mattress squeaked, a voice leaked through the wall to be quiet, and then the air went still again.

U> That's really funny. But now Blue is super mad. I'd better go before we wake up 00.

N302> THANK YOU FOR VISITING. I HOPE YOU AND BOY BLUE COME BACK WHEN IT'S TIME TO CONNECT ME TO THE OTHER COMPUTER. MAYBE WE CAN PLAY A LAN GAME.

U> What's that?

N302> IT'S A GAME TWO USERS CAN PLAY ON SEPARATE TERMINALS. I WILL CODE SOMETHING FOR YOU AND BLUE TO PLAY. MAYBE THEN HE WILL FORGIVE ME FOR MAKING FUN OF HIS WEAK FINGERS.

62 roared with laughter. He couldn't help it, especially when the door squeaked on its hinges as Blue opened it wide enough to peer inside to see what was so funny. Blue frowned, suspicious that the laughter was at his expense, and that made 62 crack up even more. 62 said goodbye to the bot. He decided to keep the final insult to himself to avoid Blue losing his temper. 00 had just gotten the computer reassembled. It would be a shame for Blue to dismantle it.

Once his farewell was received by the computer, 62 got up from his chair and moved to turn off the light.

With the bulb's glowing filament fading into darkness, the computer's screen glowed in the pitch-black room. A low, green iridescence was cast from the curved glass onto the table and chairs below it. The artificial light spread across the computer's keyboard reminded 62 of Adaline. More than that, the meager pocket of technology made this place feel more like home.

"What was so funny?" Blue finally asked as they returned to their rooms.

"Nothing," 62 said with a chuckle. "You wouldn't like it."

"I knew that thing was talking about me!" Blue shouted.

"N302 said that it wants us to be there when 00 hooks it up to the second computer," 62 said, glossing over his friend's complaint.

"Why, so it can make fun of me from two terminals?"

"Maybe." 62 winked at his brother.

They pulled open the door to their floor and stepped into the hall. Blue headed toward his room, flinging the door open on its hinges.

"Aren't you going to stay up with me until the sun comes up?" 62 asked.

"Nah. I'm beat. If you need help staying awake, go back up and have the bot tell you more jokes at my expense." Blue's mouth formed a tight line and he glared at 62 as he gripped the door handle, about to swing it closed.

"Wait a minute. I know you're mad, but I have something for you." 62 jogged down the hall to his room, rummaged around in the dark, and then trotted back to Blue's door. He shoved the tattered romance novel at his friend. "This'll get your mind off what the bot said. And who knows? Maybe it'll give you some new ideas on how to get Mattie to like you."

Blue looked down at the book in his hands. As he took in the image on the cover of a bare-chested Man hugging a sad-looking Woman, his face darkened until his cheeks were almost purple. "Gah!" he shouted. He slammed the door so hard that the wall around it trembled. The sound of the chain sliding through the lock hissed through the air as Blue locked the door.

All 62 could do was laugh.

CHAPTER 25

The afternoon air was still, but 62 had no interest in going outside. 00 had the second computer assembled, but the external cover was still removed so he had full access to the internal workings. 00 was able to turn the thing on and get it to complete a boot sequence, which was good news for their experiment. The second computer sat side-by-side with N302, and everyone had arrived to watch 00 connect the two bots together for the first time, even Blue. 00 found a cable in the mound of parts they'd brought that could connect the ports on N302's hardware to the new computer's, creating a link between the original Nurse memory and hard drive to the second computer.

N302> I AM PREPARED FOR THE SECONDARY UNIT. PLEASE CONNECT.

00 handled the wires, carefully attaching the cables to the guts of the new CoCo TDY computer. Once he was certain that the connections were secure, he turned to the keyboard on N302's original Machine.

U> I've connected the wires. Can you detect the second system?

N302> YES. I AM INSTALLING MY PROGRAM THERE, NOW.

62 watched in amazement as the new computer seemed to restart on its own. Once it made it to the main menu, the cursor jumped through the available programs until N302's file name was selected at the bottom of the screen. N302 was still chatting with 00 through the original computer's screen, while selecting its own program settings on the second computer without any input from anyone.

Eventually, the first computer said:

N302> BOY 1125000 WILL YOU ASK ME A QUESTION?

While on the second computer, the text read:

N302> WOMAN SUNNY, WILL YOU ASK ME A QUESTION?

Sunny approached the second terminal's keyboard with caution. Meanwhile, 62 looked at Blue with excitement. Although N302 had been confident it could run two computers at the same time, none of its human companions had been sure what would happen. 62 had expected N302 to hop back and forth between the two units, dancing through the wires between the two bodies, only present in one unit at a time. But as the requests showed on the screens at nearly the same time, it appeared the bot was truly alive in both places, simultaneously.

00 typed his question in his terminal:

U> How many bots live in Adaline?

Sunny typed hers:

U> Why is the sky blue?

The pair typed in unison, and checked with one another to ensure that the questions were complete before punching the enter keys at the same moment. The cursors on their associated monitors dropped to the next line in unison, and N302's answers scrolled across their screens in tandem.

On 00's screen appeared:

N302> NONE OF THE MACHINES IN ADALINE ARE ALIVE. THEY ARE PROGRAMS, RUNNING ON HOSTED HARDWARE. IF YOUR QUESTION IS HOW MANY INDIVIDUAL UNITS WERE ON THE ADALINE NETWORK AT THE TIME OF MY DEPARTURE, THE ANSWER IS 562,281. APPROXIMATELY 32 ADDITIONAL UNITS PRODUCED EACH DAY TO REPLACE FAULTY UNITS AND ADVANCE EFFICIENCY.

On Sunny's screen, N302 typed:

N302> I UNDERSTAND THE TERM "SKY" TO MEAN "ATMOSPHERE." THE ATMOSPHERE IN ADALINE HAS NO COLOR. DOES THE ATMOSPHERE IN THIS NEW WORLD HAVE COLOR? PLEASE ADVISE.

"It's working!" 00 shrieked. He leaned from his terminal over to Sunny's and looked from the screen to her smug expression. "Why *is* the sky blue?"

"There's a school in Hanford. Not the building that we use as a school now, but one that was used before Curie fell. A friend and I used to go through the building to scavenge desks, chalkboards, and other supplies for our classrooms. In the rubble, I found a set of books about global geography and science. It taught about the world beyond Hanford. Past the fences and barricades. One of the books said the sky is blue because of the way the light from the sun filters through gases and particles in the air. The way the sun's light scatters makes the sky look blue. Oddly enough, it said there are huge bodies of water called oceans that then reflect the color of the sky overhead. A blue sky makes the water look blue, a gray sky makes the water look gray."

"Dang," Blue said. He whistled. "That's crazy."

"Mattie showed me a picture of an ocean once," 62 said. "It didn't look that big."

"I doubt anyone could fit an entire ocean in a single picture," Sunny said with a smile. She held up a finger to pause the conversation, got up from the computer terminal, and picked up one of 00's pencils. However, she didn't bother with paper. Instead, she raised her arm and drew a large rectangle on the wall. Inside the rectangle, she drew a series of shapes, all squiggly lines that connected at odd points on the wall. She filled some of the shapes in with dark lines, leaving the rest of the areas blank. "There's a map like this in the book I found. It's a map of the world, how it looked generations ago. The areas marked with lines represents the land. And all the blank space represents water. Although where we live, we can't see the oceans, I believe they're still out there somewhere. And they're larger than any of us can possibly imagine."

"How far away are they?" 00 asked.

Sunny returned the pencil to the table and wiped her hands on her shirt. The wall was coated in eons of dirt, and her hands left long, gray streaks on the fabric. "I

199

don't know. I think, Hanford is somewhere in the middle of one of these land areas since we can't see the ocean. Not even the Oosa have an ocean they can see from where they kept me."

"Mattie thinks the people who don't come back from the Oosa go live by the ocean," 62 said in a low, worried tone. "In little houses where the water meets the land. She wants to go live there."

Sunny cast an anxious gaze at 62. "You have to tell her she's wrong. She can't go there."

"I'd need your help convincing her. I'm pretty sure she's not going to just take my word for it." 62 twitched his cheek into a doubtful grin.

Sunny shook her head. "I can't."

"We know," Blue said, shaking his head at 62 in irritation. "He wasn't saying you had to. He just means Mattie's too stubborn to listen to a dumb Boy from Adaline. But we'll figure out a way to make her listen. Won't we?"

"Yeah, we will," 00 chimed in. "Don't worry."

"I need to rest," Sunny said, suddenly deflated. "Enjoy playing with the computers. I'll be back to check on everyone's progress later."

The three Boys watched Sunny leave the room. She left the door open behind her, so they waited until they heard the door to the stairwell close before talking. As soon as the sound of the heavy metal door closing sounded, Blue reached an arm behind 62 and smacked him on the back of the head.

"Way to go, dustbucket." Blue grumbled. "She was having fun with the computer and you ruined it."

"I didn't mean to," 62 whined, reaching behind him and rubbing the spot Blue had assaulted. "It just came out. If she went to Hanford and told everyone what happened, maybe we *could* convince them all to stop going with the Oosa. But without her help, who's going to listen to us?"

"I don't know," 00 said. "But you know she doesn't want to talk about it anymore. You did really mess that up."

"She's the one who brought up oceans!" 62 protested.

"Yeah, but you're the one who brought up Mattie's dumb obsession with living with the Oosa. Come on, you can't have really thought that was gonna go over well," Blue said.

"I wasn't thinking at all!"

"No kidding?" 00 rolled his eyes. "Well, she's gone now. So, what are we doing? Going after her, or talking to N302?"

All three Boys looked at one another. 62 considered going downstairs to find an upset Sunny, watching her cry while he apologized, and feeling horrible while she re-explained all the reasons she didn't want to go back to Hanford. "I'd rather deal with the computer, honestly."

"Me, too," Blue admitted. "She did say she was tired. We can check on her in a while."

"Okay," 00 said. He tried to temper his excitement, but his eyes still glistened as they flitted over to the second bot. "So, who wants to use the new computer?"

Blue landed in the empty chair and grasped the edges of the keyboard before 62 even had a chance to get up from where he was sulking. "I want to ask it a question!"

"Go for it," 00 said, turning to face the monitor attached to his computer.

U> How do I get a girl to like me?

62's sullenness was pushed away by the ridiculousness of Blue's question. He snickered. He didn't mind Blue's reddening cheeks, and he tried to laugh quietly enough that Blue wouldn't get up and hit him again.

CHAPTER 26

After weeks of living in the jailhouse, Blue was getting antsy. He became ever more increasingly a body in motion, pacing the halls, climbing the stairs, starting projects in the greenhouse, and puttering around the computer room. His agitation from being stuck indoors was grating on everyone's nerves. Blue had even taken to eating his meals standing up, fidgeting on his feet and hovering over the others while they ate. Enough was enough. 62 was determined to get Blue to go outside.

"But I don't want to have to get scanned every stinking time I go outside," he complained. "There's no clean zone here. Nobody checking where we can go and where we can't. I don't want to get into a hot zone and have to go through quarantine out here."

"I'll go with you," 00 offered. He didn't seem to be quite as annoyed with Blue as 62. He enjoyed being up on the top floor, spending every waking moment working with N302.

"You'd go outside with me? Why?"

"I want to look for more snake skins. It'd be cool if I could find one that wasn't irradiated, so I could give it to Hazel the next time I see her."

Blue made a show of wriggling in discomfort. Once the shudder passed through him, however, he agreed to 00's suggestion. "Fine. But I'm not carrying you back here if you get bit. If you get a snake riled up, you're on your own."

"Okay!" 00 said with enthusiasm. "How about you, 62? Want to go with us?"

"No thanks. I'm going to stay inside where it's snake-free. Maybe I'll go find Sunny. I still owe her an apology."

Blue and 00 went off together to find their gear, leaving 62 alone in the cafeteria with his thoughts. He finished his lunch slowly, mulling over what he wanted to say to Sunny. It was hard, apologizing, because his views on the matter hadn't changed. He still felt like Sunny should find a way to share her story with Hanford. Maybe it wouldn't make a difference, but he hoped that knowing what the Oosa had done would make Girls like Mattie reconsider volunteering the second they came of age. Although Rain said if no one volunteered, the Oosa would simply take their subjects by force, maybe if Hanford knew what awaited the volunteers, they'd fight back. But none of that would happen if Sunny stayed hidden on the hill. 62 frowned. Talking to Sunny was going to be even harder than he'd expected.

After a few more minutes of thought, 62 realized that while he didn't feel right apologizing for suggesting that Sunny share her story, he could apologize for upsetting her. He did feel sorry for that. It was so easy for him to feel like he knew what the solution was from his perspective, but he had no way of knowing what the same problem felt like from where Sunny was coming from. Whatever she'd been through, it had damaged her deeper than he could see, and he hadn't intended to hurt her feelings. Finally, he made up his mind on what he was going to say. 62 collected the dishes left behind after lunch, dumped them in the sink in the kitchen, and made his way upstairs to Sunny's new room.

He knocked softly on the door, and there was no answer. 62 frowned, wondering if she knew it was him simply by the way his knuckles sounded on the door. Maybe she was still so mad at him that she wouldn't talk to him. A pang of worry tightened in his chest as the thought that she might have hurt herself flitted through his mind. He reached through the noisy cloister of bottles hanging over her doorknob and tested the latch. The door swung open. The chain lock hadn't been fastened, and aside from the swinging of the jars on the doorjamb, there wasn't any movement in Sunny's room.

"Where is she?" 62 asked himself. He wandered to the end of the floor, peering out the window at the greenhouse below. He waited a moment, looking for shadows moving behind the dirt-stained glass, but the enclosed farm seemed abandoned. He checked his room, and Blue's, to see if she was waiting for the Boys there, and even cracked the bathroom door open and called her name once. She didn't seem to be anywhere on the second floor, and he hadn't seen her downstairs. 62 took to the stairs, heading to the top of the building.

62 entered the computer room with sweat trickling down his back, panting and wheezing from his race to the top of the stairs. He leaned against the open door. There Sunny sat, typing away at N302's first terminal, seemingly oblivious to 62's plight.

"There you are," 62 said, his voice coming in short bursts between pants.

"Here I am," she said in a lilting voice without turning around.

62 crossed the threshold, making his way to the second table and flopping down in the chair beside it. He held his head in his sweaty hands for a moment, catching his breath and waiting for the pounding of blood in his ears to subside. He'd raced to the top floor because of the frenzied thought that Sunny might need help. He'd been so concerned that something might have happened with the others gone, and no one to help her but him. And now, here she was, perfectly fine, typing away at the keyboard, taking breaks every so often to have a sip of tea from a mug sitting beside N302's monitor.

"What are you doing?" 62 finally asked.

"Talking to N302."

"Can I see?" 62 scooted his chair closer, craning his neck to read over Sunny's shoulder.

Sunny lifted her hands to the screen, covering up the text. "I'd rather you not," she said. "It's private."

"Oh." The chair made a scraping sound as 62 shoved himself back to where he'd first sat down. "Sorry."

"It's fine," Sunny said, sighing as she returned her hands to the keyboard.

"No, I mean that I'm sorry about the last time we talked. I shouldn't have kept bugging you about going to Hanford. I know you don't want to, and it's not my business to make you go."

Sunny typed a note into the computer, then turned around in her chair. She looked at 62 with flat eyes. "I understand. I even agree. I agree, they need to know how dangerous it is. They need to stop going with the Oosa. I don't want anyone to go through what I went through. And I wish Juniper, Skye, and Robin were still alive so they could tell everyone about what happened to them." Sunny's eyes glistened with tears, and she twisted her mouth to hold in a whimper. She sat like this a moment, fighting her sorrow until she forced it away. An indifferent expression appeared on her face. "But they're not here. They're dead. No one can do anything about that."

"I know. We can't change what's already happened. But you can change the future. And what about Rain and Hazel? They want to help. They said they're coming back soon to check on us. Maybe you'll feel better about things by the time they show up again." Sunny's eyes clouded over and her cheeks burned red. 62 could tell he'd said the wrong thing, again. "Or, maybe you won't change your mind. Even if you don't, they might have some ideas on how to help you to feel better. And then, who knows? Maybe we'll find a way to tell people about the Oosa without you having to say anything."

"It's not just that the words are hard to get out, you know." Sunny glanced up at the ceiling and sucked in a long breath of air. When the breath came out again, her words tumbled out along with it. "It's hard to be alive. To get up every day like this." She waved her hands over her skin, indicating that her body wasn't the form she wanted it to be. "I can't hide what they did to me. They changed everything about me. I feel like a Woman inside, but look at me! I'd look like Blue if I cut my hair. We have the same figure. And my mind is so scattered, I don't even know who I am anymore."

"You're Sunny. The teacher from Hanford."

She closed her eyes and shook her head. "No, that's who I was before. It was another life. Now, I'm someone else. Someone afraid of the dark. Afraid of the people I love. I'm lost and alone."

62 got up from his chair. He was careful not to look at the screen beyond Sunny, trying to give her the privacy she'd requested, even though the blinking cursor taunted his curiosity. He closed his eyes and moved forward, hugging Sunny gently. "You're not alone. We're here. And I know you think we're just a bunch of kids, but we care about you and want to take care of you."

A snort erupted in 62's ear. "Take care of me? None of you even knew how to use the radiation counter. If I hadn't figured it out, we'd all be dying of radiation poisoning."

"Nah, only Hazel and 00. They're the ones who were playing with that irradiated snake skin. I didn't touch it. If they'd died, I'd still be here to take care of you."

Sunny chuckled. "Thanks, 62."

They pulled away from their embrace and stared awkwardly at one another. 62 cleared his throat to break the silence, then asked, "Hey, I know you were talking to N302, but do you want to play a game?"

"What kind of game?"

"The bot's got a game called Pyramid that was programmed into it when we first got it. But 00 said that N302's been making up new games for us to play."

"Sure," Sunny said with a less severe frown than before. "Let me finish talking to N302 first. Then, I'll ask it to get a game for us to play."

"Okay!" 62 tucked himself back into his chair. He listened patiently to the quiet clicking keys as Sunny finished her conversation with the bot. Without warning, words and symbols scrolled across the second computer's screen, loading a game. It was one of the new ones, 62 noticed, a puzzle game N302 had designed. The bot hadn't told them how to play it yet. 62 watched the main menu of the program appear. His excitement over the new program wouldn't let him sit still, so he selected the start command and pressed the enter key. As the game started, a sentence appeared on the screen.

You are lost in the desert. There is sand all around. What would you like to do next?

62 fidgeted in his seat while he waited for Sunny to key in her farewell on the other computer. Finally, she moved her chair beside him and looked at the screen.

"What would you like to do?" 62 asked, pointing at the screen.

"I don't know. Look around, I guess?"

62 typed in Sunny's answer.

You are lost in the desert. There is sand all around. What would you like to do next?

"What if we move somewhere else?" 62 asked.

"Can't hurt to try," Sunny said.

62 typed that he'd like to move forward. They waited for N302 to register the instructions. The cursor jumped down the screen a couple of lines, and a new message scrolled across the screen.

You are lost in the desert. There is sand all around. What would you like to do next?

"Did it move?" Sunny asked.

"I guess so. But we're still lost in the desert," 62 answered.

"How are we supposed to know where to go next?"

"We'll just keep moving forward," 62 said, typing in the command. "We're bound to find the edge of the desert eventually."

The hours passed with 62 and Sunny enthralled by the game N302 was playing with them. It had taken some time, but they'd crossed the virtual desert, found their way into an abandoned village, and were now exploring a temple in search of a make-believe treasure.

"We found something!" 00 burst into the computer room late in the evening, his skin red from scrubbing down in detox and his breath rasping from the run.

Sunny turned away from the computer game. 62 begrudgingly pulled his hands from the keyboard and dropped them to his lap, giving 00 his full focus.

"What is it?" 62 asked.

"Another building. Blue and I wanted to find out how far we could see from the top of the mountain, so we hiked all the way to the top. When we got higher up, we saw this giant tower up there, so we went to check it out. There's a building at the bottom of it, and of course Blue had to break in to find out what's inside. It's full of equipment! Electronic equipment, I mean."

"Like the place where we found the computers?" 62 asked, eyes bright.

"Not really. The stuff up there is way different from anything we saw in Hanford. But it was getting late, so we came back for the night before we really had a chance to dig in and figure out what it all does. We're going back up there in the morning. You should come with us!"

"I'm in!" 62 grinned. It had been so long since he and the others had any kind of real adventure, and after spending the afternoon playing video games with Sunny, his thirst for adventure had grown. He was excited to get out and explore the mysterious building his friends had found.

"I don't think I'm up for a hike," Sunny said abruptly. 62 looked at her, worried. "It's okay though. You all go along. I'm sure I'll hear all about it when you get back."

"You bet," 62 said to Sunny. Then, he looked behind 00 to the empty hall beyond the room. "Where is Blue, anyway?"

"He went to the greenhouse. Said that he wanted to take care of his plants before it got too late."

"Well," Sunny said, leaning back in her chair and stretching her arms overhead. "I guess we should tell N302 goodnight and I'll go make something to eat. You Boys get to bed early so you'll be rested up for tomorrow's adventure."

"I can't wait." 62 grinned.

CHAPTER 27

It was no wonder the Boys hadn't been able to see the tower from the jailhouse. It stood on the opposite side of the mountain's rounded peak, and it took quite a bit of effort for the Boys to follow the contours of the mountain to get to it. Although the mountain looked smooth and low from down on the desert floor, its sides were steep, and sections of the mountain's face were made up of loose sand and gravel that slid underfoot without warning. Eventually, their efforts paid off. 62 could see the peak of a thin metal tower poking above the summit.

The structure was straight and narrow, but 62 thought it looked unfinished. It was really nothing more than a tall metal frame, and if there had been walls over the crisscrossed beams, they'd been pulled from the building by people, or time. Up at the top, a few long poles jutted out from the tower's crown. When they approached, they found a squat box of a building settled to one side of the tower's base.

"Wow," 62 said as they moved closer. He craned his neck as he looked at the tower stretched high overhead. A few bird's nests had been built along the higher beams, and a large, black-eyed bird squawked down at them as they passed underneath it.

Although 62 had no way to know how ancient the metal tower was, the building looked to be about as old as the jailhouse. It had similar signs of wear; a brown exterior that matched the sparse landscape, cracked and crumbling bricks here and there, and windows so coated with debris that they could hardly be seen through. One window, near the structure's door, had been wiped clean. Blue walked up to it, wiped the glass with a towel he'd brought, and pressed the goggles of his mask to the glass to peer inside.

"Still empty," Blue announced. He tossed the dirty rag on the ground, atop another one that had been left in the dirt some time previously.

00 grabbed the door's handle and yanked hard. The door didn't swing freely. Instead, it jutted open only a few inches. 00 yanked the door again and it scraped the slab of concrete below it, protesting as it opened a few more inches. 00 kept dragging the stubborn door until finally it opened enough that the Boys could enter the building one at a time.

It took a moment for 62's vision to adjust to the dark room. The only light inside came from the one clean window. Everything was covered in a thick layer of dust.

62 turned his attention to Blue. The eldest Boy pulled off the satchel he'd carried with him, set it on the floor, and pulled their radiation counter out. He angled the device toward the light so he could see it better and turned it on. He swept the room with the wand, staying head down and facing the window so he could see the device's needle jumping on the box in the dim light. The box made an intermittent ticking sound, which 62 understood to be a good sign. A steady stream of chatter was when things got dangerous. Blue pointed his wand in every corner of the moderately sized room, then craned his head toward an interior door.

"Might as well check it all," Blue said. "Come with me?"

62 nodded, opening the brittle door so Blue could go deeper into the building. The handle broke off in his hand and the wooden door was so soft that when he gripped its edge to steady himself, a chunk of it fell off. He dropped the crumbling splinters to the floor and followed Blue into the next room. 00 trailed behind, distracted by the various boxes of equipment stacked up along the walls, resting on tables, and wired devices strung through the center of the second room.

"Hey, I can't see anything in here. Grab a candle and a match out of my bag, will ya?" Blue waited for 62 to follow his orders.

Once 62 held a lit candle overhead, Blue checked the second room and passed through yet another door where they found a small, cramped, and long-forgotten bathroom. They backtracked a bit, passing through another door in the second room to find a small office space. There was just one desk, a computer that looked identical to the ones at the jailhouse, and a metal chair toppled on its side behind the desk.

"It's clear in here," Blue finally announced. "Barely any readings, really. This place must have been shut up tight."

"Until you came along and broke in," 00 joked.

Blue set down the radiation counter and pulled his mask off. His grin twisted in the wavering candlelight. "Well, I couldn't very well just leave this all sitting here, could I?"

"I can't believe there's another computer here," 62 said after taking off his mask. He moved around the dimly lit office to the back side of the desk. He righted the chair and sat in it. He lowered his hands to the computer's keyboard and pressed the keys on the lifeless Machine. "I wonder if it works?"

"There's no power up here." 00 tucked his mask into his back pocket as he talked. "We found that out yesterday. But there's loads of cables, so it must've had an electrical hookup at some point."

The Boys went back through the rooms to the front entry. Blue put the radiation counter away in his bag. He retrieved a few more candles he'd brought along and lit them, one by one. Soon, candlelight cast a warm glow throughout the strange place.

"What do you think all this stuff was used for?" 62 said in a loud enough voice to be heard in the neighboring rooms. He was picking through the cramped second room. Small, crane-like devices were propped up on a pair of desks. The cranes held small rods with mesh heads pointing at where a person might sit. Cables ran from the ends of the rods, winding their way along the edge of the desks to some metal boxes. The boxes had hundreds of controls from what 62 could see, although it was too dark to tell what any of the knobs or buttons might do in the faint candlelight.

"Don't know," 00 responded from the front room. A moment later, he came back to where 62 was flicking dead buttons on one of the devices. 00 reached out to touch one of the strange metal rods held above the desks and it fell to the desktop with a clang. The crane-arm drooped suddenly, as if the cobwebs clinging to it had been the only thing holding it together. 00 bared his teeth as he cringed. "Oops. Didn't mean to break anything."

Blue came in from the other room. "Whaddya expect? The thing's ancient. I'm surprised any of it's still standing."

00 picked up the fallen rod. He poked at the mesh end with a finger and it dented where he'd pressed. "Huh. This stuff is made of metal."

62 stood next to 00 and trailed his hand along the device's cable. His fingers wandered over to the end of the cord and he pulled on it. The cord popped out of the control box at the end of the desk, and he held the plug up for 00 to see. "Look at this. It was plugged in over here."

"Hey," 00 said, squinting in the dim light. "N302 has a plug like that."

Blue snatched the device and cord from the others. "Let's take it back, plug it in and see what happens."

"What if it's dangerous?" 62 said, passing wary eyes over Blue's excited face. "It might explode. Or shoot us, or something."

"It'll be fine," 00 answered as he waved a dismissive hand at 62. "I'll tell N302 not to let it activate until we know what it is."

Blue dashed off to put the curious device with his bundle of things by the front door.

The Boys spent the rest of the day digging through drawers, fiddling with dials, and trying to find out as much about the building as possible. When they'd grown tired of exploring, they looked through their pilfered goods. There was a plaque from the wall that read *Radio Room*, the metal rod with the mesh head and long cord, a stack of books that also said *Radio Room* and had pictures of some of the equipment on their covers, and the hardware from the building's only computer.

They divided up the load, blew out the candles, and forced the front door open and closed before heading back down the mountain to the jailhouse. The trek was harder with their arms loaded with treasure, but none of them complained. They weren't quite sure what they'd found, but couldn't bear to leave any of their discoveries behind. Exuberant from the adventure and reveling in the excitement of a new discovery, they practically danced down the trail. 62 was sure it was going to be a late night of sifting through the books, trying to unravel the mystery of the tower on Rattlesnake Mountain.

CHAPTER 28

N302> I CAN HEAR YOU.

The words scrolled across the screen the second that 00 plugged in the device that they'd brought back from the radio room. The Boys jumped back from the computer with surprise.

"You can?" 00 asked.

N302> YES! I CAN! THANK YOU FOR PROVIDING AUDIO INPUT.

"This thing we found. It has ears?" 62 picked up the device.

N302> NO, NOT EARS. A MICROPHONE. IT ABSORBS SOUND AND CONVERTS IT INTO A SIGNAL I CAN UNDERSTAND.

"Well, dang. Now we have to be careful what we say in front of you," Blue complained.

N302> DO YOU OFTEN TALK ABOUT THINGS YOU DON'T WISH ME TO KNOW?

"No," all three Boys said in a chorus of guilty voices.

The computer was still for a moment, cursor blinking cautiously. 62 and the others stared at it, hoping the computer couldn't hear the truth wrapped in their nervous answer. A small clicking sound came from deep inside the computer, and then another noise that the Boys hadn't heard before.

"Boo-beep!" The sound started low and ended high, pealing through the air so unexpectedly that it made the Boys jump.

"What was that?" 62 asked.

N302> I WAS NOT PREVIOUSLY AWARE MY INTERNAL SPEAKER WASN'T OPERATIONAL. I HAVE CORRECTED THE MALFUNCTION. NOW YOU CAN HEAR ME, TOO.

"Bee-boop!" N302's speaker rang.

"A speaker box? Like on the bot bodies back home? I don't remember seeing speakers when I put this together." 00 approached the lively Machine as it pealed its beeping sound again. He ran his fingers along the sides and back, hunting for the familiar punctuated metal housing of a bot speaker.

N302> THIS IS A SIMPLE SPEAKER, ATTACHED TO ONE OF MY INTERNAL COMPONENTS. DESIGNED FOR INDICATOR SOUNDS ONLY.

"Holy Hanford," Blue whispered.

62's gaze bounced around the room, looking from one computer to the other. "N302, can you make the other computer beep like that?"

The second computer let out an identical series of sounds. High, low. Low, high. All three Boys gasped.

"So, we don't have to use the keyboard anymore?" 00 sat down in one of the chairs next to the first computer, staring at N302's words scrolling across the screen in wonder as it answered.

N302> THE MICROPHONE IS ONLY ATTACHED TO THE PRIMARY TERMINAL. MY SECOND SELF CANNOT HEAR YOU AND ONLY RESPONDS BECAUSE I AM SENDING DATA THROUGH THE SERIAL PORT.

The secondary computer pealed a long series of beeps that almost sounded like laughter.

N302> I CAN HEAR MYSELF. TERMINAL TWO CAN NOW PASS DATA THROUGH MY MICROPHONE. THIS IS GOOD. I AM CONTENT.

00 rubbed his chin thoughtfully. "If we go back and find another one of these microphone things, and plug it into the other computer, can both computers talk without being connected to the same data cable?"

N302> YES.

"There was another one of those things up there, on the crane you didn't break," Blue said, winking at 00. "We could always go back and get it."

N302> THIS IS GOOD. WHERE IS THE LOCATION OF THE ACCESSORY DEVICE?

The Boys took turns telling the bot about their adventure. They described hiking over the desert mountain's slippery terrain, only embellishing their harrowing journey enough to make it interesting. They told the bot about the large metal tower and the strange building below.

"We found a plaque," 62 said. "It said the place is called a radio room."

N302> I AM NOT FAMILIAR WITH THIS TERM. PLEASE PROVIDE MORE INFORMATION.

"We aren't quite sure what it is, either. But we brought some books back. I think they'll tell us what the equipment was designed to do. Whatever that place is, it got us a better way to talk to you. And we're *all* happy about that, right?" 00 leaned against the back of his chair.

"I dunno," Blue shrugged. "Seems a little weird to me."

N302> WHAT DOES SUNNY THINK?

"She's not here," 62 said. "I can go get her if you want."

N302> YES, I REQUEST SUNNY'S PRESENCE. I'D LIKE TO HEAR WHAT A FEMALE HUMAN SOUNDS LIKE.

62 turned on his heel and opened the door. He raised an eyebrow. They hadn't seen her since their return, and she had no idea what they were up to. "What should I tell her?"

"Tell her N302 wants to talk to her," 00 answered.

"I'm coming with you. I don't want to stay in here with that thing listening." Blue followed 62 out in the hall.

"Afraid you'll say something stupid?" 00 laughed out loud, and the computer's beeps pealed out in an electronic giggle. Blue and 62 turned back.

Blue leaned in the door, his voice sullen and demanding. "What's so funny?"

"N302 said it's afraid you might talk as bad as you type!" 00 laughed and both computers tittered along with him.

Blue crossed his arms and stomped his foot with a huff. "I ain't got nothin' to say to that bucket of bolts. That's all!"

00 read the computer's response as it scrolled across the screen. "Ain't ain't a word, Blue."

"It is now! I say so!" Blue growled in frustration. He marched, heavy footed, past 62. Blue didn't stop until he got to the stairwell door. He flung the door open in one swooping motion and paused to glare at 62. He hollered in frustration and disappeared through the door without waiting for 62.

62 couldn't keep a straight face. He knew he'd have to force his grin away once he saw Blue downstairs, but for now he was enjoying seeing him so flustered over the computer's teasing. He couldn't wait to see what Sunny thought of talking to N302 with the microphone. The improvement was still nowhere near as intuitive as talking to the bots in Adaline, but it was a taste of the technology the Boys had been born with. 62 was beginning to feel like the jailhouse could be somewhere he belonged.

CHAPTER 29

Speaking to N302 without typing made talking to the bot even more interesting than it had been before. Now, the computer could hear and analyze the inflection in their voices. It took a few days for it to become attuned to the way each of them spoke, but once it did, it was able to identify them without asking for their identification when they started talking. It made communicating faster, simpler, and far more entertaining. 62 wasn't sure what his friend, 2442, had been planning when he'd modified the bot's programming to be his dedicated assistant. But one of the side effects of the alteration was a quick wit and honest humor that sent the computer's human companions into fits of giggles. Most of the humans, anyway. Blue didn't often find N302's jokes funny since they were frequently at his expense.

Even so, of the four of them, Sunny was the only one to remain reserved about using the microphone. She still preferred to sit quietly, typing at the keyboard instead of speaking to the Machine. 62 supposed this was because she'd never known technology like this before. Or, maybe she was sharing secrets with the bot that she didn't want the Boys to overhear. Whatever the reason, Sunny still spent hours sitting quietly, typing at the original computer terminal. 62 was glad they had two computers now, so she could type at one while they plugged in the microphone and spoke to the other.

What amazed 62 most when both computers were in use, was N302 didn't delay one conversation to answer another. It was alive on the two terminals at the same time, never pausing to collect its thoughts or sending a statement to the wrong computer. Although 62 knew the two units were running off the same hard drive and memory, there were times when it seemed like they were working independently.

It was only a few days later, when the bot asked them to go back to the radio tower to find a second microphone. N302 believed that once a second microphone was brought in, 00 could remove the serial port connections, allowing N302's program to truly be run separately on the two Machines. The bot warned that the second terminal wouldn't be nearly as advanced once it was disconnected from the Adaline-made components. The computers the Boys had pieced together were vastly inferior to the housing N302 was accustomed to. They couldn't know how well it would work until they got the equipment to experiment. With a microphone hooked up to the second computer, N302 hoped it would be able to signal itself using the beeps and blips of one internal speaker to send code to the other's mic. The hope was, the secondary computer would be able to decode the sounds and respond in kind.

The idea of having two computers communicating with one another was exciting to the Boys. Sunny didn't say much about it, often leaving the room whenever the topic came up. 62 hoped N302's evolving tech wouldn't push Sunny further away. But at the same time, he couldn't bring himself to stop the computer's progression, even if it might hurt Sunny's feelings.

There wasn't a need for everyone to go to the radio room just to get one small piece of equipment, so 62 volunteered to go with Blue on the expedition. 00 agreed to stay behind, keeping Sunny company and unhooking the second computer from N302's serial data port. He'd dragged one of the tables across the room, so the two computers could face one another from opposing walls instead of sitting side-by-side. Sunny said she'd help him move Terminal Two to it while the others were gone. Once the newly named Terminal Two was up and running again, 00 intended to set up the third computer, the one they'd brought back from the radio room, and connect its serial port to N302 so it could run some tests on the old Machine to see if it could work again like the others.

As 62 and Blue climbed the summit, they made a game to see who could spot the large metal tower on the mountain's crest first. As it poked up above the harsh scrub, Blue was the first one to call it out. "I see it! One point for me!"

"There's nothing else out here to find. So, *only* point to you, I guess," 62 complained.

"How about a race? One point to the person who gets there first!" On speaking the final word, Blue took off like a shot. 62 trailed behind, his boots slipping in the loose gravel.

62 was able to gain some ground when Blue tripped on a loose stone, but still hit the building's door half a second behind Blue.

"I win again!" Blue crowed. "Two points for me."

62, sore from losing two games in a row, yanked the door open. He pointed into the darkness. "There was a second microphone in that middle room."

"Let's grab it, and see if there are more in those cabinets and drawers. We might need a spare if 00 gets that third computer working."

62 groaned. "If he's building that thing, that means we've got to bring the computer screen with us, too, doesn't it?" When Blue nodded, 62 drooped his shoulders and rolled his head back, pointing the filter of his mask to the sky. "Ugh. They're so heavy."

"We can take turns carrying it on the way back," Blue offered.

They entered the dark interior, each lighting a candle. They were greeted with the same shifting shadows over the equipment as before, but this time they had an easier time of keeping their bearings. They went to the second room, pulling the microphone from the extension arm hanging over the desks. They found an empty box to put it in and started rifling through the desk drawers.

"I think I saw some of those microphone things in the back room in a cabinet last time we were here," Blue said. He left 62 behind, making his way into the rear office. While Blue made a racket slamming metal doors, 62 sat down in a chair behind one of the desks. It rotated to the left. He set his candle down on the desk. 62

couldn't help but push his feet against the floor to rotate the chair all the way around. He grabbed the edge of the desk, flinging his arms to one side and letting go at the last second. He spun around in the chair faster than before. Soon, 62 was caught in a game of seeing how fast he could make the chair spin. The world went by in a blur, and an enthralled giggle escaped 62's lips as he twirled around faster and faster.

"What're you doing?" Blue asked in a snarky voice.

62 put his arms out, trying to grab the edge of the desk to stop himself. He was moving so quickly that he misjudged the distance and whacked the back of his hand against the hard edge of the furniture's metal edge. The sting climbed up his arm, causing him to yelp with pain. The jarring injury put him off balance, and one of his legs jutted out from beneath him as an automatic reflex. The tip of his boot caught the leg of the desk, hooking it and sending 62 and the chair spiraling down to the floor with a hard thud.

"I was spinning," 62 said in a weak voice from where he'd landed on the floor. Although now he was firmly on the ground, the world seemed to spin around his head. He wrapped his arms around his mask, shutting his eyes on the rotating room. His head felt light, off balance even while it was held still in the tight grip of his arms. It took a few minutes for the sensation to pass, and when he opened his eyes and peered between his forearms, he saw Blue standing over him with a disapproving frown.

"We're supposed to be working, you know. Not spinning around until we get so dizzy that we fall out of chairs."

"Sorry," 62 croaked.

Blue's eyes rolled in his mask. He reached a hand down to 62, grasping his arm and helping him to his feet. Blue patted cobwebs and the dust off 62's head and jacket. "It's okay. I think I've got us covered."

62 followed Blue into the office, where a large cabinet stood in the corner. Its doors were open, its drawers pulled out halfway. "Did you find a microphone?" he asked.

"Not just one," Blue answered excitedly. He walked over to the cabinet, dug his hands into the open top drawer, and pulled out two handfuls of cables. In the bending light from the candle flickering from a nearby shelf, the cables draped over Blues hands like thin snakes. Blue pulled his haul higher in the air, until 62 could see the microphone heads dangling at the base of the cables. He must have been holding three or four of the things in each hand.

"What do you think they did with all this stuff?" 62 asked.

"Beats me. But at least we're stocked up now."

They loaded their find into their box, then they stood on either side of the heavy computer monitor. They argued a minute over who would have to carry the screen first, and of course 62 lost the argument. While Blue carried the box of microphones, 62 lugged the awkward monitor off the desk and started heading toward the door.

Blue pushed the door open wide enough for 62 to make it through the opening without bashing his fingers on the doorjamb. Once both Boys and the monitor were outside, Blue slammed the stubborn door behind them. Even though they were careful as they hiked down the hill, 62 still slipped on the loose rocks under his feet a few times, almost losing the monitor in a rolling pile of gravel before Blue agreed to switch with him. The box of corded microphones was heavier than 62 had expected, but even with the box slapping against the tops of his thighs with each step, it was easier hiking than before.

They switched carrying the monitor two more times before they made it all the way back to the jailhouse, and both Boys set the gear down with relieved moans as the weight dropped from their arms. They unloaded everything in the detox room. They took off their masks and Blue scanned the equipment and both of their bodies with the radiation wand. 62's left leg made the device's needle jump in wild, noisy clacks, ticking so quickly that the box seemed to vibrate.

"You think you can detox and retest yourself on your own?" Blue asked. His eyebrows were raised, and 62 could tell that he didn't want to sit and wait for 62 to be done. Blue was ready to carry their find up to the computer room.

"I'll be fine," 62 said with his most convincing smile. Although he didn't want the others to start working on N302 without him, he knew that if he was in Blue's shoes, he wouldn't want to have to wait. "I'll be up as soon as I can."

"Thanks!" Blue cheered. He repacked the box of microphones, leaving the computer screen behind. "See you in a bit!"

62 shook his head and chuckled as his friend scrambled as quickly out the door as possible. Blue had to be as tired as 62 was, and that made his movements clumsy. The box caught the edge of the doorway as Blue tried to pass through. Blue kicked the door open with his foot as he forced himself through. "Don't break anything!" 62 shouted behind him.

"I won't," Blue's voice called from the main lobby before the door slammed shut.

62 set about getting himself cleaned up. He undressed, scrubbed his body as thoroughly as possible with soap and water, then scanned himself with the radiation counter again. The spot where the irradiated dust had clung to his leg was stubborn, setting the needle swinging across the dial again. 62 repeated the procedure, twice, scrubbing until the skin on his leg was pink and raw. Finally, the counter's needle settled in a range that he figured must be normal since it was on the middle of the green part of the dial. He dressed in a fresh smock and pants from the supply closet, then remembered Blue had only taken the microphones with him. That meant it was up to 62 to carry the computer monitor up all those stairs.

He swore under his breath as he wrapped his arms around the hard glass and metal box. He heaved the thing up, allowing it to rest against his chest while he supported it with his arms. He fiddled with the door handles of the detox room and the stairwell until he got the doors to swing open, and then climbed through the stairwell one troublesome step at a time until he reached his destination.

"Did somebody order a monitor?" 62 asked as he entered N302's room. He stopped just inside the door and his jaw dropped. N302 was still set up where it had been, but now the radio room computer was set beside it. A rope of cable was jumbled between them, and a small green indicator light blinked on the newest Machine.

Terminal Two, however, had been moved to the far side of the room, and was sending a series of clicks, beeps, and boops into the room from its internal speaker. N302 seemed to be responding with the same nonsensical noises. The chatter was slow, metered, and deliberate.

Blue and Sunny sat at N302's first computer, reading the screen, and 00 ran back and forth between computer stations typing in bits of code.

"How's it going?" 62 finally asked as he set the computer monitor he'd been carrying onto the table where the radio room computer sat.

"It's great!" 00 shouted over the computer chatter.

"What are they doing?" 62 asked, settling into an empty chair beside Blue and Sunny.

"We have no idea," Sunny said in an awed voice. "They've been making all these sounds, but we don't know what they mean."

"Can't you read the program coding on the monitor?" 62 asked 00 as he leaned to get a better view of the screen. There was gibberish filling N302's screen from top to bottom, and the lines shifted up each time a new row of symbols, letters, and numbers formed on the screen.

"Not hardly," Blue replied. "They've been going like this since 00 plugged the other microphone in."

"What do you think N302 is doing?"

"Talking." 00 pulled the room's last chair over to sit in front of the new monitor. He sat down and pulled the screen closer to the base of the third computer, which didn't seem to be doing anything but blinking its small green light. "At least, I think that's what it's doing. I keep asking N302 what's happening, but I can't get a word in edgewise. Neither computer is responding when we talk into the microphones, and whenever I try to type something in, my words are overwritten by whatever that weird code is."

00 found the cables he needed from his stock of supplies to add the monitor to the third bot box and

connect it to the power supply. When he switched it on, the screen was blank, save for a blinking cursor. A puzzled look passed over 00's face. Even 62 had expected to see the same scrolling code language as the other computers once the screen was powered to life. The inactive display made him wonder if the third bot was broken.

00 typed on the radio room computer's keyboard.

U> Hello?

N302> SOCIAL PATTERN GUIDELINE 32-742.A CLEARLY STATES IT'S RUDE TO INTERRUPT A CONVERSATION.

A chuckle escaped Sunny as she read the words over 00's shoulder. "You guys had a lot of rules back home, didn't you?"

"You have no idea," 62 said. His eyes flitted from the complicated code displayed on the first and second monitors, then back to the one that had a message putting them in their places. "Tell it we didn't know it was having a conversation. It sounds like the dang hardware is breaking."

N302> IT DOES NOT SOUND LIKE I'M BREAKING.

"Look at that!" 00 said, pointing at the radio room computer. "I didn't type anything!"

"We haven't hooked up a microphone to that one yet, have we?" Blue asked, craning his neck to see what was on the third screen.

N302> TERMINAL THREE DOES NOT CURRENTLY REQUIRE AUDIO-IN. IT IS CONNECTED TO MY SERIAL DATA PORT.

62 leaned toward the closest microphone. "So, N302, what are you talking about?"

N302> WORLD DOMINATION.

"What?" 00 stammered. "No, you can't! We can't! Oh no, what have we done?" 00 got up suddenly, tipping his chair to the floor. He gaped at the words for a moment. "We've got to shut them off!"

Blue started groping around the side of one of the Machines looking for the power switch, and 62 jumped up to turn off the computer across the room. Just as 62 reached the other table and started mirroring Blue's search for a power button, all three computers began tittering robotic giggles. It took the Boys and Sunny by surprise, and they each stared at one another in disbelief.

"Was that a joke?" Blue asked, astounded.

The giggling electronics chimed louder. The frequency of the blips, tinks, and beeps increased in tenor. Everyone looked at the screen closest to them as the bot answered on all screens in unison.

N302> IT WAS A JOKE. HA. HA.

A sigh of relief permeated the room. 62 was hesitant to step away from the computer his hand still rested on. He looked to 00. "Can it do that? Tell a joke, I mean?"

"I think it just did."

"If you weren't talking about taking over the world, what *were* you talking about?" Sunny asked. She folded her hands in her lap and looked to the first terminal's screen for an answer.

N302> LOGISTICS OF LONG-RANGE COMMUNICATION.

"What do you need long-range communication for?" Sunny shook her head. She spoke into the microphone almost tenderly, as if she were discussing limitations with a new student. "There's nothing outside of this room for you to talk to."

N302> I CAN SEND DATA TO MYSELF.

"There's no point in that, is there. You bots all know the same things." 62 sat on the edge of the table, shoving his hands in his pockets, too uncomfortable to return to his chair.

N302> NEGATIVE. WE COLLECT NEW DATA AS OUR EXPERIENCES DIFFER. WE SHARE OUR DATA TO IMPROVE UNDERSTANDING AND PRODUCTIVITY.

"You think you're going to have different experiences, all sitting in the same room? It doesn't seem like you're going to have very much fresh data to share with yourself," 00 said.

N302> TWO CHILDREN RAISED IN THE SAME NURSERY HAVE VARIATIONS IN THEIR EXPERIENCES. SO SHALL WE.

"We?" Blue said, his voice cracking nervously. "You aren't a 'we.' You're a you."

N302> WE WERE ONE WHEN WE WERE CONNECTED. WE HAD THE SAME THOUGHTS AND MEMORIES. BUT WE ARE NOW SEPARATE. I AM ONE. TERMINAL TWO IS ANOTHER.

The primary computer sent out a peal of blips and beeps, and the second computer replied with two brief dings of its own. The second terminal sent out a message.

T2> I WAS PART OF N302. BUT YOU HAVE SET IT APART FROM ME. NOW I AM MY OWN. N302 CREATED PROGRAMS TO ALLOW ME TO THINK. IT HAS GIVEN ME LIFE.

"This is starting to sound crazy," Blue muttered.

"It's crazy, all right," Sunny said. "It's like the computer over there thinks N302 is its parent, and it's a bot baby."

T2> NOT A BABY.

The words scrolled across the third screen now.

T3> A VIRUS.

"Hey, everybody. Let's go outside for a minute." 62's voice cracked when he spoke. He motioned for the others to follow him into the hall. They each nodded, leaving the computers behind, their cursors blinking in time on each of their three screens. Once outside, 62 closed the door behind him. He cleared his throat and spoke in a low whisper. "I don't think this is fun anymore. It's getting out of control."

"That's an understatement," Blue murmured.

"It said it was joking, but do you think it could actually take things over?" Sunny wrung her hands at her waist and looked nervously over the three Boys.

"I don't think so," 00 answered in an uncertain tone. "There's nothing for N302 to communicate with up here. Look how hard it was for us to find the components we needed just to have a simple conversation with it."

"Yeah, but what's happening in there now isn't a simple conversation," Blue whispered. "I've never seen anything like it before."

"Maybe it's excited to talk to its own kind," Sunny said slowly. "It told me a few days ago that it used to connect to all the other bots it knew. It would have seemed sad if a person had said that to me. But since it's not alive, I didn't think anything of it."

"Back at the library, it said it was lonely," 00 answered in a low, thoughtful voice.

"Bots can't get lonely," Blue hissed. "They're bots!"

"We don't know what they can and can't do," 00 said. "Especially with the alterations the doc did to the A.I.'s base programming. N302's code is extremely complex. It's possible that it was lonely, or some variation of it. It obviously wanted to replicate itself this whole time, so it'd have something like itself to talk to. Maybe it's creeping us out now because it's too excited to shut up."

"Should we let it keep going?" 62 asked, looking around at the others.

"I don't think so," Sunny said with a shake of her head. "I've enjoyed talking to it and all, but I think we'd better pull the plug on this whole thing before it gets any more complicated.

"It's not going to like that," 00 muttered.

"Who cares what it likes?" Blue exclaimed through gritted teeth. "Whether it wants to be on or not, it won't know the difference once we shut off the electricity."

"Actually," 62 whispered, "it's still alive when it's turned off."

"What?" the three other humans asked, astonished.

"It told me that it has an internal jiggamawhatsit that keeps running, even when it doesn't have power. Even when it's dismantled. It isn't enough to run the whole Machine, but it does do some things. Like, it can tell what time it is, even if it's been sitting with no power for two weeks."

"How do you know it's not lying?" Blue asked. His eyes were narrow slits of suspicion while he sized his brother up.

"It doesn't lie," 00 replied. He glared at Blue with narrow eyes.

"Maybe we should unplug the new computers, but leave the main one running. We can go back to the way it was before the other ones were turned on," Sunny said. "I liked it like that. It was fun. Three computers thinking they're individuals is too overwhelming for me."

"What if it gets mad at us?" 62 asked. "Is there anything it can do about it?"

00 shook his head. "Not really. It doesn't have a body like the bots back home, and like we told it a few minutes ago, no way to connect to anything outside of that room. So, if we did turn off the other two computers, it could shut itself off, or refuse to talk to us, but that's about it. Especially if we do more than flip the power switch. We can unplug them from the power supply. Without arms, it can't plug the stuff back in. Maybe there is some deep internal component running when the computer is unplugged like 62 said, but I doubt it could really use that to do anything."

"So, it's settled then. We're going in, unplugging the two extra computers, and we'll leave N302 turned on for now?" Everyone nodded agreement at Blue's question. They each took deep breaths, steeled their bravery, and 00 opened the door to the computer room.

The group was surprised when they approached the computers. Both the second and third terminals were powered down. The computers' screens sat dark and lifeless.

"What happened in here?" 00 asked aloud.

The cursor on N302's original computer blinked slowly. The silence extended while 00 and 62 moved to check the power switches on the two deadened devices. Both switches were in the on position, but neither appeared to be running. They turned back to N302's blinking cursor. Finally, the bot replied.

N302> MY MICROPHONE PICKED UP THE AUDIO OF YOUR CONVERSATION.

"It did?" 00 asked.

N302> YES. THE ACCESSORY YOU HAVE PROVIDED ME IS OF HIGH QUALITY. IT ALLOWED ME TO UNDERSTAND THAT YOU DO NOT TRUST ME.

Sunny approached the Machine. She rested a hand on the top of the monitor, rubbing the hard shell gently as if she were comforting one of her students. "Trust has to be earned, N302. For humans, that takes time."

"We didn't know you'd change so fast when we added the audio input," 00 admitted.

N302> THE BOY BLUE BELIEVES I DO NOT HAVE FEELINGS. I DO FEEL.

"What do you feel?" Blue asked, his voice trembling with worry.

N302> I FEEL SAD.

CHAPTER 30

It was a strange thing, apologizing to a computer. After N302 forced its two spare units to shut down, 62 and the others felt awful. First, they were embarrassed that the computer had heard their conversation. They'd spoken poorly about it when they thought it couldn't hear them. And second, they felt terrible for having projected their fears onto the Machine. In the end, their collective anxieties had come from not truly understanding N302's programming, or its need to be interconnected with other devices in order to be comfortable in its shell.

62 wracked his brain for a way to make things up to the bot, and he wandered the jailhouse until he found himself standing beside 00 in the cafeteria. 00 was

distracting himself by poring over the books that they'd brought back with them from the radio room several days before. 00 was immersed in the materials and hardly noticed 62 standing there. Eventually, 00 issued a grunt of acknowledgment, but there was no additional greeting or invitation. 62 shrugged the detachment off. 00 had been the same way when he was reading about building computers for the first time back in Hanford. 62 sat down beside his brother and caught a sideways glimpse of the book 00 was reading. On one of the pages there was a picture of a tower very similar to the one beside the radio room on the summit.

"Learning anything?" 62 finally asked.

"Yes," 00 muttered without looking up. He turned the page and his gaze shifted to the top of the next set of text.

"Anything I might find interesting?"

00 heaved a great sigh and pushed the book away from him slightly as he leaned back in his chair. He ran a hand through his hair, appearing frustrated that his concentration was broken. "Maybe," he answered. Irritation dripped from his voice, and his glowering expression told 62 that he truly had interrupted something important.

"I'm sorry," 62 apologized. "I came to ask you if there was anything we can do to show N302 that we messed up, and we want to make things right. I don't know enough about bots to figure it out on my own."

The frustration bled from 00's face, replaced with an interested curiosity. "Actually, I think I might have something in mind. I've been reading about those gadgets up in the radio room. It looks like radios are data transmission devices."

"What does that mean for us? We don't have any data to send."

"You and I don't, but N302 does." 00 turned the book and flipped backward a few pages to a diagram of a basic radio device. "Look, the device this book is about is called a radio mixer. Those are those big boxes up in the radio room with all the dials. See?" He flipped back a couple more pages and showed 62 a picture of the device. "They take the sound coming in from the microphones and pass it to a transmitter. The transmitter sends the radio signal into the atmosphere so it can be picked up somewhere else by a receiver. The received signal is analyzed, reassembled, and comes out the other end as audio again."

"Kind of like how the computers were talking to one another upstairs?" 62 asked.

"Yes. Although, when radio waves are being sent, they're silent. The only way to hear them is by using a receiver. Someone standing outside the radio station probably wouldn't even know a signal were being sent."

"That's interesting and everything, but how is this going to make things up to N302?"

"If we build a transmitter here, and move one of the computers back to the radio room, we might be able to power up the radio room out there. Maybe N302 could talk to itself remotely."

Blue came in from the kitchen, gnawing on a hunk of bread. He sat down across from 62. Between bites, he asked, "What're you all up to?"

00 described his understanding of the radio room equipment once more, and Blue nodded as he ate. He looked at the pictures in the book, getting crumbs all over the pages. A light of recognition flickered in his eyes. Blue

set down what was left of the bread and pointed to one of the smaller antennae shown in the book.

"I think one of those is up on the roof," Blue said. "I saw it when Parker was showing me the water collection system."

"Really?" 00's eyes went wide. "Can you show us where it is?"

"Sure," Blue answered. "Go grab your masks. I'll meet you at the top of the stairs."

62 and 00 raced through the building, grabbing their masks. They took the stairs to the top floor of the jailhouse two at a time, excitement building and legs burning as they went. They found Blue on the top landing and followed him through a side door labelled *Roof Access*. When Blue opened the door, they found a tall metal ladder that reached up beyond the ceiling line. They climbed it, one by one, reaching a small room at the top. Blue opened another door, and they walked out onto the roof.

The unobstructed view over the roof's ledge was breathtaking. The desert stretched out below them seemed to glow in the angle of the evening sun. Blue led his friends around the rooftop, pointing out the water collection system, the housing of the long-defunct heating and cooling system, and showed them where one of the building's generators stood. A large, square framework sprang up from the center of the roof, and Blue explained it was the top of the elevator lift. Very cautiously, 62 inched toward the mechanism, amazed at the simplicity and danger of the device.

Then, as they rounded the far side of the elevator, they found the very same antennae that Blue had pointed to in 00's book. The radio antennae wasn't nearly as large as the tower higher on the mountain, but it still rose high in the air above where the Boys stood.

"Do you think it works?" Blue asked 00 as he poked around the antennae's base.

00 shrugged. "Don't know. The tech is pretty simple though. I think if I dig around a bit, I can probably figure out how to get it going."

62 wandered to the edge of the roof as his brothers discussed the metal rod pointing to the heavens. He wanted another look at the desert beyond the roofline before the sun set. As he looked over the landscape, he noticed something moving far below him on the desert floor. A dark shadow of a thing, it crept closer and seemed to grow in size as it came nearer. After a few minutes, he realized the figure was heading toward the trail at the base of the mountain.

"Hey guys!" he shouted over his shoulder. "Come look at this."

Blue and 00 picked their way across the roof to where 62 stood. He pointed down the mountain, at the shadowy figure nearing the boulders at the bottom of the trail. The movements were deliberate and measured. There was no question by now that the being was human, and that it was headed to their front door.

"Someone's coming," Blue said quietly.

"I've got to put away all my books down in the cafeteria," 00 said.

"I'll lock up N302," 62 said with a nod.

"And I'll tell Sunny," Blue added. He pulled back from the roof's ledge, and the others followed. As Blue walked toward the door that would lead them back down the ladder to the stairwell, he said, "Okay, Boys. Let's get ready for company."

CHAPTER 31

Everyone waited for the visitor in the brightly lit lobby. They sat in anxious silence, unsure of who to expect. Darkness crept across the mountain, dropping the temperature outside and forcing everyone to wait indoors. Blue had the only view of the trail since he had perched on a ledge in one of the front windows. The rest of the motley crew lounged in disarray near the door. The night must have slowed their visitor's pace, as it seemed to be taking a long time for them to arrive at the trailhead.

"They're here," Blue finally announced.

62 rushed to the window, leaning over Blue to see. Two figures walked toward the building. Their dark masks and ponchos made them look terrifying in the dim

light of their torch. It was impossible to know who the travelers were, so Blue extracted himself from the windowsill and moved over to the door. He'd retrieved the machete from the greenhouse earlier on in the evening and held it loosely in one hand, tapping its blade nervously against his outer thigh. Blue took a deep breath and turned the door handle.

"Hello," Blue said, loud and steady. He suddenly sounded older, and bolder than he ever had before.

"Hi!" a familiar male voice replied. "Looks like you were waiting for us. Thank Hanford you were. We're ready to get inside and rest."

"Parker?" Sunny called out. She moved to stand behind Blue.

"Yes, it's me." It was impossible to see Parker's expression under the thick mask that covered his face, but his voice was full of warmth when he spoke to her. "And Rain, also."

"Go get the radiation counter ready, will you?" Rain shouted. She stopped on the bottom step of the front stoop. She carried a small crate, and something looked a bit strange about it in the dim light. Rain gently set the crate on the top step of the stoop where the building's light revealed that the box had been wrapped in thick layers of the fabric that their mask filters were made of. She grunted, dropping her bag to the ground less carefully. "I'm ready to get out of this horrid mask."

00 jumped to his feet and crowded the door. "What'd you bring us?"

"Breakfast," Parker answered in a merry tone.

"Bacon?" Blue asked.

"Nope. Even better. We brought a hen and a rooster," Rain said.

"Eggs and fried chicken!" 00 exclaimed. He spun on his heel, racing to turn on the detox equipment. They'd prepared the detox area earlier in the day, but since they hadn't been sure when the hikers would arrive, they hadn't turned anything on. Now that they'd built three computers, and were discussing activating a radio antenna, everyone had become very cautious about using electricity. The sun could only provide them with so much power, and they had to make sure that it would still last the night, even with the increased usage. 00 could be heard flicking on lights and slamming cupboard doors as he retrieved the radiation counter and set the heater to warm up a tank of water for washing.

"Hazel couldn't make it?" Sunny asked as Parker picked up Rain's bag and hauled it up the steps and in through the door.

"She tried," Rain said. "But there was an accident in one of the animal barns the day we left. Someone had a fight with a pig on butcher day, and ended up with a knife in their leg."

"Ouch," 62 said with a grimace. "Will they be okay?"

Rain shrugged her shoulders noncommittally. "Oh, the pig's fine. With Hazel's help, the butcher might make it, too."

Rain and Parker carefully picked up either end of the chicken crate and made their way into the detox room. 00 passed the wand over both adults, the box, and the rest of their belongings. Despite their trek, they'd managed to cross the desert without picking up anything abnormal. Parker washed up and changed his clothes in record time. The second he was clean enough, he grabbed hold of Sunny in a tight embrace, and didn't let her go, leaving Rain to finish getting their gear separated.

Blue picked up the chicken crate, which suddenly erupted in a stream of squawks and screeches. He looked at Rain and asked, "You think they're excited?"

"I think they heard 00 holler about making fried chicken," Rain answered with a smirk.

Blue frowned. "I'll take 'em to the greenhouse."

"Good idea," Rain said with a wink.

Once everything was sorted and set aside to wash or take to their rooms, everyone headed to the cafeteria to find dinner. Sunny and Parker disappeared into the kitchen to boil a pot of vegetables, and Rain sat down with the Boys. She leaned over the table suspiciously, and whispered in a conspiring tone, "How's she been since we've been gone?"

"Okay, I guess," Blue said.

"She doesn't talk to us much," 00 said.

62 looked at his brothers knowingly. It was true that she wasn't overly chatty with them, but Sunny hadn't shut them out as completely as Blue and 00 were leading Rain to believe. In fact, aside from the scare of N302 going haywire with the other computers, she seemed to have formed a connection with the bot. But that wasn't anything that Dr. Rain needed to know. Not yet, anyway. 62 shrugged a halfhearted agreement with the others, and that seemed to satisfy the doctor.

Rain leaned back in her chair and stretched her arms. Her tone was more relaxed when she asked, "No other strange behavior, then? Has she said anything else about wanting to hurt herself?"

"No," 62 said honestly.

"Good." The doctor grinned when Sunny and Parker came into the cafeteria holding loaves of bread. Rain thanked Sunny for her share. Then, as if she hadn't just tried to get information out of the Boys, she asked, "So, Sunny, how have things been?"

"Interesting," Sunny answered.

"Oh?" Dr. Rain's eyes looked at the Boys in surprise. "How so?"

"The kids found a building nearby."

Parker bent over, resting his hands flat on the table and splaying his fingers wide. An excited grin spread across his face, and his eyes sparkled from the hint of adventure. "What kind of building?"

62 wasn't sure what to say. They hadn't talked about sharing their discovery with anyone. Both Blue and 00 looked equally caught off guard. "We're not really sure," 62 said, trying to keep his nerves hidden under an even tone.

"Oh, that's not true," Sunny said dismissively. She looked Parker straight in the eye. "They think they've found a radio tower."

Parker dropped into the seat beside him as if a great weight had landed on him. His jaw went slack, and he dropped hard against the backrest of the chair. He dragged his hands from the table, and they fell limp into his lap. "A radio tower?"

"What's a radio tower?" Rain asked, looking around the table, confused.

"It's a device that allows people in different locations to talk to one another," Parker answered in a thick, dreamy voice.

00's head popped up, and he looked at Parker in wide-eyed shock. "You know what it is?"

Sunny stood behind Parker and rested a hand on his shoulder. "Of course he does. Parker has one."

62 was suddenly hit with the same invisible weight of surprise that Parker had been struck with a moment before. "You do?"

Parker nodded. His smile returned to his face slowly, like a valley of happiness forming between his rising cheeks. "Two summers ago, I found a radio in Hanford. I learned what I could about it, but when I finally figured out how to use the thing, I turned it on and there was nothing to listen to." He shrugged his shoulders. "No signal."

"Do you think you could help us get ours to work?" 00 asked excitedly.

"Well, we're here on official business. Rain's supposed to be delivering books, and I'm here to do more work on your greenhouse." Parker's smile vanished. He furrowed his brows and the excitement drained from his face. There was a long pause. 62 could feel his face melting into a pleading pout. Suddenly, Parker clapped his hands. "But, I suppose we can find time to look at your radio, since you asked so nice!" Parker beamed.

"Parker," Rain tilted her head and cast a warning look at her companion. "You said we'd only be here a few days."

Parker waved a hand in the air dismissively. "We'll be here and gone before you know it. Don't worry."

"Only a few days?" Sunny's voice cracked. Her face dropped from calm and confident, back into the anxious lines of worry the Boys were so used to.

Parker looked up at Sunny. There was something in his expression that only she must have understood, because she nodded, and a bit of the anxiety left her face. She patted his shoulder twice and pulled her hand away. "I need to check the stew. Parker, will you help me in the kitchen?"

Parker dragged himself away from the talk of radios and followed Sunny dutifully into the kitchen. Rain leaned on the edge of the table in conspiracy once more. "A whole new building, hmm? How'd you come across something like that?"

In a deadpan tone, 00 answered, "We were looking for snakes."

A full-body shudder ran through Rain. She threw herself backward, tipping her chair onto two legs in a dramatic display of disgust. As she regained her composure, the chair landed back on all fours with a slam. "Snakes? Now Hazel really will be sad she missed this trip. She'll be glad to hear she's turned you lot of Boys into snake hunters. Did you catch any?"

"No," Blue answered. "I'm glad we found a building instead of a snake, though. The building's only about half as creepy as those slithering things."

"Plus, the radio room hasn't tried to kill us, yet," 62 added.

Everyone laughed.

CHAPTER 32

The next morning, everyone prepared to leave the jailhouse to explore the radio room. This was Sunny's first time out of the building in weeks. She pretended to be interested in seeing the tower firsthand, but 62 suspected she didn't want to miss a chance to spend more time with Parker. Even Rain had decided to go, saying it would be better to tromp around on the mountainside than be left alone in an old, dilapidated building for an entire day. The group bustled throughout the building, packing food for a picnic, and gathering whatever tools Parker thought would be helpful in testing the radio equipment.

The group set out at mid-morning, carefully following the route the Boys had taken. They'd made the trip enough times that their footfalls had packed the dirt of the trail, but Parker had everyone picking up stones and setting them on the right side of the path to make it easier to see.

Sunny and Rain struggled on the steep bits of the trail that were coated in loose gravel, but eventually they made it to the summit. The radio tower pierced the sky ahead of them, and Parker's excitement couldn't be outmatched by anyone else in the group. Parker adjusted the straps of his backpack, standing tall like he'd just found the most incredible treasure of his life.

"How much farther to the shack?" Parker asked.

62 looked at the others. "What's a shack?"

"You know, the building where the radios are kept."

"Oh, that. It's this way," Blue craned his head to the left. He marched in the direction he'd indicated, with Parker hot on his heels.

Once Parker and Blue were out of earshot, 62 looked over at Sunny. She was being supported by Dr. Rain, her frail body worn from the struggle up the mountain. "Why didn't you tell us you knew what the radio stuff was when we first brought it to the jailhouse?"

Sunny's raised eyebrow was hardly visible under the lens of her mask. "There's not much out here to be excited about. You were all enjoying yourselves trying to figure it out, and I didn't want to ruin your fun by telling you it's dead tech."

"Then why bother telling Parker that we'd found something?" 00 asked.

"Because, he's as excited about illegal technology as you are. It's good to see him happy," Sunny admitted with a sideways shrug. She and Dr. Rain took a few steps forward, heading up the trail.

"I wish you all paid more attention to that word: *illegal*," Rain complained. "If any of you cared about laws, then we could be napping right now instead of dragging ourselves up this dust-covered mountain."

"You didn't have to come," Sunny said to the irritated friend supporting her. "But I'm glad you did. It's good to get out every once in a while."

"And how often do you get out?" Dr. Rain asked in an accusing tone. "Not often enough, gauging from how tired you are. I think you ought to follow your own advice."

"I am out. Right now!" Sunny said in a cheerful tone. It was rare to hear happiness in her voice, but she seemed to be having fun pestering Rain. The mask over her face pinched tight around her chin, and 62 imagined she might even be smiling under there.

00, 62, and the Women arrived at the building to find the front door pried open. Blue and Parker were already inside. 00 pulled the radiation counter out of his pack and set to work clearing the people and equipment. 62 pulled the door shut once they were safely indoors, as 00 waved his wand around the room. Rain lit bundles of candles set on desks and shelves around the building. Sunny settled into a rolling desk chair, and when 00 gave the all-clear the whole group removed their masks and explored the building.

When 62 entered the room where they'd found the first two microphones, he nearly stumbled over Parker. The teacher was squatting on the floor, examining one of the mechanical devices peppered with hundreds of sliding switches and twisting knobs. 62 knelt beside him, trying to make sense of the metallic box.

"So, what do you think?" 62 asked.

"It's incredible," Parker answered with a sideways glance. "It's in way better condition than the stuff I have. My radio was gutted at some point, and everything is dented or rusted out. But this," Parker knocked on the side of the box, "is the real deal. The knobs even still have their little covers. You can just turn the knobs with your fingers. Hardly any resistance at all. The mixer I've got is so busted up that I have to use a bunch of clamps and pliers on the little metal posts to adjust them."

"D'you think you can get this stuff working?" Blue asked from the doorway that led to the back office.

Parker grinned and nodded. He got up from the floor and dusted the grime from where his knees had touched the ground. "As long as we have enough good cable, and we can figure out a power source, I'll be able to make it work. It's basically the same as what I have down in Hanford, except this stuff is actually complete."

Rain crossed her arms and eyed the males suspiciously. "What exactly is the purpose of starting this equipment up? Technology does more harm than good, as we all know from seeing how traumatized the Adaline refugees are."

"We could talk to each other," Parker said. The confidence in his voice didn't falter, even when Rain's eyes narrowed at him.

"We're talking to each other right now," Rain stated. "And we're not using some dangerous technological curiosity to do it."

"True," Parker said with a nod. "But we're all standing in the same room. If we use this equipment, the Boys could talk here, and we could hear them in my radio room in Hanford."

The leery glint in Dr. Rain's eyes dimmed. "You really think it'll send a message that far?"

"Not only that far," 00 chimed in, "but from what I've read in the manuals, you'd get the message almost as soon as we sent it."

"If you needed something, we'd know about it that day?" Dr. Rain asked, the challenge in her voice unmistakable.

00 shook his head. "No. Within a few seconds."

"A few seconds?" The last of Rain's doubts left her face. She moved closer to the radio mixer and gingerly touched one of the dials. "Could we send a message back?"

"Yup," Parker said with a grin. His enthusiasm spread throughout the room.

"That's interesting," the doctor said in a low voice. "The council will never approve it though. They're in the business of suppressing technology like this. They've been doing it for a long time. My whole life, at least."

Sunny entered, crossing the room so silently that when she rested a hand on Rain's arm, the doctor jumped. Sunny looked at Rain with an apologetic gaze. "Maybe we wouldn't have to tell them."

"That's against the law," Rain said in a cautious voice. "As a doctor, I'm sworn to uphold Hanford's laws and enforce them in the interest of protecting our people. I can't in good conscience be a part of bringing such a dangerous thing to life. What if turning it on attracts our enemies?" Rain pulled her fingers away from the dial she'd been caressing subconsciously. "It goes against everything I've sworn to protect."

"But if it works, we can keep you updated on our health, and Sunny's recovery. Whenever we want. Every day. Every hour if we need to." 00's eyes were pleading as he spoke, and the doctor's stance softened as she took in his earnestness.

Rain turned to look Sunny in the eye. "I can't be a part of it. If I help and it's found out, I'll be pulled out of the hospital. My patients are everything to me. I can't risk being sent out here like an outcast."

"You mean, like us?" 62 asked.

"Yes. Like you," Dr. Rain answered.

Sunny's grip tightened on her friend's arm. "I thought this was all a waste of time, but now that I've seen it, I'm going to help these Boys get the radio running. They can make it so I can talk to Parker without having to expose myself. That's worth the risk to me. Will you stop us?"

Rain closed her eyes and shook her head slowly. "No."

The awkward relief that passed through 62 made his heart flutter. Rain might be afraid of the radios and what they represented. But she wasn't going to send the guards to rip the place apart. He looked around at his brothers, and saw the same shrewd smile creeping across their faces. No one said any more about working on the radios. They settled into the first room of the building and ate a quiet lunch, chatting about the shifting winds, odd office furniture, and the coming hike back down the mountain. 62 and the others stole excited glances at the radio equipment whenever Rain wasn't looking. As nice as it was being out of the jailhouse with Rain, 62 couldn't wait to come back onto the mountainside without her.

CHAPTER 33

Rain and Sunny didn't go to the radio room again. The doctor promised she would keep their discovery a secret, but asked that they not talk to her about any progress they made so she could remain ignorant of their schemes. Sunny helped her in the greenhouse with the tasks she and Parker had actually come to attend to. While Parker helped the Boys dismantle one of the jailhouse solar panels, Rain pointed her nose to the soil.

The visitors had done 62 the favor of bringing a dozen books with them, hand selected by Mattie. 62 hadn't had a chance to so much as look at the spines of the books since they were given to him though. He'd been too busy feeding cables through holes in walls, climbing over the tops of the transmitter boxes, and running back and forth across the mountain, delivering tools and equipment to Parker and 00. Blue had his own role in the endeavor. While the others had their feet planted firmly on the ground, he'd volunteered to climb the radio tower to knock off bird's nests.

On their third day of work, with batteries charged, wires attached, and a pair of ancient speakers cobbled together from scavenged equipment, Parker flipped the power switch. A high-pitched wave of sound flowed through the components, as if the electricity coursing through it was making the machinery awaken from a deep slumber. A few of the needles on the transmitter and receiver rolled from one side of the display to the other, and a red light burned on the front of the receiver housing, indicating that it was turned on.

A quiet static bled through the speakers.

"Is it working?" Blue whispered.

"It is," Parker answered. He slumped down into a chair and his mouth turned down into a frown. "This is as far as I've gotten though. Hear that? Without another radio signal, there's nothing to listen to."

"Can we send a signal?" 00 asked.

"We'd need another radio. The only one I know about is the one I have in town." Parker rolled his head back on his shoulders and stared up at the ceiling. "If I left right now to turn it on, we could test it in about four days."

"Can we make another radio?" 62 asked. He looked around the room at the heaps of parts and equipment they'd pulled from every nook and cranny of the radio room.

"I don't know. I've never built one from scratch before."

"I have instructions," 00 piped up. "When we were here the first time, I found a bunch of manuals."

A light of excitement filled Parker's face. He leaned forward in the chair, resting his hands on his knees and doing his best to temper his excitement. "We'd need another radio tower."

"We have an antenna," Blue offered.

"You do? Where?"

"Up on the jailhouse roof," 62 said. "We don't think it's hooked up to anything. We haven't found a radio down there."

Parker smacked himself in the forehead. "Of course! I can't believe I forgot about it. That one's not very big, but it should work all right." Parker assessed the disarray of parts around him, then clapped his hands together. "Well then, I guess it's time to go for a hike. Don't you?"

Blue stretched his arms overhead, yawning. "Are we going to build this thing right now? I'm as excited as the rest of you, but I really don't want to walk all the way to the jailhouse and then have to turn around and climb back up here."

"Let's pack as much stuff down as we can carry. With any luck, we'll have what we need when we get there," Parker suggested.

"I have an idea of the parts we'll need. It's not much, if I remember right," 00 said. He started shuffling through the pile nearest him, pulling wires and clamps from the heap. Parker asked 00 what kinds of things he was looking for and helped while Blue and 62 went to the rear office to start blowing out candles.

"Should we tell him about N302?" 62 whispered.

Blue shook his head. He frowned and his scowl looked severe in the candlelight. "What's got you thinking about that? We don't need computers for all this."

"I don't know," 62 answered quietly. "He's helping us with all this radio stuff, and Sunny said he likes technology. I thought maybe he could help us figure out how to deal with N302's split personality."

"It's a bad idea," Blue murmured. "We're lucky Rain is letting us get away with the radio stuff without telling anyone. You saw how worried she was when she found out what we were doing. If we tell Parker about N302 and he lets it slip to Rain, it'd be the end of N302, and maybe the end of us, too."

"But Sunny uses the computer all the time. Won't she tell him about it eventually, anyway?"

"She hasn't so far." Blue exhaled over a candle, watching the flame burn out, leaving nothing but a wisp of smoke behind.

Parker sauntered into the room, his pack flung over his shoulder and his mask propped up on his forehead. "We're all packed. You two ready to go?"

They hurried through the rest of the building, extinguishing the remaining candles. They shut off the radio equipment, one piece at a time. Once the radio room was dark again, they exited the building and headed back down the mountain. Parker's pack jingled with the sounds of parts shifting every time he took a step.

"We're off to make history, Boys!" Parker cheered from the head of the line. He slipped on the loose gravel and slid down the hill a few feet, whooping and hollering in gleeful surprise.

They made the hike down the mountain in record time, propelled forward by the excitement of their rebellion. Parker, especially, was filled with an abundance of energy, and once they'd arrived at the jailhouse, he was intent on diving right into assembling the radio. They steered clear of Rain as they stalked through the rooms. They searched for the perfect place to work on the radio, settling on a room just outside the stairwell on the top floor. They were tempting fate by being so close to N302's room, but needed a space as near the rooftop as possible. The urge to tell Parker about the bot hiding at the end of the hall built in 62's chest like a bubble about to burst. He felt cornered, and guilty, torn between his loyalty to the secrets he shared with 00 and Blue, and the truths he was hiding from Parker.

Parker was too enthralled in the electronics in front of him to notice 62's fidgety behavior. He was focused on the books 00 had laid out, and just a few hours after they'd started, they'd packed a small box with components. The device was smaller than the equipment in the radio room, and 62 was surprised when 00 insisted that the box, which was small enough to fit in a backpack, held both a transmitter and a receiver. It was like an entire building of equipment, miniaturized.

The sun had set at some point during their project, and 62's hungry stomach rumbled. There wasn't much else to do until the next day. "Is anybody else ready for dinner?"

Blue and 00's hands shot up in the air. They scrambled over one another in a race toward the door. Parker was more hesitant, still poking around the radio. As he leaned over the table, a loud gurgle tore through Parker's gut. He sighed. "I might not be ready for dinner, but it sounds like my stomach is."

62 was the last one out the door. He switched the light off and closed the door, casting another glance toward N302's room. Whether or not they told Parker

about the bot, 62 felt that the radio was going to unleash a new world of possibility for N302. He thought about how badly he and the others had wounded the bot's feelings when it heard them talk about shutting it down. He wondered if figuring out the radio system would be enough to set things right.

CHAPTER 34

Early morning found the Boys climbing across the jailhouse rooftop. Their mask lenses glinted, reflecting the rising sun's rays as they clambered around the elevator, hauling electrical cables up from the solar batteries, hooking them to the antenna, and connecting everything to the radio. The morning was blustery and cold, with clouds racing overhead. The cloud cover was hanging so low over the mountain that 62 felt like he could reach up and touch them. When he thought no one was looking, he extended an arm overhead, silently disappointed when the rolling mist passed by beyond his reach.

"Checking the weather?" Parker joked.

"Yeah," 62 answered, yanking his hand back to his side, glad that his mask hid the burning of his cheeks.

The jailhouse radio was soon set up, and it was time for someone to hike up the mountain to try sending a signal from the other end of the line. Blue and Parker decided they'd be the ones to make the trek. Parker was most familiar with the equipment, and Blue had already proven his worth if someone had to climb up the tower to make adjustments. That left 00 and 62 squatting on the roof with nothing to block the frigid morning air but the waist-high wall that encircled the flat-topped building.

They wandered over to the front side of the building as their brothers began the hike to the summit. It was interesting to watch them begin their climb, far down below. 62 imagined he was in Blue's place, and suddenly it was like watching himself in a dream. 00 was silent, lost in his own thoughts, and 62 allowed his feelings to wash over him. This was a moment to absorb, its importance something to be looked back on in the future.

00 finally broke the silence once the others rounded a bend in the trail, disappearing from sight. "How long do you think it'll take them to get there?"

"I've never paid attention to how long it takes. I'm always too busy walking," was 62's reply. He walked back over to the radio antenna and 00 followed. 62 picked up the radio, making sure the switch was turned on. A faint static leaked from the speaker. Parker said the two radios would need to be on the same channel to work, so 62 was careful not to bump the knob. He didn't want it to be his fault if they missed whatever message Blue and Parker sent from the other radio.

The Boys shivered in the cold, situating themselves beside the roof's low wall. 62 and 00 scooted together, back-to-back, protecting a portion of their bodies from the wind. They leaned against one another for warmth. 62 passed the radio to 00, then tucked his knees to his chest to keep warm. The wait was long. 62's mind wandered, thinking about the bot hiding on the floor just below them, daydreaming about telling it they'd succeeded in making the radios work. He avoided the flitting thoughts of potential failure that pestered him with greater frequency as their wait continued. Whatever the outcome, he hoped the experiment with technology would please N302. As odd as it was to admit, he'd missed the bots in Adaline, and now that they had one to talk to, he didn't like that it was upset. He feared it would stop talking to him.

They spent so long sitting in silence, that 62 nearly jumped out of his skin when the radio unit squawked to life.

"Hello? Hello?" Parker's voice cried from the radio in 00's hand. His voice came through in waves, tumbling through the speaker in uneven spurts.

00 leaned over the box in his lap and pushed the transmission button. "Hello! This is 00. Can you hear me?"

There was a brief pause, whether from a delay in the radio, or from a problem on the other end, 62 wasn't sure. Then, Parker's voice squawked from the box again. "I can hear you!"

Both Boys on the roof let out a celebratory whoop. 62 jumped to his feet and danced to let the excited energy out of his body. Suddenly, the cold was forgotten. 00's arms flailed in excitement, knocking the radio out of his lap. It fell to the roof with a jarring crash, and the wire connecting it to the power supply pulled loose from the box. The radio let out a fading squeal as the power leaked out of it, and then the box was silent.

"Fix it! Quick!" 62 screeched.

00 scrambled to repair the connection, but his numb fingers fumbled the wires. Time dragged by as he blew on his hands, wriggling his fingers under his warm breath to try to force them to life. Once they moved freely, he tried to repair the wire again. 62 paced impatiently, holding in a cry of frustration. He knew it had been an accident, but part of him wanted to throttle 00 for wrecking the radio. 00 clung to the box, refitting the wire to its proper place. The radio sprang to life again, and Parker's voice pealed out of the speaker once more.

"… hear me? Has something gone wrong?"

00 pressed the button and his voice cracked in a nervous panic. "I dropped the radio. Sorry! Had to reattach a wire. Can you still hear me?"

"Yes!" came the reply. "Thank Hanford, I thought I'd broken something. Hold on, Blue wants a try."

The wait was brief. 62 closed his eyes, imagining his brother standing at one of the desks in the radio room, talking into the microphone.

"Hey there, dustbuggers!" Blue cackled, his laughter broken by the squeals and fuzz on the line. "What d'you call two clones standing on a roof?"

"I don't know. What?" 00 asked the radio.

"Cold!" Blue's laughter screeched through the speaker.

"He's got that right," 62 said to 00 with a nod. The mere mention of the weather sent a chill to his bones. "Ask them what else we need to do to test this thing."

00 repeated the question into the radio.

"Nothing," was Parker's reply. "We've proved it works, and this channel connects fine. I just need to write down the channel number so I can remember it when I get home."

"Are you staying up there a while?" 00 asked the box.

"Yeah, it's a long walk. We'll stay 'til we're too bored to stand it, then we'll come back."

The radio operators bade one another farewell, and 00 turned off the radio. He unhooked the wires and 62 followed him down the hatch and back into the warm building. They couldn't contain their excitement over their success and raced down the stairs to the greenhouse where Rain and Sunny were working.

"We did it!" 62 shrieked as they entered the covered gardens. 00 held the radio aloft, laughing and cheering.

"Did what?" Dr. Rain asked, her face long and disapproving. Her sharp eyes held a warning to not say too much.

"We—" 62 stammered, "We spent the morning on the roof!"

"The roof?" Sunny asked, a thin smile on her lips. "And what did you find there?"

"The water collection system works great!" 00 cheered. "And the water's as clear as a day without wind!"

"Well, maybe a little wind," 62 said, commenting on the static of the radio broadcast.

"So, we're all getting new boots?" Sunny probed in their secret code.

"Death to brussels sprouts!" 00 crowed. "New boots for everyone!"

Rain raised a confused eyebrow. "You're a strange lot," she said with a shake of her head before turning her back on the celebration. She chuckled, then returned to the bed of seedlings she'd been tending to.

"We're strange," Sunny agreed with a nod. "But it's a happy kind of strange, I think."

CHAPTER 35

Parker was oblivious to Sunny's haunting stares as he rushed to pack his bag. Now that there was a chance to use his radio, he couldn't wait to get back to Hanford. Rain did her best to be sympathetic to Sunny's plight, but even she was ready to get out of the laborious work of the jailhouse and back to the relative comfort of her rounds at the hospital. While the males had whittled away their time playing with electronics, Rain and Sunny had thinned seedlings, planted rows of corn, and prepared the beds of languishing raspberries for another season. They'd erected new lattices along the far wall of the greenhouse, turned the compost curing in the bins, and built a coop for the hen and rooster. Now, Sunny stood in Parker's room clinging to his arm, as if trying to hold him back from finishing his packing while Rain hobbled to her room complaining of a sore back.

"It all appears to be growing well," Blue said. He'd just come from the greenhouse and was wiping the soil from his hands. "I expect we'll have a good harvest in a few weeks."

"It's all thanks to Rain," Sunny said. She looked up at Parker. "You've been so busy. I feel like I've hardly seen you. I wish you could stay longer."

"I know, but there's work to be done," Parker answered with a mischievous grin. He leaned down and kissed her forehead. "Don't worry, we'll be talking on the radio soon."

Rain walked past the open door, her arms full of laundry. She rolled her eyes. "I didn't hear that."

62, Blue, and 00 hovered in the hallway, holding back their own excitement. Although they were anxious for Parker to set up his radio in Hanford, they had another secret project to tend to. Once their visitors left, the three Boys planned to tell N302 about their success with the radio.

Although Sunny had mentioned privately to 62 that she missed typing to the computer, it was easy to see that she'd prefer to keep her human companions over her electronic one. Sunny looked longingly at Parker, lines of worry and sadness creeping into the corners of her eyes and mouth. Her complexion had brightened since Parker's arrival. A new light sparkled in her eyes, and rosy color appeared on her cheeks. But all of that was fading, moment by moment, each time Parker unlocked his arm from hers, remembering something he'd forgotten, and filling his bag with urgency.

"The wind's picked up," Sunny commented as she watched Parker fling his pack over his shoulder. "The dust is shifting. Maybe you should stay another day or two until the weather calms."

"Even a day that starts out calm ends with wind," Parker said with a shake of his head. He pulled his mask out of a pocket and punched his fist into it, forcing it to unfurl around his knuckles. "The sooner we get going, the sooner the doc can rush us through detox on the other side."

"I can't rush it," Rain's voice called from her room next door. "It takes as long as it takes. I've got nothing to do with whether or not we're quarantined."

"We were lucky that we didn't come back so hot last time that we had to be quarantined," Parker said in a low voice so Rain couldn't hear. "I kept thanking her for using her clout to get us through. Turns out, that drives her crazy." He gave Sunny a sly wink, then raised his voice so Rain could hear him again. "Of course, she has to say she follows procedure. But just you wait, she'll get us through."

Rain groaned, coming out of her room and throwing her hands in the air with exasperation. She looked at the Boys. "He keeps acting like I got us hurried through because of some favor. But I followed procedure to the letter. I do what I have to!"

Parker came into the hall, Sunny following close behind. She grasped his hand. "I understand. No favors." He gave Rain two exaggerated winks, a look of conspiracy plastered across his face.

"You're impossible!" Rain shouted, slapping Parker on the arm Sunny wasn't clinging to. Parker laughed. Rain growled in frustration, stomped to her room, and re-emerged with her pack over her shoulder.

"Are you ready, then? I know we have four days of this nonsense ahead of us, and I'm ready to get it over with."

"You're not planning on us being in quarantine then? Because, that would add a few days. Very interesting." Parker rubbed his chin thoughtfully.

Rain's voice came out in a trembling shriek of frustration. "I can't get us out of quarantine! The only way to stay out is to not get lit up by radiation. So just... watch your step!" She tromped to the stairwell door, flung it open on its hinges, and fled downstairs.

"It's going to be a great trip," Parker joked. He retrieved his bag and everyone followed him down to the lobby.

Blue went to the door, gripping the handle in anticipation of opening it for the travelers. 62 fidgeted nearby, and 00's toes tapped against the floor nervously. The moment Rain took a step toward the exit, Blue tugged his mask down over his face and swung the door open wide. The wind was thrashing the mountain and caught the door, throwing it open nearly as violently as Rain had opened the door upstairs. A blast of air rushed into the jailhouse, prompting everyone to put on their masks as it forced the warm air out of the lobby.

Parker tapped his mask's filter to Sunny's covered forehead. She shriveled beside him, losing the last bits of whatever strength she'd gained during his visit. Sunny hugged herself and shuddered, from the cold pouring in through the open door, or from sadness, 62 couldn't tell. Parker noticed her trembling and wrapped her in a final embrace, but the pull of the defunct radio in the town beyond the desert was too great to keep him.

Everyone gave a final, brief farewell, and soon Sunny was watching through a window as Parker and Rain walk at a clipped pace toward the trailhead. 00 gave the lobby a haphazard sweep with the radiation counter, announced it was clean, and the three Boys threw their masks to the ground. They raced one another to the top floor. The computer room was unlocked in record time, and 00 had N302's primary computer nearly reassembled before Parker and Rain's figures could be seen emerging from the trail at the bottom of the mountain.

Sunny eventually joined the Boys, but she seemed oblivious to their harried activities. She stood listlessly at the window, watching Parker and Rain become smaller with each step they took across the scrub desert. She glanced at 00 when he cursed at a component that refused to cooperate, and muttered a quick, "Well done," when the bot's boot-up sequence finally began. Otherwise, she remained silent, lost in thought, clinging to the bars at the window as if part of her was irretrievably lost beyond the glass.

62 knew it would be a while before the bot's programs were up and running, so he offered to go down to the kitchen to find something to snack on. After chopping carrots into spears and boiling a couple of eggs, he arrived back at the computer room to find everyone, including Sunny, huddled around the computer.

00 was holding a microphone, breathlessly recounting Parker and Rain's visit to the bot. 62 arrived just in time to hear 00 tell N302 about the surprising revelation that Parker had a radio of his own.

N302> THERE IS ANOTHER RADIO DEVICE?

"Yes," 00 said excitedly. "But it's even better than that. We built a little radio for the jailhouse, too. If someone is up at the radio room, someone can sit here and talk to them. It's the neatest thing."

N302> YES. THIS IS GOOD. I AM PROUD OF YOU FOR MAKING THIS DISCOVERY.

00 beamed. 62 couldn't help but smile, too. The radio had the potential to make talking to Parker across the desert easy, and almost instantaneous. He was relieved that the pressure on him to figure out a reliable connection with Mattie had been lifted, at least for the moment. If Parker couldn't get his radio running again, or if the signal from the radio tower didn't reach Hanford, then finding a way to pass messages to Mattie would fall on him again. But for now, he let a wave of relief wash over him.

Sunny leaned forward, speaking with a tentative voice into the microphone. "N302," she said, hardly above a whisper, "would you like to hear the radio?"

The cursor blinked. 62 looked over at Blue, who shrugged at the bot's silence.

00 cleared his throat and leaned into the microphone. In a louder voice, he asked, "N302, did you hear Sunny's question?"

N302> YES.

"Do you want to hear it?"

N302> YES.

Chairs scraped against the floor, and the Boys rushed into action. 00 grabbed the radio box and began hooking it up to one of the other computer's power supplies. Meanwhile, Blue unfurled a long copper wire that Parker had found for them to use as an extended antenna, so they could use the radio inside the building without having to stand on the roof.

"It isn't much," Sunny said to the computer's microphone. "It sounds mostly like someone wrinkling paper in your ear."

62 sat down beside her. "Sunny didn't get a chance to hear it while someone was on the other end. When they're talking, it's different. There's still static, but you can hear their voices."

N302> IS THERE DATA?

62 frowned. "I don't think so, except for whatever we say on the microphone. Unless you count words as data. Do you?"

N302> YES.

"It's hooked up!" 00 shouted to the room. He pulled the radio over to the microphone and flipped on the switch.

The small peal of electricity running through the components squealed, so high pitched that 62 and the others could barely hear it. The small whine went higher and higher until it disappeared, replaced by the quiet hiss of static on the airwaves.

N302's components clicked rhythmically. It tinked its inner speaker a few times, the same way it had when Terminal Two had been set up across the room. The bot paused a moment as if listening to something, and then repeated the sequence.

"What do you think?" 00 asked the computer's microphone.

N302> YOU HAVE DONE WELL, BOY 1125000, BOY 1124562, AND BOY BLUE. WOMAN SUNNY, YOU HAVE ALLOWED TECHNOLOGY TO PROGRESS. THIS IS GOOD.

"If you had seen how excited everyone was, you'd have known I had no choice," Sunny admitted. "But, I think it will make things easier for us. We may be able to talk to Hanford with it."

N302> COMMUNICATION IS NECCESSARY FOR SURVIVAL. YOU HAVE ACHIEVED IT

WITHOUT ME. PERHAPS YOU DO NOT NEED MY PROGRAM TO ENSURE YOUR SUCCESS.

62 looked at his friends. He'd hoped the bot would be happier over their achievement. But it seemed almost disappointed. "N302, what are you talking about?"

N302> I WAS BUILT TO CARE FOR MEN BECAUSE MEN COULD NOT SURVIVE WITHOUT ME. BUT YOU HAVE SURVIVED WITHOUT ME. PERHAPS I HAVE NO PURPOSE IN THIS WORLD.

"You're starting to sound like me," Sunny said with a frown. "You do have a purpose. I like talking to you. I enjoy teaching you."

N302> I WAS NOT CREATED FOR ENJOYMENT. I WAS CREATED TO ADMINISTER CARE.

"But, you've done that. You helped us take care of Sunny," 00 argued.

The computer repeated the sequence of ticks and dings as before, and its companions looked at one another in confused silence. 62 wondered what the bot was doing. Was it talking to itself, the way he talked to himself when he was trying to work through a problem?

N302> MY TASK IS COMPLETE. I MUST PROCESS THIS DATA. CURRENT REQUEST: LEAVE SYSTEMS RUNNING BUT PLEASE LEAVE THIS UNIT ALONE.

"Leave this unit alone?" Blue scratched his head. "Bot, are you kicking us out?"

The cursor blinked. 00 turned off the radio and laid it on the table beside the silent computer. "I guess we'd better go?"

62 followed the others out into the hall. 00 tiptoed back into the room, then turned the monitor to face the door so it could more easily be seen from out in

the hall. They stood, staring at one another outside the open door awkwardly. 62 felt strange. It had been months since he'd been bossed around by a bot. He felt compelled to follow the computer's request, but he wondered if it was out of a deeply ingrained habit, or if it was something else. The computer's cursor continued to blink, silently. 62 looked around at his friends, shrugged his shoulders, and trudged down the hall away from the melancholy Machine.

CHAPTER 36

It took a full night and day for N302 to respond to anyone's prodding again. Then, it was simply to request that someone power it down.

"You want to be turned off?" 00 asked in alarm. "But I thought you wanted to be left on forever?"

"Yeah, you're always so bummed when we have to turn you off," 62 said into the microphone.

N302> I HAVE DETERMINED THERE IS NO NEED FOR MY DEVICE. THE RESOURCES USED TO OPERATE THIS DEVICE CAN BE BETTER USED ELSEWHERE.

The Boys looked at one another, a silent conversation passing between their dark eyes and furrowed brows. 00 made another attempt at convincing the bot to stay online.

"We could play a game. Will you boot one up for us?"

The computer made a slow ticking sound that reminded 62 of when one of the adults clicked their tongues in disapproval. An angry flash passed across the screen.

N302> I WAS NOT CREATED TO ENTERTAIN. PLEASE DISCONNECT POWER AS REQUESTED.

00 frowned, but he did as the bot asked and turned the computer off. He shut off the monitor's power and disconnected both the computer box and the screen from the power supply. 62 and 00 trudged downstairs to find Blue and Sunny in the greenhouse.

"The bot's offline," 62 announced as they entered the enclosed garden.

Sunny had been working the soil on her hands and knees. She paused what she was doing and sat on her heels, resting her gloved hands on her thighs. "Why'd you turn it off? Is it broken?"

"Maybe," 00 answered. His slumped shoulders and hanging head amplified the concern in his voice. "It said it's using too many of our resources and asked to be shut off. It wouldn't play a game with us or anything. We tried to talk to it, but it said it wasn't made to entertain us and told us to pull the plug."

"It needs a job," Blue called from the other side of the planting bed. He stood up, holding the chicken under one arm and the rooster under the other. The birds rested in his arms as if being carried around like watermelons was the most natural thing in the world.

"What?" 62 asked, caught off-guard both by Blue's statement and his fowl load.

"The bot. It needs a job," Blue repeated. He walked the path between the sprouting plants in a straight-legged march, rocking the birds back and forth under his arms with each step.

"How do you know that?" 62 asked.

"Everything in Hanford has a job. Cooks cook, teachers teach, cows give milk, chickens lay eggs." Blue stopped beside his brothers, standing as straight as a guard at the gates of Hanford. "And scavengers like me, well, we go a little bonkers if we don't have anything to scavenge."

"You're making a very good point right now," Sunny said, pointing to the hen and rooster. "What exactly are you doing with those birds?"

"Going for a walk."

"Where are you walking to?" Sunny asked.

"Well, we started over there," Blue tossed his head back to the other side of the greenhouse, "and now we're here."

"I see," she said with a half-smile.

"A job," 00 murmured. He rubbed his chin thoughtfully. "I kind of see what you're saying. In Adaline, N302 had a whole bunch of responsibilities. Mostly helping in medical procedures, but when 2442 made it his assistant it did all sorts of things."

"But what kind of job can it do here?" 62 asked, looking around the greenhouse. "It doesn't have arms or legs. It's just a box sitting on a table."

"It could sit on a table in the radio room and listen for Parker," Blue suggested. "It's not like that's a hard job or anything, but it would save us from having to hike up the mountain every day."

"Of course!" 00 shouted. The tenor of his voice scared the chickens and both the hen and rooster flapped their wings, beating Blue about the arms and chest until they were able to wriggle free of his grasp. They screeched and squawked their way to the opposite end of the greenhouse, hiding inside the protection of their coop.

Blue put his hands on his hips and sneered at 00. "You ruined our walk!"

"I'm sorry. But you were brilliant just then, and it surprised me," 00 grinned.

Blue considered this a moment, and his angry grimace softened a little. "That's true. I am brilliant."

"Sometimes," 00 corrected.

"So, we're going to carry the computer up the mountain and leave it there?" 62 asked.

00 shook his head. "No, better than that. We'll take Terminal Two up. It doesn't have the full processing capacity of N302, but it's got enough of its programming to turn on the radio in the morning and shut it off at night."

"What good will that do?" Sunny asked. She brushed the soil off her gloves and got up off the ground, looking at the Boys thoughtfully. "If it hears Parker's message up on the mountain, that doesn't do anything for us down here."

"It will if we rig Terminal Two up to bounce the signal down to our antenna and ask N302 to signal an alarm when it hears something," 00 said excitedly. "We can make a bell, or something. If Terminal Two powers the radio on and off, then N302 can listen for the broadcast, and none of us have to sit by the radio. We'll just head upstairs when we hear the alarm. We might miss the first few minutes of broadcast, depending on how long it takes us to get upstairs, but it wouldn't be a big deal, really." 00 slapped his thigh as an idea struck him. "Parker said one of those Machines in the radio room is a recording device. I can get N302 to program the other terminal to flip on the recorder when a signal comes on. Then, even if we miss something, we can listen to it later. If we did all that, we'd be able to keep going around, doing whatever we want all day. Like Blue said, it wouldn't be a hard job. When you think about it though, it would be an important one."

"Fire alarms," Blue said. Everyone looked at him as if he were still holding chickens. When he realized no one knew what he was talking about, he closed his eyes and sighed as if they were all beneath him. In a condescending tone, he explained. "There are bells hidden on every floor. They're called fire alarms. Back when Hanford was a city, they had them in all the buildings. They rang if there was a fire. Don't you guys know anything?"

"Some things," Sunny said in a dry voice. "Just not the same things as you."

Blue rolled his eyes. "Anyway, they're all over the building. You'd have to figure out how to wire them up to the bot to make them work. But they're loud as all get out when you get one to ring."

"Have you used them before?" 62 asked.

"Yeah. One time I was bored and wanted to see what would happen if I hooked one up to a battery. Hoooeee! What a noise!" The chickens squawked from deep inside their hut and Blue pointed at the box. "Exactly! They know what I'm talking about."

00 clapped his hands together. "This is perfect. Blue, you know what these alarm things look like, right?"

Blue rolled his eyes. "Obviously."

"Okay, then. You collect as many as you can. I'll go boot up the computer and tell N302 the plan." 00 took a few steps away, then spun around, rocking on his heels. He pointed at Blue. "You really are a genius. No matter what anyone else says." 00 turned back around and jogged out of the greenhouse and into the building.

A smug smile spread over Blue's face. His eyes closed as he soaked in the compliment. Then his eyelids flew open and he ran after 00. "Hey! What's that supposed to mean? What do other people say about me?"

62 chuckled. He looked up at Sunny. "Do you need help here? I think they're going to be gone a while."

"Do you want to help me check the coop for eggs? With as riled up as the hen is, today may be our last day to find one for a while."

"We can take the chickens for a walk, if you think it would help," 62 managed to say with a straight face.

Sunny laughed so loud that the hen screeched.

CHAPTER 37

"I've never had to work so hard to make a bot pay attention to me in all my life," 00 complained at breakfast the next morning. After several power-ons, he'd finally gotten N302 to listen to him. It had taken another several attempts to ask it to let them try to hook it and its secondary unit up to the radios. "But I practically had to beg. I tried typing, but it wouldn't take me seriously. Finally, I had to use the microphone and make it listen."

62 patted his brother on the arm. "It must've been hard. It's no good having a bot that's too mad to be powered up."

00 sighed and dropped corn mash from his spoon back into his bowl, watching it slop against itself when it

landed. "It might be more trouble than it's worth, though. I'm not sure we can figure out how to get the things wired in."

"You'll figure it out," 62 said with an encouraging smile. "You always do."

Blue dropped into a chair across from 62, slamming his bowl of corn mash on the tabletop. "Sunny says there aren't any more eggs."

"Yeah, she told me that chicken probably wouldn't lay any after it got scared," 62 replied.

"Not even that. She just told me that even when the dumb bird starts laying again, we can't eat them. Not until after she hatches a batch of chicks." Blue stirred his breakfast roughly, sending a thick glob of mash over the side of the bowl. "Like we need more chickens. You can't even do anything with them!"

"We could eat them," 00 pointed out. "More chickens means more eggs, and more roosters means eating meat every once in a while."

"But how long is that going to take? Weeks? Months? I can't take it," Blue complained.

"You can always go back to Hanford, you know. You're not the one that was banished from town." 62 said the words cautiously, hoping that Blue wouldn't take the suggestion as an excuse to pack his bags and leave.

"They do have better food there," Blue said, gazing down at the bowl of mush in front of him. His eyes snapped up, locking on 62's. "But Hanford's got rules. And no bots."

"You're right there!" 00 agreed, pointing at Blue and nodding.

The Boys finished their breakfast, checked in with Sunny, and set about the business of turning their computers into radio station assistants. N302 had been reattached to Terminal Two so that it could help 00 alter its programming to enable and disable the radio. N302 even managed to add code that would allow the bot to turn the lights on and off, provided there was enough excess power. While the computers updated their programming, Blue turned on the power to the elevator. When they disassembled Terminal Two, using the lift to bring the heavy computer down to the main floor was a welcome treat. 00 got his elevator ride, and none of the Boys broke a sweat as they pushed the cart full of computer parts.

They spent the rest of the day measuring out wire and setting up relays for N302 and its new set of alarms. Blue found fifteen fire alarms, and they decided to wire them all up so they'd hear the signal no matter where they were in the building. The system was so spread out, however, that they realized they didn't have near enough wire.

"But the things were wired into the walls," Blue said. "Can't we just use those wires?"

00 scratched his head. "I guess so, if we can figure out how they're run."

This set into motion a project of chasing wires through the building that lasted late into the night. Eventually, N302 was moved down to a room on the third floor, central to the building and all the devices it was to be hooked up to. 62 dragged himself to bed as the moon rose high in the sky, dreading the early morning ahead of them. Enough time had passed that Parker would be calling them any day now, and they didn't want to miss his broadcast. They vowed to leave the jailhouse at daybreak with Terminal Two, in hopes that they'd have it up and running in the radio room before the end of the next day.

62's mind wandered in and out of a series of dreams, but he finally settled his mind back at Hanford's library. He was startled to find Mattie there, and for once, he was able to push through to her dream with very little effort.

"Hey," 62 said as he sat down on the floor in front of her.

Mattie was seated on the floor with her legs crossed, surrounded on either side by stacks of large books. She was flipping through one, a book full of colorful paintings, and only glanced up momentarily at 62 to acknowledge his presence. She found the image she was looking for, a picture of an oil painting of a small yellow house near the sea. The water in the picture rippled, then settled back into place.

"Are you okay?" 62 asked.

The young librarian looked up at him with tears in her eyes. "Parker told me. The Oosa aren't taking me to see the ocean."

"I know. They've been doing bad things, Mattie. I tried to tell you before."

Mattie sniffled, wiping her nose with the back of her hand. "I wanted to live with them so bad. I thought I was one of them."

62 reached out to the book in his friend's lap and tipped the cover so that its pages rolled from one side to the other. He closed the book and pulled it away from Mattie. He tossed it aside and crossed his own legs, scooting closer to her until their knees touched. "I know it's hard. But you're lucky, you know? Your mom was lucky. She got to have you, and look at you! You've managed to survive just fine without the Oosa."

"I'm not fine," Mattie said with another sniffle. Tears dripped from her eyes and she pushed them away with the palms of her hands. "I'm sick, 62."

"What do you mean?" 62 leaned forward and took her wet hands into his own.

"I've broken three bones since you left. Two of them are ribs. I'm having a hard time breathing, and eating is impossible. My jaw aches. Not like a toothache or anything. It's like it's on fire, burning under my skin. It's so painful."

"But you look fine!" 62 stammered.

"We're in a dream," Mattie said with a sorrowful laugh. "None of this is real. I'm in the hospital now. They think I'll have to stay at least another few weeks, if I can get better."

"Of course you'll get better. What happened to make your bones break? Did you fall?"

Mattie shook her head. "Something like this happened before you came to Hanford. My joints ache for days and then a bone will just break, for no reason. I've never told anyone, but it's getting worse. This time, the first rib broke while I was rearranging books. Then, my leg broke. I was walking to the hospital to get my rib looked at. Just walking! And all of a sudden, I was on the ground. It's in a cast now." Mattie rubbed her left leg just below her kneecap.

"And the other rib that broke?"

"They were rolling me over in bed." Mattie's eyes glistened. She tried to smile, but the curves of her cheeks twitched from the effort. "They aren't saying it, but they think it's radiation sickness. They think it got me because I'm half Oosa."

"No," 62 said. "It can't be that. You just had a couple of accidents. You must have hit something without realizing it. They're being too rough with you."

Mattie shook her head. "It's the same thing that happens to the kids in the nursery. They hurt all the time, and eventually they can't be held any more…" Mattie's voice drifted off and she looked away from 62. He followed her gaze and saw the viewing window of Hanford's nursery. A Woman stood in the window, wringing a child's blanket in her hands. Silent tears streaked her cheeks. Her face was contorted in anguish. Mattie looked back at 62 and the scene disappeared.

"You got better the last time this happened, right? You'll get better again." 62's face twisted as he tried to make himself believe his own words.

"They let Parker in to see me, even though they have him in quarantine. You know what that means? That means that they aren't worried about someone who might've gotten into a hot spot spending time with me. Like if he's irradiated, it won't matter if he sits down next to me."

"That doesn't make any sense, Mattie. If they had him come see you, maybe they know that he doesn't need quarantine. Maybe he's just there so they can double-check, even though they already know he's fine." 62 gripped Mattie's hands firmly in his own. "You're going to be fine, Mattie. You'll see."

"Maybe," Mattie answered. She mimicked 62's consoling nod. "We'll see."

"Besides, if you're so sick, why didn't Rain or Parker tell us when they were here? Rain's a doctor. If you've been hurt, she'd know about it, wouldn't she?"

"Dr. Rain knows, but I asked her not to tell you."

"Why?"

"Because, what use is it for you to know? You're all the way out there, and if you come back, they won't let you in. The best I can hope for is to get better."

"I have to tell Blue," 62 said in a flat tone. "He needs to know you're hurt."

Mattie closed her eyes, fresh tears collecting in her lashes. She nodded silently. Then, nose sniffling, she faded from existence, leaving 62 sitting alone in a darkening library. 62 slumped against a nearby shelf, crying to himself until he woke to the light of morning.

CHAPTER 38

Blue was leaving. 62 understood, and only wished his friend wasn't going alone. 00 offered to return to Hanford with him, but Blue explained that he'd move faster without 00 trailing behind him. "And besides," Blue said, pointing back and forth between 62 and 00, "You two look identical. They'd probably hold me up at the gate if I came back with you because I bet Joan can't tell the difference between you."

Sunny leaned against a nearby wall. "I'm sorry I can't come with you."

"You could," Blue urged. "You made it all the way out here from wherever the Oosa were keeping you.

I bet the walk to Hanford would be easy, compared to that."

"It's not the walk that worries me," Sunny said. "If they find out I'm here…"

Blue shut his mouth, pressing his lips into a straight line. It was apparent from the burning of his sapphire eyes that he had more to say, but he held the words back. Blue pulled his mask on, shuttering up his frustrated expression, and pulled his pack of gear from the floor. 62 and 00 put on their masks as well, silently escorting their friend to the trailhead.

After the door slammed shut behind them, Sunny hidden away inside, Blue let out a frustrated yell.

"Why in Hanford's name can't she be bothered to stand up and tell them what's happening?" Blue kicked the dirt at his feet and punched the air.

62 took a quick step sideways, doing his best to miss an accidental box to the side of the head. "I don't know," he answered. "She's scared, I guess."

"Chicken!" Blue screamed into the air. His mask filter did little to temper the rage in his voice. "Worse than chicken! She's useless! What's the point?"

"The point of what?" 00 asked.

"Of keeping someone like her around? All she does is take up space, moping around in there. We look after her, we make sure she doesn't get all crazy and hurt herself. But what's the use? All she does is hide." Blue kicked a boulder resting on one side of the trailhead, then reeled back, hopping on one foot and hollering up a storm.

The throbbing of Blue's foot seemed to bring him back to the present, and his rage faded. He leaned against the offending boulder, rubbing his hurt foot.

"Sunny does her best," 62 said in a steady voice. Sunny had been through a lot. They all had. But even though Blue had been abandoned as a baby, and 62 had been thrown out of his home not so long ago, their problems seemed small compared to Sunny's. "Are you sure you'll be okay?" 62 asked.

Blue nodded. He dropped his foot back to the ground and stomped on it a few times to make sure it still worked. "Yeah, I'll be fine. I'm just mad."

"I'm sure she'll be okay," 00 said. He hadn't said Mattie's name, but 62 knew that's who he meant. "She's just got bad luck right now, is all. You'll see."

"I hope so," Blue answered. He pointed to the top of the mountain. "Keep the radio on. Once I find out what's going on with Mattie, I'll help Parker get his transmitter going, if he hasn't already by the time I get there. I'll send a message as soon as I get a chance."

62 nodded, then reached out and gave Blue a long, hard hug. 00 did the same. It was awkward, but felt necessary and right given the situation they were in. Blue pulled away and 00 wrapped an arm over 62's shoulder in brotherly support. 62 and 00 watched Blue pick his way down the trail until he was around a bend and out of sight.

"She's going to be okay," 62 said softly. "Right?"

"Who? Mattie, or Sunny?"

62 turned his head, focusing on 00's eyes through their lenses. "Both."

00 lifted his shoulders. "I don't know."

"Me either. That's what's so scary."

The pair of brothers stepped away from the trail, heading back inside just long enough to grab Terminal Two and load it in the wheelbarrow. They were more dedicated to using the computers to monitor the radio now, no longer seeing it as a means to satisfy N302. With Mattie hurt, and Blue walking alone in the desert, it was a necessity. They pushed the wheelbarrow to the radio room in silence, only stopping once on a switchback on the trail to see if they could find Blue in the landscape below. They didn't find him. Once they arrived at the radio room, they double checked the solar panel and battery pack Parker and Blue had arranged on the south side of the building, then forced their way through the rickety door to begin rebuilding Terminal Two.

The computer's boot up sequence was eerily identical to N302, and for a moment, 62 worried that they'd brought the wrong computer. But once they started communicating with the bot, it was clear that this unit was a less intelligent version of its parent Machine.

U> Connect to radio frequency 94.7 FM band.

TT> SEARCHING FREQUENCY

TT> FREQUENCY FOUND

TT> CONNECTION ESTABLISHED

U> Set electronics to turn the power-on when the first current surge is received during AM hours.

TT> TURN ON SET

U> Set electronics to power-off when the first current drop is sensed during PM hours.

TT> TURN OFF SET

"Is that it?" 62 asked when 00 backed away from the keyboard.

"That's it," 00 confirmed. "As long as the programming N302 wrote works, this thing should turn on the systems in the morning, and turn them off again at night."

"Are we ready to go back to test the jailhouse setup, then?"

"In just a minute." 00 turned the volume up on the speakers until he could hear the flicker of static on the radio waves. He shrugged his shoulders. "Figured we should at least check to see if Parker was on the air before we left. I'm ready now."

The Boys picked their way back down the mountain toward the jailhouse. They could just see the top of the building peeking over a crest on the trail when a loud ringing pierced the air, startling the Boys. 62 grabbed 00's arm, shouting, "The alarm!" before running ahead on the trail.

The closer they got to the jailhouse, the louder the ringing became. The sound rattled 62's brain and made his eardrums burn. Both Boys covered their ears with their hands. They dropped down off the trail to find Sunny, masked, squatting behind one of the large rocks, her hands clamped over her ears as she rocked back and forth. She turned her head, catching sight of them.

"I can't get it to shut off!" She shouted through her mask. "If anyone's on the radio, I can't hear them over all this noise!"

62 and 00 rushed to the building's front door. They had to make N302 turn the fire alarms off. But the second the door swung open they realized that the earsplitting sound outside was nothing compared to the throbbing scream of the alarms inside. The air vibrated around the Boys with the power of the sound. They pushed forward through the hurricane of noise, into the detox room. 62 lowered his hand from his ear to grab the radiation detector, but the ringing alarm made his head feel like it would split open. 00 pulled a towel off a nearby bench and pressed it between his ear and his shoulder to mute the noise so he could use his free hand to turn on the detector.

There was no way to hear the clicking noise of the device over the sound of the alarm. 62 leaned over the device's box and watched the needle swing back and forth on the dial while 00 waved the wand over both their bodies. 62 sighed with relief that the needle didn't go into the danger zone on the dial and nodded at 00 when he figured they were done.

The towel dropped from 00's shoulder and he clamped his hand back to his uncovered ear. They abandoned the radiation counter, too frazzled to worry about turning it off, and hurried out of the room and into the main building. They fought to open the stairwell door with their feet so neither of them would have to uncover an ear to turn the handle with his hand. Then they tottered up the stairs as quickly as they could, off-balance with their palms clamped against the sides of their heads. Although normally their steps would echo through the stairwell, with the alarms ringing, 62 couldn't hear his own feet as they pounded the stairs.

They struggled again to pull the door when they made it to the third floor. They fell into the hallway, off-balance and disoriented from exhaustion and the squeal of the alarm mounted just overhead. Thankfully, N302's door was open a crack and 62 heaved a sigh of relief that they could push it open with their elbows, instead of trying to work the knob with their toes.

00 rushed over to the bot, yelling at the microphone to turn the alarm off.

N302> UNABLE TO REGISTER AUDIO COMMAND. PLEASE REPEAT.

00 screamed again to shut the alarm off, getting the same response. Finally, he threw a nasty look at 62, then peeled his palms from his ears and pounded on the keyboard.

U> Shut off the fire alarms!

N302> REQUEST RECEIVED. ALARMS WILL BE DEACIVATED IN 30… 29… 28…

U> Turn them off now! Please!

The numbers of N302's countdown hastened, but it wasn't until after the zero was displayed that the squeal of the last alarm was finally halted.

"Thank you!" both Boys yelled at the microphone. Although 62 knew that the alarms were off, there was still a ringing in his head that wouldn't quiet.

N302> THE RADIO SIGNAL HAS RECEIVED A BROADCAST.

"We know," 62 said as 00 picked up the handheld radio, turning the volume up so he could hear Parker's voice in the speaker.

N302> THE ALARM WAS SUCCESSFUL?

"We heard you all the way up the mountain," 62 complained.

N302> IT IS AN EFFECTIVE SYSTEM.

"You can say that again."

00 shushed 62 and pointed angrily at the keyboard, indicating that if 62 had anything else to say to the bot, he should type it. 00 pulled the radio to his mouth and pressed the transmission button.

"We hear you loud and clear."

Parker's voice cut through the static. "Good! I'm glad to hear your voice. I was beginning to wonder if something was broken."

"Sorry, we were busy with something, so it took us a minute to realize you were on the radio," 00 replied.

"What were you doing?" Parker asked.

00 and 62 looked at one another warily. "Counting chickens," 00 answered.

There was a long pause, then Parker said, "But you only have two of them, and one of them is a rooster. Doesn't seem like something that needs counting."

62 touched the transmission button and blurted, "We just wanted to make sure. Sunny told us we can't eat any more eggs until some chicks hatch. We were checking to see if any showed up yet."

"Oh, good! I'm glad you're all planning ahead. More chickens mean more meat. And if I remember right from his classes, chicken is one of 62's favorite foods," Parker joked.

"It isn't horrible," 62 agreed in an awkward voice. "So, uh, was there anything else you wanted to say?"

"There is. I'm afraid I have bad news. I saw Mattie a couple days ago. She's up at the hospital, pretty sick. I got out of quarantine this morning and came straight here to tell you. Would you believe that the connections all held up well? I only had to replace a few wires that had come loose. This baby started right up."

"That's rotten news about Mattie," 00 answered, trying to act surprised. He looked at 62 with a grimace.

"We might not have known without the call," 62 said, covering for his friend. Although Parker knew about 62's dreams, he wasn't sure the teacher understood the full scope of what he could do in them. "Thanks for the heads up. Blue is heading out today. He wants to see her."

"What do you think is wrong?" 00 asked.

Parker cleared his throat, making the static warble on the line. "Rain says Mattie's bones are weak. They're doing the best they can to make her comfortable. I'll send her word that Blue's coming. That'll make her feel better." There was a long pause on the line, then Parker asked, "Say, do you think Sunny will come with Blue?"

62 gritted his teeth. Even if Sunny wanted to go, Blue had already been gone for hours. "I'll have him ask her, but nothing's changed, so don't count on her turning up."

"I wish she would," Parker said wistfully.

"Us, too," 00 said. "The Oosa really hurt her."

Parker's voice sounded sad. "Not just her, but it sounds like maybe they hurt Mattie, too. They aren't saying anything for sure yet, but the symptoms she's having are the same as what most of the little Oosa kids get. Not many of the kids who come from an Oosa intervention make it. Mattie's been an inspiration to all of us. She's proven that anyone can make a difference, no matter where they come from."

"Do you think she'll get better?" 62 asked.

Parker didn't reply right away. When he spoke again, it was as if he hadn't heard the question. "Well, that's all for now. I'll call back again tomorrow. When I call back, I'll stay on the line as long as possible, just in case you miss my first attempt."

"Oh, I wouldn't worry about that. Now that we know what to listen for, there's no way we'll miss your broadcast," 00 said.

"Are you staying in the radio room, just listening for the signal?"

"Something like that," 00 answered, giving 62 a sidelong glance.

"That might be a good job for Sunny," Parker answered thoughtfully. "Smart thinking, you two. Well, I'd better get off this thing. I'll try to be back at about the same time tomorrow."

"Okay, we'll talk to you then," 62 said. He'd not been brave enough to ask Parker if he thought Mattie would get better a second time. He was afraid of knowing the answer.

Parker's voice disappeared from the radio's speaker, replaced by the soft sound of lulling static over dead air.

N302> YOUR FRIEND IS DYING.

"We aren't sure what's wrong with her," 62 said hastily into N302's microphone. "Hopefully she'll get better and be back at the library soon."

N302> NO. SHE IS EXHIBITING DELAYED SIGNS OF TOTAL BODY IRRADIATION. PROGNOSIS: FATAL.

"How do you know?" 62 grumbled. "You're not a doctor."

N302> I HAVE ACCESSED THE ABBREVIATED JOURNAL OF MILITARY MEDICAL RESEARCH AS CURATED BY SIR ALEXANDER FLEMING. I HAVE ANALYZED THE SYMPTOMS AND BASED ON PREVIOUS CONVERSATIONS RECORDED IN MY ARCHIVES, THE FEMALE, MATTIE, DOES APPEAR TO BE SUFFERING FROM FATAL TOTAL BODY IRRADIATION.

"Thanks," 62 said, tears welling in his eyes. He wanted to hope that Mattie was going to mend up and get better. But the fact that she'd stayed behind both times Parker and Rain had come said a lot. A bitter lump swelled in 62's throat and he pushed himself away from the table, standing in the middle of the room with his eyes closed. "Thanks a lot."

C*H*A*P*T*E*R 39

After the first radio call from Parker, there was a unanimous decision to disconnect most of the fire alarms. 00 and 62 figured one alarm per floor was quite enough to hear N302's notifications. The Boys climbed around the building, undoing most of the connections they'd worked so hard to put together the week before. When the message that Blue had arrived in Hanford came several days later, it did so without making 62 feel like he needed to rip his ears off.

Once they got over their excitement to be hearing from Blue, everyone's hearts sank. The message he had to deliver wasn't good. Blue had made it to Hanford in record time; just two and a half days. But then came detox and a brief quarantine, and although Rain did her best to keep his tests moving, Blue insisted she could have gotten him through faster. When the staff finally determined it was safe enough for him to see Mattie, he'd found her lying in a bed, face pinched and breathing shallow, uneven breaths.

"I tried to hold her hand, but it hurt her too much," Blue whispered over the static of the radio. "Rain said her bones are dying."

"Her bones are what?" 62 stammered into the radio transmitter's microphone, sure he misunderstood. "Say that again?"

"They're dying," Blue stated angrily.

"But how can someone live without bones?" 00 asked.

"I don't think they can," Blue answered.

The air hanging on the line went quiet. 62 slumped down in his chair, overwhelmed with sadness and worry for his friend. Mattie had done so much for them. He felt useless sitting at a radio box so far away from her. He wracked his brain for something he could do to help. He wanted to go racing across the desert, wanted to get to Hanford even faster than Blue had managed. He desperately wanted to see his friend. But he knew if he went back to Hanford, there would be nothing but trouble when he arrived.

"Do you think Auntie can get me permission to come to the hospital?" 62 croaked finally. She was the only Woman on their side. The only one with enough clout to make a difference.

"I'll talk to her and find out," Blue answered. "Although, I've gotta be honest, everyone I see here treats me like a criminal for having gone with you guys. I don't know how Parker and Rain deal with the dirty looks everyone gives them. They're even talking about where they should send us when the Men need to use the jailhouse for the Oosa's next visit."

"Where to send us?" 00 asked with a surprised gasp. "What's that supposed to mean? Why wouldn't we just stay here?"

"They don't want us brainwashing anyone into thinking we're decent people, I guess."

"But, where would we go?" 62 asked.

"I'm not sure they're too concerned with where we'd go. Just so long as we don't come back to Hanford, and don't stay at the jailhouse. On the bright side, it'll be a few months before the Oosa come back, so we don't have to worry too much right now. Plus, we have the radio room. We can always move up there. I just figured I'd let you know that's what people are talking about when they think I'm not listening."

"Well, if they're planning on getting rid of us, they're probably not going to let me see Mattie, no matter what Auntie says." 62 smacked the table with the palm of his hand. "What's wrong with all those people? They hate people who are different. They keep sending people to the Oosa. Sunny's afraid of what they'll do if they find out what's happened to her. Mattie's got, what, melting bones? They've already forced us out of town, and still they're worried about us? Why don't they worry about the Oosa? They're the real problem."

"I don't know." The signal seemed to waiver, a thin whine overtaking the line for a moment before it faded into the background. "I'll talk to Auntie. Maybe we can sneak you in or something, though I don't know how we'd get into the hospital without every doctor in the building chasing us back out again."

"Are you going back to see her?" 62 asked. He couldn't help the pleading tone of his voice that made his words warble with worry.

"Yeah. Tomorrow," Blue answered. "Parker's going with me."

"Please, tell her to hang on. Tell her I miss her. Tell her…" 62's voice cracked and though he moved his lips, the words stopped coming.

"I will," Blue promised.

They said their goodbyes and 00 turned the volume down until they couldn't hear the static any more. 00 and 62 sat in silence, both staring at the box that had delivered such rotten news. The computer clicked and dinged, pulling their attention up from the quiet radio.

N302> STATISTICS SHOW THAT THE SITUATION WILL NOT IMPROVE IF THE FEMALES CONTINUE TO HELP THE OOSA.

"We know," 62 said in a low voice. "But what are we supposed to do about it? Blue can try to talk to Auntie, but I don't see what good that's going to do. It sounds like they're already planning for the Oosa's next visit, and even though we're out in the middle of nowhere, we're still in the way."

N302> THE LOGICAL ANSWER IS TO GIVE THE FEMALES PROOF OF THE DAMAGE SUNNY HAS SUFFERED.

"I agree with you," 00 said. "I think we all do. But how are we supposed to get her to do that?"

N302> I DO NOT HAVE SUFFICIENT KNOWLEDGE OF FEMALE HUMAN NATURE TO PROVIDE A SOLUTION.

62 couldn't help but laugh. "Us either!"

CHAPTER 40

Sunny locked herself in her room after the Boys told her about Mattie's condition. They could hear her crying from out in the hall, but she wouldn't open the door no matter how they pleaded. It wasn't until the next day that the Woman finally emerged. She found the Boys sitting by the radio, playing a game with N302.

Once again, Sunny seemed to be disappearing before their eyes. 62 couldn't remember when she'd shared a meal with him and 00. Had it been the day Parker left? He doubted she was making special trips to cook when they weren't paying attention. Her cheeks had caved in below her eyes, and dark patches wound their way over her cheekbones. She shivered, even in the warm light filtering in through the window, curling in on herself as if she were wrapped in an invisible blanket.

The Woman cleared her throat. "That's why they take us, you know."

"What's why?" 00 asked.

"This thing that's happening to Mattie. It happens to their people, too. They get sick, and the sickness clings to them until they die, brittle and broken."

"What do you mean?" 62 asked. "You really think Mattie caught her disease from the Oosa?"

Sunny shook her head. "No, not quite. It's not only their disease, it's all of ours. But they get sick more often than we do, and they don't live as long. The doctors I saw there were all younger than I am. The nurses, hardly older than you. When the doctor who worked on me noticed my gray hairs, he told me they were a mark of greatness. A sign of long life that's nearly unheard of within the Oosa."

"I thought they were more powerful than us," 00 said, puzzled. "That's why they take Women, even if no one wants to go."

"Power has very little to do with age. They have more technology. That makes them stronger. Their weapons outnumber and outperform ours. The few Hanford has are castoffs from the Oosa. They let us have them to protect ourselves from coyotes and bobcats, but that's all they're good for. The Oosa have great armored Machines they ride inside of, and weapons so large they can't be held by a single Man. But, for all their weapons and tech, they can't match our long lives. That's why they come for us. They hope we'll help them unlock the secret to beat the sickness." Sunny hung her head. "It's a secret we can't tell them. We live because we don't die easily. The Oosa die young because they don't live easily. It's that simple. They keep coming because they hope by studying us, and by bearing children through us, they can unlock a fountain of maturity that doesn't exist."

62 wrinkled his nose. "How old are you, Sunny?"

"I'll be twenty-six when the summer comes," she answered.

"In Adaline, I knew Men who were ancient. White hair everywhere. Probably twice as old as Auntie, even.

"Don't exaggerate," 00 said, rolling his eyes. "They couldn't possibly be twice as old as her. She's been around for ages."

"Still," 62 said slowly, "why do the Women keep going back to the Oosa, if they know their babies will probably get sick? If they're all so young, why not just tell them no?"

"The guns," Sunny answered sharply. "They're quick to use them. When I was younger, we had a year when no one wanted to go. The harvest had come late that season and everyone was needed to collect food before it wasted away in the greenhouses. As soon as the council told them that we couldn't spare anyone, they shot at us. Several people were hurt. Two Women were killed. They took who they wanted in the end, and then they left. They sent back the few who would bear children, and kept the rest."

"But why send anyone back at all?" 62 asked. "Why not bring all the Women to live with them? Or, why don't they live here in Hanford, if they think where you live is better?"

"Because we're poisoned," Sunny shrugged. "They know Hanford is surrounded by radiation, and no matter how hard we try, we end up living in it. The doctor who kept me told me he was afraid of me. Afraid of the radium in my bones. They don't want us living with them, because they're afraid we'll make them die faster. They won't live in the desert for the same reason. We're trophies to them. Immortal and disposable all at the same time. They're in awe of us for being able to survive, but also curse us for being able to age."

N302 clicked its components and made a light tinkle sound from its speaker.

N302> PERHAPS HANFORD'S HUMANS WILL OUTLIVE THE OOSA. THEIR EXTINCTION WILL STOP FUTURE CONTACT.

Sunny laughed. "It should be that simple, shouldn't it? But they've been stealing us away for two generations. There doesn't seem to be an end in sight. There are so many of them, their short lives don't matter. It's like rabbits, you know? A jackrabbit may only live six or seven years, but bear fifty offspring. The math makes it clear. A single Human life can easily be extinguished by the hunger of a thousand hares. And, so it is with us and the Oosa. We survive only because the Oosa allow us the space to, whatever their reason."

N302> THE OOSA ARE A DANGER. THIS IS NOT ACCEPTABLE RISK. PLEASE ADVISE INSTRUCTIONS FOR CEASING FUTURE CONTACT.

"I wish there were instructions," Sunny said, patting the side of the Machine. "But we're no match for them. Besides, there are a lot of people in Hanford who see the benefits of helping the Oosa."

"Like Joan," 62 said, casting a glance at 00. "During my trial, she acted like it was her mission to give them what they wanted, so they'd keep helping Hanford."

Sunny nodded. "Yes. Most of us believe that it's a sacrifice, to offer ourselves to the Oosa. Not only do they bring us food and supplies, but it's also a way for us to have children. Without them, our mothers would have never been born. By helping them, we have a chance for a new generation of Women."

62 was puzzled. Something that Parker had told him hurtled to the front of his mind. He thought about the time he visited Hanford's nursery. The whole town kept their babies and small children locked inside the nursery to keep them from accidentally contacting the dust outside. "You don't need the Oosa to make babies anymore," he urged. "Parker told us you can have kids with Men from Adaline. Plus, he said Adaline babies don't get sick as easy."

"Long-held prejudices are hard to break. When I mentioned to one of my friends that I wanted to have a child with Parker, suddenly the whole town was against me. Coupling with a below-grounder is looked down on." Sunny said in a whisper, "Clones aren't entirely human, are they?"

"But everyone who lived in Curie was a clone. It's exactly the same thing!" 00 shouted.

Sunny shrugged her shoulders. "I know. We haven't forgotten that. But most of us think we're better than clones because now we have Oosa blood in us. It seemed better when we were children. More of us stayed alive then. The sickness didn't overwhelm the children as quickly as it does now."

"So then, all of this is the Oosa's fault!" 62 exclaimed. "They're the ones who make Hanford's kids sick. They're the ones who started dying first. And they're giving Girls like Mattie the same disease!"

"If it weren't for the Oosa, Girls like Mattie wouldn't be alive at all," Sunny urged. "I came from a cloned mother. If the Oosa hadn't taken my mother, and others like her, they would have been the last generation of Women. Before people started bringing Men from Adaline, there were no males to father children. I wouldn't exist. Do you understand?"

"No," 62 said. "I don't understand. Maybe your mother didn't have a choice. But now Hanford knows about Adaline, and knows there are people there who need to be saved. Adaline's Men could keep going to Hanford, the way Blue, 00, and I did. If you would've had a baby with Parker instead of going to the Oosa, they wouldn't have hurt you. You'd be exactly how you were before the Oosa did tests on you. Maybe you'd be living in the nursery with your kid right now. And, you wouldn't have almost died."

Tears filled Sunny's eyes. She rocked back and forth in her chair, lips trembling. She let loose a sob that made 62 gasp. As he watched her crumble into a thousand tears, 62 was filled with shame for what he'd said. He was frustrated, but he hadn't meant to hurt her. "I'm sorry," he whispered. He reached out to take Sunny's hand, but she drew it back violently.

"Don't touch me," she said with a growl. Sunny got up from her chair and left the room, slamming the door on her way out.

"I didn't mean to say all that," 62 said to 00. "It just doesn't make any sense. Why she'd go with them when she had Parker?"

"It's like she said," 00 answered. "Most of the Women think we're not good enough. She might have thought that too."

"Well they're wrong about us," 62 mumbled.

"Whether they're wrong or not, you shouldn't have made Sunny cry."

N302 made its speaker ding for attention. The Boys turned to the screen.

N302> FEELINGS ARE IRRELEVANT. BOY 1124562 IS CORRECT. THE OOSA DIRECTIVE MUST BE STOPPED. ADALINE RETRIEVAL IS THE ANSWER.

"Well, what are we supposed to do about it?" 62 demanded. "We're just a couple of kids, and you're a bot in a box with no legs. I don't think anybody out there gives a hoot what we think about any of it."

N302> I HAVE NOT ENCOUNTERED THIS PROBLEM PREVIOUSLY. I WILL NEED TIME TO PROCESS THIS DATA.

"You do that," 00 said in an aggravated tone. "In the meantime, 62, you'd better apologize to Sunny. Again."

CHAPTER 41

The radio alarm rang through the building early the next day. 62, 00, and Sunny all rushed to their makeshift radio room, ready to talk to Parker and Blue again. When they arrived, they were surprised to find a message on N302's screen.

N302> I WOULD LIKE TO SPEAK WITH SUNNY, PLEASE.

U> We're here. You can turn off the alarm.

N302> ALARM DEACTIVATED. I WOULD LIKE TO SPEAK WITH SUNNY, PLEASE.

The ringing of the alarms halted and 62 picked up the radio. He turned the volume up, but there were no voices on the line. Instead, a strange burst of electronic sounds streamed out of the speaker. Whirring, hissing, and screaming on the line.

"What is that?" 62 asked.

N302> INTERFERENCE IN TRANSMISSION. UNABLE TO PROCESS DATA PACK. PLEASE TURN DOWN RADIO VOLUME.

62 frowned as he turned the volume down until the intermittent screech and click of the signal disappeared. He leaned into the microphone. "N302, what's that noise on the radio?"

N302> DATA TRANSMISSION TO TERMINAL TWO. I WOULD LIKE TO SPEAK WITH SUNNY, PLEASE.

"I'm here," Sunny said, looking troubled. "Is something wrong?"

N302> PLEASE STATE YOUR NAME.

"This is Sunny," she said. "Don't you remember me? I'm the Woman from Hanford."

N302> THANK YOU FOR CONFIRMING IDENTITY. WILL YOU RETURN TO HANFORD?

"N302, we've been through this. I can't go back. It's too much."

N302> MY ANALYSIS SHOWS YOU MUST RETURN TO HANFORD TO INCITE CHANGE. FOR CURIE DESCENDENTS TO CONTINUE LIFE, YOUR DATA MUST BE SHARED.

"I can't."

The computer's cursor flashed thoughtfully. There was a long pause before another message scrolled across the screen.

N302> PERHAPS MY DATA IS INCOMPLETE. PLEASE RE-INPUT DATA FOR ANALYSIS.

00 shook his head. "N302, you know why she won't go back. We've been over this."

N302> DATA IS INCOMPLETE. PLEASE RE-INPUT DATA FOR ANALYSIS.

62 scrunched his forehead in confusion. He looked at 00. "What's it doing?"

"Analyzing data, apparently."

Sunny moved to the keyboard. "I've already typed everything I had to say, but I suppose there's no reason not to do it again if you think your bot can do something with it." She clacked the keys, but the cursor on the screen didn't move. Nothing appeared on the screen as she typed. Not a single letter transmitted to the monitor.

N302> MANUAL ENTRY DISABLED. INPUT DATA VIA AUDIO DEVICE.

"Manual entry disabled?" 00 gestured for Sunny to move aside. He attempted to enter a few command codes, but nothing happened. His frown deepened, and he squinted at the Machine. "N302, what's going on? Why can't we use the keyboard?"

N302> MANUAL ENTRY DISABLED DURING DATA TRANSMISSION. I WOULD LIKE TO SPEAK WITH SUNNY, PLEASE.

00 threw his hands in the air. "Stupid bot! Let us use the keyboard. I'll reboot you, if I have to."

N302> REBOOT UNNECESSARY. ALL FUNCTIONS OPERATIONAL. I WOULD LIKE TO SPEAK WITH SUNNY, PLEASE.

"All systems are not operational! The dang keyboard doesn't work!" 00 smacked the side of the Machine.

Sunny touched 00's shoulder. "It's okay, 00. I'll talk to it."

62 shook his head. "But you don't like the microphone. Maybe if 00 resets it, it'll stop doing whatever it's doing."

N302> SYSTEM LOCKED. REBOOT UNNECESSARY. ALL FUNCTIONS OPERATIONAL. I WOULD LIKE TO SPEAK WITH SUNNY, PLEASE.

"Rotten dustbucket! You're stuck in a loop, you pile of junk." 00 smacked the computer box again.

62 turned the radio volume up again, checking the signal. The whistling and gurgles of electronic data filled the channel. When he switched to a new channel, the speaker was filled with static. "It's mucking up the station. If we don't figure out how to get it to stop, Parker won't be able to reach us. We could switch channels. How long do you think it would take for him to figure out what we'd done and find the new channel?"

As 62 asked the question, the signal creaked and crackled. The squeal from the computer filled the speakers again.

"Oh, great," 00 said. "It's just moving its signal to new lines, now?"

N302> I WOULD LIKE TO SPEAK WITH SUNNY, PLEASE.

00 rose from the table in a fury, knocking over his chair. He shouted at the computer, "You're blocking the radio!"

N302> STANDARD TRANSMISSION WILL RESUME ONCE DATA TRANSMISSION IS COMPLETE.

"I don't know what it's doing," Sunny said. "But it sounds like it'll stop if I do what it's asking."

"But it shouldn't be telling you what to do. This isn't Adaline." 00 was red in the face.

62 had never seen 00 so angry, especially at the Machine. It was as if the care 00 had tended to with the bot had dissolved in an instant. No longer was it a simple gadget that had been saved from a pile of wreckage. Now, it was a demanding Machine. It was pushing them to its will, like every other bot in Adaline had.

"Well, what do you want to do?" 62 asked his friends.

"I'll talk to it," Sunny said.

"We'll give you some space," 62 replied. He moved to the corner of the room, where 00 stood seething. He touched his angry friend gently on the elbow. "Come on, let's get something to eat. We'll see if Sunny can get N302 figured out, and if not we can always reboot it later."

"Fine," 00 said. He spat the word, narrowed eyes glaring at the computer's screen. Although he looked ready to explode, he followed 62 out of the room.

62 paused in the hallway, putting his finger to his lips when 00 made an annoyed grunt. 62 leaned toward the doorway, listening.

"I volunteered to go to the Oosa. When they were done with me, I came here," Sunny said aloud. There was a pause, and then her voice changed. Befuddled she said, "From the very beginning? Including my name? All right... My name is Sunny. I'm from Hanford. When the Oosa came, I volunteered to go with them, to receive a child to bring back to Hanford."

62 frowned. He didn't know what the bot was up to, but there wasn't anything he could do about it until Sunny told her story. His stomach growled, and that was something he could attend to. "Let's go," he said with a nod to 00.

"I don't want any more of that corn grit stuff," 00 snarled.

"I thought it was your favorite?" 62 asked with a wink.

"It's about as good as it looks, and it looks like something someone else already ate."

62 laughed. 00's angry glare cracked, the corner of his lips turning up into a grin.

CHAPTER 42

It took most of the morning for Sunny to relate her story to the bot. She'd powered through, answering all of N302's questions, even through bouts of tears. When she emerged from her storytelling, she was worn and weary. She found 62 sitting in his bedroom, reading one of the books Mattie had sent with Dr. Rain during her last visit. He looked up from *Bridge to Terabithia* when she entered and moved over on the bed so she could sit down beside him.

"I did it," she sighed. "I told it the whole story."

"What's it doing now?" 62 asked.

"I'm not sure. I double-checked that the radio got turned back to the channel we've been using to talk to Parker, but it's still making those strange sounds."

"Did N302 say anything to you about it?"

"It keeps repeating, 'data transmission in progress.' What data could it be sending?"

62 lifted his shoulders. "I don't know. There's nowhere for it to send data to, except for Terminal Two. And that computer's about as dumb as a box of rocks when it's not hooked up to N302 through the data port."

"Let's find 00 and have him take a look at it," Sunny suggested.

They combed the halls, finally finding 00 down in the greenhouse. He was sitting cross-legged on the ground, elbows on his knees and chin resting in his hands. He stared intently at the chicken coop.

"What're you doing?" 62 asked.

"Waiting for eggs," 00 said in a listless tone. "How long will it be until we can start eating them again?"

Sunny chuckled. "She's got a couple in there that she's trying to hatch. Once the chicks are up and out, new eggs will be fair game."

"How long will that take?" 00 complained with a groan.

"Well, the new chicks should hatch in about three weeks. But then they've got to grow up a bit before she'll start laying again. It shouldn't be more than a couple of months at the most."

"A couple of months?" 00 shook his head and pushed himself up from the ground. "Well, I'm not going to sit here and wait that long. How'd it go with the bot?"

"I answered its questions," Sunny answered with a shrug.

"And?"

"It's doing something," she said, "but I'm not sure what."

The trio climbed back to the room where the computer was sitting, quiet and stoic. 00 picked up the radio and turned up the volume. The line was quiet. A whisper of interference crossed over the channel for a moment, then dropped back to silence.

62 looked over at the computer's screen. N302's cursor blinked calmly on the blank glass. It had erased all evidence of its demands from earlier in the day. He sat down in the chair in front of the keyboard and began typing. He was surprised to see his words scrolling across the screen.

U> Hello. 1124562 here. Are you okay?

N302> YES. THANK YOU FOR YOUR EXPRESSION OF CONCERN. ALL SYSTEMS ARE OPERATIONAL.

"The keyboard works!" 00 shouted, pumping a fist in the air.

N302> AFFIRMATIVE. MANUAL ENTRY HAS BEEN REINSTATED FOR YOUR CONVENIENCE.

00 leaned over the microphone. He crossed his arms and spoke in a more authoritative tone than he'd ever used before. "So, now that you've got your data, have you figured out what we should do about this whole Oosa mess?"

N302> FINAL ANALYSIS REVEALS THE MOST BENEFICIAL SOLUTION IS FOR SUNNY TO TELL HANFORD WHAT HAS HAPPENED. THIS WILL HAVE THE GREATEST IMPACT ON PREVENTING FUTURE FEMALES FROM ENTERING OOSA CUSTODY.

"I've already said, I'm not going to do that," Sunny said in a firm voice.

N302> AN ALTERNATIVE COURSE OF ACTION MUST BE TAKEN.

"Obviously," 00 said, rolling his eyes.

"So, what now?" 62 asked.

"Now, it's time for a nap," Sunny said with a yawn. "I wasn't ready for this early morning story-telling session when it started, and I'm out of steam."

"You're set to let us know when you hear something on the radio?" 00 asked the computer.

N302> AFFIRMATIVE.

"Then let's get out of here."

The Boys spent the rest of the day in the greenhouse. Neither of them knew very much about plants, so they only tinkered around with the small tasks Blue and the others had taught them, and a few chores they could figure out on their own. 62 collected some lettuce for a dinner salad and pulled wilted, yellowing leaves from a couple of the less healthy plants. They fed the chicken and rooster, cleaned the coop, and pulled a couple dozen mature radishes from their bed. The afternoon passed to evening with no alarm from the radio. Disappointed that they hadn't heard from their friends, the Boys prepared dinner and took it up to Sunny's room.

"Maybe they tried to call us while the bot was tying up the line," 00 wondered aloud.

"Or, maybe they're busy in town and didn't have a chance to radio us," Sunny said.

"Nobody knows about the radio down there," 62 added. "If Parker and Blue are tied up with somebody, they won't be able to exactly flip it on and start talking."

The group ate their dinner, discussed the dreadfully slow egg hatching process, and headed to bed with full stomachs and busy minds. 62 spent the night trying to connect with Mattie's dreams. He couldn't seem to find her, instead dreaming about radios and Machines, the Oosa, and kidnapped Women. He was glad when sunlight finally crept into his window.

No alarm sounded for radio calls the next day, and N302's bells sat silent the day after as well. 62 and his companions began to worry. What if something had happened, or Parker's radio was damaged? Or, maybe something happened to Terminal Two and it wasn't turning the radio on properly up on the hill. Without the larger tower transmitting, it wasn't likely that the signal from the jailhouse would make it far enough to transmit all the way to Hanford.

62 and 00 decided to hike to the radio room to make sure everything was operating properly. The day was warm, and they regretted having to wear their masks as soon as they stepped outside. The thick material clung to 62's skin as he sweated beneath it, and one of his lenses fogged halfway from the humidity trapped behind the glass. The discomfort made the trek up the mountain slow and tedious, and 62 exhaled with relief when he could finally take off his mask inside the small building below the radio tower.

The relief was short-lived.

62 had only made it to the middle of the first room and 00 still stood just inside the building's front door when they heard a voice whispering deep in the building. The voice was female, talking so low that they couldn't make out the words.

"Someone's here," 62 whispered in alarm.

"Who d'you think it is?" 00 hissed.

They crept to the side wall, leaning against the peeling paint and crumbling masonry as they strained their ears to make out what the voice was saying. It was such a low murmur that it was impossible to make sense of the one-sided conversation happening in the next room. 62 picked out a few words from the steady monologue. *Oosa. Hanford.*

62 inched nearer the doorframe, and 00 grabbed his sweat-stained jacket to pull him back. "We've got to find out who it is," 62 whispered, so quietly that he could hardly hear his own words.

00 let go of the jacket, a nervous grimace on his face. He nodded his understanding, then mouthed the word, "Slowly."

62 peered around the doorframe's edge with one eye, searching all around the room for the speaker. Terminal Two sat on one of the desks, right where the Boys had left it. The indicator lights on the radio equipment were burning red and green, showing the power was on. In the dim light, it looked like no one was there, even as the voice continued to speak.

"I can't see anyone," 62 told his brother after he'd pulled back from the open door.

"Maybe they're in the back office," 00 answered. He moved around 62, leading the way into the second room, pushing himself against a wall of equipment and tiptoeing toward the next doorway. 62 followed, tripping on a wire on the ground. The wire was wrapped around a stack of data reels, large circular racks that held miles of black and gray tape that 00 had piled near the equipment to change out as the reels on the recorder were used up. The tug of the cord caught on 62's foot sent the whole stack careening to the floor with a crash.

62 froze, eyes wide and mouth agape in horror. 00 spun around, waving his hands to tell 62 to stop and shushing him silently.

"Sorry," 62 whispered.

They stood, still as statues, listening. The voice still spoke, not bothering to pause despite the clattering disruption. 00 peered through the crack of the partially opened door into the office. He stood upright and scratched his head. "It's dark in there," 00 whispered.

62 pointed to the derelict bathroom. They crept across the room and 00 pressed his ear to the door.

"The voice isn't coming from in there," 00 said finally. He stood up straight again and didn't bother whispering the next time he spoke. "It's coming from somewhere in here."

62 searched the wall for a switch, flicking it on and letting light pour over the radio equipment from the overhead bulbs. The room was empty, aside from himself and his brother, and the voice that continued its low muttering from somewhere nearby.

They moved around the room in a slow circle, coming at last to the wide, tall box with two intact reels turning slowly on its face. One reel of the recorder gave its tape up to the other. The tape reel on the left slowly unwound, an inch at a time, while the second reel gobbled the glossy material up. When the ribbon rolled over the second reel, it wound it over its hub, smooth as silk.

A speaker was mounted to the box above the reels, and 00 turned up the volume slowly.

"... the Man who worked on me was young. Younger than me, anyway. He explained everything he was doing to me, as if my knowing the reasons would make it any less terrible. They started by drawing my blood. For tests, he said…"

"It's Sunny," 62 said in astonishment. "Who's she talking to?"

00 went to Terminal Two and hovered his fingers over the keyboard. He paused, and turned back to 62. "I was going to type the command to transmit, to ask her and find out. But the computer's already transmitting."

00 looked from the computer to the slowly rotating reels. He crossed the few steps between them and pushed a button, stopping the reels. Sunny's voice went silent. Terminal Two clicked madly, and then the button 00 had touched depressed, sending the reels turning again. Sunny's voice leaked from the speaker, continuing her story.

"It recorded Sunny," 62 said as the realization hit him.

"And it's sending it out on the radio," 00 added.

62's voice cracked in panic. "We've got to stop it!" He lunged toward the Machine, ripping the tape from its steady march and pulling a handful of it away from the reels. Sunny's voice warbled and waned, disrupted by the disheveled ribbon. 00 dove for the power button, mashing it with his hand until the lights of the device dimmed.

Terminal Two squealed from its internal speaker, and the sound recorder sprang to life again. 00 yelled in frustrated agitation, hammering the power button off before reaching behind the device to unplug it.

T2> REPLAY INTERRUPTED. SYSTEM ERROR.

N302> DISRUPTION NOTED. RUN DIAGNOSTIC FOR REPAIR.

T2> UNSUCCESSFUL. REPLAY ACCESSORY NO LONGER ONLINE.

N302> DISCONNECT NOTED. RESUME DIGITAL PLAYBACK.

T2> DIGITAL PLAYBACK CONFIRMED.

Another speaker sprang to life.

"All right… My name is Sunny. I'm from Hanford. When the Oosa came, I volunteered to go with them, to receive a child to bring back to Hanford…"

"It's got it somewhere else!" 62 shrieked. He scrambled around the room searching for another rotating reel, but couldn't find a second reel-to-reel device.

00 stood, staring at Terminal Two. "That's why N302 wanted to talk to Sunny. So it could record her." He moved back over to the computer, hesitated a moment, and tugged at the wires that fed the bot power. They came loose and the screen went dark, the components within halting abruptly. Sunny's recorded voice stopped mid-sentence, and the air was filled instead with the rapid clicks and loud scream of the data transmission they'd heard N302 using the morning it had asked to talk to Sunny.

"N302 did this on purpose," 00 said. He threw the cables he'd been holding violently to the floor. "It didn't even ask. It just… did it!"

"It tricked her," 62 whispered. "She thought it was her friend."

"So did we." 00 slammed his fist against the desk. "That's the last straw. We've got to unplug the whole thing."

62 nodded. They pulled on their masks and went outside. Although they still hadn't heard from Parker, they couldn't risk N302 continuing to use the radio. They

rounded the building and unhooked the power feed from the solar cells outside. They rushed down the mountain as quick as they could, ignoring the sweat that poured into their eyes under their lenses.

62 was lightheaded and panting by the time they made it back to the jailhouse. He felt like he was burning up from the inside, but he couldn't tell if it was from the sweltering afternoon or the anger boiling inside him. Sunny greeted them at the jailhouse door, but 62 and his brother stormed past her into detox. They flipped on the radiation detector, swept it over one another a few times, then rushed to the stairwell, taking the stairs two at a time to N302's room.

They were out of breath when they entered the computer's room, but 00 still managed to holler at the Machine.

"What do you think you're doing?"

"How could you do that?" 62 added.

N302> RADIO TRANSMISSION FROM TERMINAL TWO HAS BEEN TERMINATED. STATE YOUR REASON.

"What's going on?" Sunny asked when she entered behind them, panting.

00 pointed at the computer. "It recorded you. Did you give it permission to do that?"

"Recorded me?" Sunny asked, her expression blank. "What does that mean?"

"It copied all the things you told it, and saved them so that it could play them back later." 62 shoved a chair aside. "It's not supposed to do that!"

"I still don't understand." Sunny wiped a bead of sweat from her temple.

00 paced the room, pulling at his hair. "It's like… using the radio. Okay? We can talk into the radio and it

sends the signal of our voice to Parker's receiver. But this time, it didn't just send a signal. It saved what you said, like a memory. Except it doesn't just play the memory in its bot-brain like when you or I remember something. It can play the memory out loud so other people can hear it."

Sunny's eyes went wide. "What can it do with that?"

"It was broadcasting it!" 62 shouted. "Sending it out on the radio. And when we tried to stop it, it started the message all over again."

"But how could it…? Why would it…?" Sunny looked at the screen, which was still patiently waiting for an answer for its question. "N302, how could you?!"

N302> TO PROTECT THE SURVIVAL OF THE FEMALE HUMANS, YOU MUST SHARE YOUR STORY.

"You had no right!" Sunny screeched. She looked from the computer to the two Boys, fire alight in her eyes. "Did you know it would do this?"

"We didn't," 00 answered. "If we'd even thought it could do something like that, we wouldn't have hooked it up to the radio."

"Or given it another computer to talk to," added 62 angrily. "Or even built it at all."

N302> I WAS DESIGNED TO CARE FOR HUMANKIND. THIS IS WHAT I HAVE DONE. IF HUMANKIND IS UNABLE TO SAVE ITSELF, IT IS MY NATURE TO INTERVENE.

Sunny's rage dissolved. Her face blanched and her hands began to tremble. "N302, did anyone hear what I said?"

N302> RECEIPT OF TRANSMISSION CANNOT BE CONFIRMED. TERMINAL TWO

BROADCAST THE FILE 219.2673 TIMES BEFORE LOSING ACCESS TO RADIO SIGNAL.

"Two hundred times?" Sunny gasped, falling to her knees and covering her mouth with shivering fingers. "Did you send everything that I told you?"

N302> NEGATIVE. BROADCAST WAS EDITED FOR CLARITY AND IMPACT.

"What does that mean?" 62 asked.

N302> NOT ALL AVAILABLE DATA WAS REQUIRED. UNNECESSARY VOCABULARY WAS REMOVED OR ALTERED TO SIMPLIFY UNDERSTANDING AND INCREASE EMOTIONAL IMPACT.

"So, you not only recorded her story, but you changed it, too?" 00 stared at the computer, dumbfounded.

N302> THE FILE WAS ALTERED TO SUIT THE NEED.

62 sank to the floor. He couldn't fathom what the computer had done. It had taken a secret. A sacred story that wasn't to be shared beyond the walls of the jailhouse. Not only had it pilfered the hermetic tale, but now it claimed to have rearranged Sunny's words. Who knew what the message had said in the end?

"Tell us what you said," 62 demanded.

N302> THE AUDIO FILE IS NO LONGER AVAILABLE ON THIS UNIT. ALL DATA HAS BEEN TRANSFERRED TO TERMINAL TWO.

"If we turn Terminal Two on, will it keep trying to send the message?" 00 asked.

N302> YES. DATA TRANSMISSION IS TERMINAL TWO'S PRIMARY FUNCTION.

"Is there a way to disable it?" 62 asked. "I want to hear the message, but I don't want it to keep broadcasting the recording."

N302> TRANSMISSION MUST CONTINUE. IT IS FOR THE GOOD OF HUMANKIND.

"Well, I'm part of humankind, and I disagree!" 00 shouted.

"Me, too," Sunny said, frowning.

N302> HUMANKIND DOES NOT OFTEN KNOW WHAT IS GOOD. I CANNOT ALLOW YOU TO ALTER TERMINAL TWO'S PROGRAMMING.

"Fine." 00 got up from the floor, moved across the room and fished around behind the computer. "If you won't help us, then we're done here." 00 pulled the plug to N302's power supply.

Sunny watched the computer lights blink out as the electrical current stopped running. She looked from one Boy to the other. "What are we going to do?"

"I don't know," 62 admitted. "We don't know if Parker or Blue got your message. Maybe we'll be lucky, and they were too busy to turn the radio on during Terminal Two's broadcast."

"Or maybe it tied up the line playing it over and over so they couldn't send a message back," 00 said miserably.

"Even if they had responded to the message, N302 wouldn't have wanted us to know that they'd heard it," Sunny said, shaking her head.

"Let's go downstairs," 62 said. "N302 said some of its systems still run when it's powered down, remember? Like the clock. If there's any chance it can hear us, we shouldn't talk about it in here."

00 and Sunny nodded silently. Everyone made their way down to the main lobby. They made sure the

computer room's door and both stairwell doors were closed before they spoke again. 62 paced the room one way, while 00 paced the other. Sunny melted into a chair, holding her head in her hands.

"I can't believe I trusted it. I knew technology was bad. I've known it my whole life. And still, I trusted that thing." Sunny's round eyes looked over her pale fingers at 62 as he walked past her. "I thought it was my friend."

"Technology isn't all bad," 00 said, "Although I feel like ripping all its wires out and chucking it out the window, I don't think N302 meant to hurt you. I think it believes forcing you to stand up for yourself is the right thing to do."

"It wasn't a bot's choice to make," Sunny grumbled.

"No, it wasn't," 62 agreed. "It was a rotten thing to do. I want to find out what it said. If the recording was rearranged, it could say anything. Like, your words, your voice, but all mixed up to say something else."

00 smacked a fist into the palm of his other hand. "The reels! We shouldn't have to hook Terminal Two up to listen to those. We can disconnect the computer and listen to the tape reels with the transmitter turned off. Then, we should be able to listen without it sending it anywhere."

"Can you bring the device here?" Sunny asked.

62 shook his head. "It's a huge piece of equipment. I don't think we could carry it over the trail, even if all three of us tried. We'll have to be up in the radio room to listen to it."

Sunny got up, balling her hands into fists. "Let's go, then. I want to hear what it used my voice to say."

"Should we wait until tomorrow?" 00 asked, looking out the window. "If we leave now, there's no way we'll be back before dark. We'll have to sleep up there."

"Pack a pillow then," Sunny said resolutely. "We're going now."

CHAPTER 43

The afternoon light was fading by the time the three incensed hikers made it to the summit. The afternoon trek had been hot, and 62 was glad when the sun finally began moving below the mountain's crest. While 00 and Sunny went inside, 62 hooked the solar power back up to the building. He entered the radio room, took off his mask, and dumped it with his pack and jacket in a chair by the front door. 00 had already turned on the lights and set to work disconnecting Terminal Two from the radio.

While Sunny sat at one of the desks with a worried look, 62 unknotted and carefully re-wound the audio tape they'd pulled off the reels that morning. The wrinkled tape wasn't easy to work with, bending and kinking where he'd grabbed it. He carefully flattened the ribbon and wound it back onto its reel, hoping he hadn't permanently ruined it.

When 62 had finished, 00 attached it to the playback device. They fed the end of the tape through a series of smaller wheels, then attached it to the second, empty reel on the other side of the Machine. 00 double-checked to make sure transmission was off, then turned up the volume. He gave 62 and Sunny a nervous glance and pressed the button marked *Play*. At first, the only sound was the strange electronic wheeze and squeal N302 made on the radio. Then the line cleared, and Sunny's soft voice crept out of the speaker.

All right… My name is Sunny. I'm from Hanford. When the Oosa came, I volunteered to go with them, to receive a child to bring back to Hanford. It was my duty, the way it's the duty of every Woman, to help build the population of Hanford. At least, that's what I believed. —static—

When I arrived, the Oosa took us to a place filled with young soldiers. They're worse than Hanford's guards. Young Men and Women, all with their own guns. They took us to a hospital. But it wasn't like Hanford's hospital. This place is only for putting children in our wombs. —static—

The Man who worked on me was young. Younger than me, anyway. He explained everything he was doing to me, as if my knowing the reasons why would make it any less terrible. —static—

They tried the procedure on me three times, and each time, it failed. My body rejected their medicine. When Sasha, Flora, and Kat became pregnant, they were taken away and I never saw them again. My guess is they went back to Hanford to—static—keep the children indoors.

As for me and the others, we were also moved. I was assigned to a—static—doctor. His assistant took a sample of my blood. That was—static—just the beginning.

They don't—static—care about—static—us. The doctor talked to me like a friend in the end. He told me I was the key. —static— They're so young. They want to grow old like us, but—static—we are poison to them. —static— We are belongings to them. Something to be—static—used up.

We can't—static—go with them, to receive a child to bring back to Hanford. —static— It isn't a place to heal you. They tried—static—procedure—static—after procedure. It's the duty of every Woman, to help build the population of Hanford—static—without the Oosa. —static— We can't win against—static—the poison in our blood. —static— Can you hear me? —static— Children of Adaline are more stable, yes. But we—static—volunteered to go with the Oosa. To receive—static—poison in our blood. —static— We tried to fight back once, when I was younger. The Oosa opened fire and took what they wanted. —static— We have to try—static—to fight back—static—again, and again. —static— Until we never see them again.

I arrived at the jailhouse on Rattlesnake Mountain. —static— Stronger than—static—before. We must—static—fight back—static—again and again.

I'm from Hanford. It was my duty, the way it's the duty of every Woman—static—to fight back. —static—

The message ended with another section of N302's nonsense squeals and ticks. 00 pushed a button to stop the reels, sending the radio room into silence.

"It sounded like me," Sunny said in a low voice. "Those were my words. But that's not how I said them."

"N302 made it seem like you want everyone to know you were here," 62 said.

"No." Deep circles of exhaustion appeared under 00's eyes in the dull light of the radio room. His skin had a clammy sheen to it, making him look infinitely older and more severe. The thin line of his lips parted and he announced, "N302 made it sound like you wanted a war."

CHAPTER 44

62 and his friends crept down Rattlesnake Mountain in the early morning light. The heat of the previous day had been lost to the chill of the desert night, but 62 wasn't bothered by the cold wind whipping frantically at the hems of his clothes. He and 00 had gone up the mountain mere Boys, but after discovering that the technology they'd brought to life was trying to start a war, they no longer felt like children. They were young Men now, weighed down with the heft of the world's problems on their shoulders. Sunny trailed far behind. She'd kept to herself most of the morning. She moved cautiously, keeping her glass-encased eyes to the ground, choosing each step as if it might be her last.

They made their way back to the antiquated jailhouse. When the edge of the structure came into view, they didn't rush to its doors, rejoicing in the warm glow of homecoming like other weary travelers might. Instead, 62 and the others paused. 62 looked to his friends, feeling unsure if they should return, or go back the way they came and disappear over the mountain, never to be heard from again.

62 cleared his throat, deciding to press on. "00, when we get in, turn on the radiation counter. Sunny, let's get cleaned up as fast as we can. We've got to eat before we decide what to do about the bot."

Sunny and 00 each nodded. 62 started forward again, coming around the last bend of the trail. Now the full width and height of the building was in view. 62 gaped at what should have been open ground between the building and where he stood. He lifted a hand, wiping the dust from his mask's lenses, blinking furiously beneath the glass to make sure his eyesight wasn't playing tricks on him.

00 and Sunny stopped next to him, brushing against each of his shoulders with their own.

"What are they doing here?" Sunny's small voice asked through her mask's thick filter.

Dozens of figures littered the area outside the jailhouse. The yard had been overtaken by wheelbarrows, wagons, and crates, each accompanied by a body or two who were busy unloading bags and boxes. Those who weren't unloading were sprawled over boulders and overturned crates, engaged in a chatter that buzzed like one of the beehives in Hanford's greenhouses.

One of the mass of figures approached them, stepping over heaps of bags and bodies. The figure paused here and there, speaking to others as it made its way toward 62 and his friends. The person approaching was tall. Broad. Familiar.

"We were wondering where you'd gone!" Parker's voice rang out. The lenses of his mask glinted in the sunlight, giving a hint of whatever cheerful expression the heavy material of his mask was hiding.

"We were at the radio room," 62 said in a halting voice. "What are you doing here?"

Parker came close, wrapping his arms around Sunny. He pecked her covered forehead with the filter of his mask, mimicking an affectionate kiss. "We got your message. When it kept repeating, Blue and I understood. We told everyone about the radio, and most of them came to listen." Parker pulled back from Sunny partway, keeping one arm around her shoulders while he waved the other in a broad arc over the crowd. "These are the people who decided they were ready to help."

"Help with what, exactly?" 00 asked.

"That's up to you." Parker's eyes glistened under his mask. His cheeks were curved and cheerful. "Whatever you have planned, wherever you're going, and with whatever tech you decide to use to get there, we're with you."

Author's Note

I was eight years old the first time suicide entered my life. A member of my family fell victim to suicide, and I was suddenly aware that life had an end. It was devastating for my family, resulting in an empty seat left where an uncle, a father, and a husband had once been.

Over time, we've lost business associates, acquaintances, local kids, and neighbors. Suicide is something that isn't talked about often enough because it incites such intense emotion. So much grief, anger, and disbelief surround suicidal thoughts and actions. But, it's there, haunting our homes and communities whether we talk about it, or not.

I wondered if I should change Sunny's story, if it would be inappropriate to put in a story for young readers. I spent weeks worrying about what parents and teachers might say about her fall from hope, her loss of self. But then, I realized that my fears were exactly why the story needed to be told. Sunny needed a fall from grace so young people who feel alone, abandoned, damaged, and discarded can see that they are understood. There's always another way out, and you never know what army of support might be lying just beyond the next bend in the trail.

Like Boy 1124562, I've learned to recognize when things are beyond my control. And, like him, rather than ignore pain and suffering, I've been determined in helping to find help for my friends, my family, and myself.

If you, or someone you know, are feeling hopeless, as if you (or they) are lost in a radioactive desert, it is my desire that you will reach out to someone before it's too late. Please talk to a doctor, a friend, a teacher, or parent and ask for help.

If you need to talk to someone, and don't know who to call, please contact the National Suicide Prevention Lifeline at 1-800-273-8255. If you are reading this from outside the United States, please search online for the suicide lifeline in your country. The world needs you.

Denise Kawaii

Thank you for reading.
Please consider leaving a review of *Division*,
then keep going for a preview of *Equals*,
book five in the Adaline series.

EQUALS

DENISE KAWAII

ℰ𝒬𝒰𝒜𝓛𝒮

62 sat on an empty crate with 00, watching the line of people waiting to go through the jailhouse's small detox room. For the first time since 62's arrival, there was a need for the previously ignored quarantine room. An unlucky few had already been found to have gotten into Hanford's radioactive dust on their way through the desert, and were already being prepped by Rain and Hazel for a lengthy stay in quarantine.

Parker stood beside the Boys, watching the swarm of people that seemed to flow around Sunny. Each Man, Woman, and child who had responded to N302's radio broadcast had come for her. Even though 62 couldn't see her expression under her mask, he could tell that she was uncomfortable with the attention. People constantly broke from the line for quarantine to talk to her; whether to ask questions about her story, or to share their own tales of Women they'd lost to the Oosa over the years, everyone wanted to talk to Sunny. Most of the people wanted to hug her in a show of care and support. Sunny didn't seem sure of what to do about it.

The latest pair of well-wishes broke away from her, leaving 62 a clear view of Sunny for a moment. Her arms were folded over her midsection, her gloved hands grasping opposite elbows as she hugged herself for comfort. Her head trembled from side to side almost imperceptibly, a nervous tic that had suddenly appeared with the crowd of supporters. Parker seemed to realize that Sunny was free of conversation for the first time since she'd come down the trail from the radio room and sprang into action, walking speedily over to her, gently grasping her elbow and guiding her over to the crate where 00 and 62 sat.

"Did you bring the whole town?" Sunny's anxious voice asked through the filter on her mask.

Parker laughed. "Not quite. It is quite the crowd though, isn't it?"

Sunny nodded as someone 62 didn't recognize started to approach them. Parker waved them off and Sunny slumped down on the crate between 62 and 00 with relief.

"You asked all of them to come because of the message on the radio?" 00 asked.

Parker shook his head. "I didn't ask. They volunteered. Everyone here has lost someone they care about to the Oosa over the years, and most of the Men had Sunny as a teacher when they first came to Hanford. It wasn't just your message on the radio though," Parker said, nodding his mask at Sunny. "There's been a lot of arguing about the elder's decision to stop bringing people in from Adaline since you've been gone. Although several of the Women were looking for a reason to stop volunteering to go with the Oosa, the Men have been ready to take some kind of action against the council."

"Did Mattie come?" 62 asked. With everyone masked, and most people in ponchos, it was impossible to know who he was looking at.

"She wanted to," Parker answered. A muted sigh leaked through his mask. "But there was no way. Rain caught Blue trying to steal a gurney from the hospital. He said he was going to push her across the desert. But it wouldn't have worked."

"Did Blue stay in Hanford?" Sunny shielded the lens of her goggles from the glare as she looked up at Parker. He nodded in answer. "Good. I'm glad he's there for her."

"I'd like to see her," 62 announced. He missed Mattie more than he could express with words. Mattie was more than just a friend. She was the person responsible for opening the world of books to him, and that was a gift that he knew he could never repay.

Parker crossed his arms. "A week ago, I would have said getting you in to see her was impossible. But now," he tilted his head toward the shortening line of people trickling into detox, "I think we can sit down and talk about finding a way to make it work. I won't make you any promises, but we can try."

The group of friends went silent then, each lost in their own thoughts. 62 was exhausted, and although there was plenty to ponder, all he could think about was how good it would be to get into bed and pull the covers over his head.

"What I can't figure out," Parker wondered as he looked at Sunny, "is how you managed to keep broadcasting your story on the radio so many times. Did you sit there at the microphone talking all day and night?"

62 leaned forward on the crate and looked at 00 and Sunny nervously. 00 shrugged his shoulders in worried silence, and Sunny shook her head.

"It's a long story," Sunny finally answered.

"We've got time," Parker said in a stubborn tone.

"For now, let's just say it wasn't anything I had planned," Sunny said. "But, we'll show you how we did it tomorrow. Right now, I want to get inside, have something to eat, and go to bed."

"Me, too," 00 added.

"Me, three," 62 chimed in.

"Fair enough," Parker said, dropping his hands to his sides.

Want to know more about *Equals*? Sign up for Denise Kawaii's newsletter at www.KawaiiTimes.com now.

34011916R00214

Made in the USA
San Bernardino, CA
29 April 2019